A Journey of Souls

by

Michael Mckinney

Table of Contents

Chapter One: The Astronomer

On a cool April morning in Lancaster Pennsylvania, a funeral home is hosting a number of people who have come to show their respect to the deceased. His name was Calvin Milner, and he had more friends and admirers than he knew. Calvin was a very unusual man. An early and nearly fatal brush with death when he was seventeen had profoundly influenced him. He was the sole survivor of a terrible car accident that had killed three others. The experience had left him physically, psychologically, and spiritually shaken. After months of deep reflection, he had resolved to live a life of service and altruism, whatever that might come to be. Calvin Milner saw in his escape from death a providential sign calling him to a life of helping others. At seventeen he was mature enough to know such a commitment would play out over a lifetime, and that he could only start by recovering his strength, both physically and mentally. It was as if Calvin Milner in his teens suddenly had the maturity and discipline of a 40 year old.

After recovering from his accident, he studied assiduously, finished high school and worked his way through college. He eventually became a high school teacher, and developed a reputation for caring as much about his students' well-being as their academic performance. His quiet, unassuming demeanor made those around him feel completely at ease, and he made friends easily. Calvin Milner maintained an active interest in science, and taught that subject competently in his many years as a public school teacher.

Most of his career was spent teaching in his home town, in the very same high school he had attended years earlier as a student. A counselor as much as a teacher, his association with high school students made him acutely sensitive to the shifting emotional and psychological challenges of adolescence. Though he couldn't possibly solve all the personal problems of those he counseled, his unflagging readiness to listen to all who came to him for advice was gratefully remembered by those who crossed paths with him.

Calvin Milner was also an avid amateur astronomer. As president of the local astronomy club, he would organize, and host monthly star gazing outings at his home in the country. These trips, affectionately called 'Cal's Astro Excursions' were particularly memorable for those who attended. As a boy, Calvin had spent many nights in the dark Pennsylvania countryside with his small telescope viewing the sky. As an adult he became committed to sharing his love of astronomy with others, and so one night a month he would set up his 24" reflecting telescope, hosting friends, students, and all others for a night of serious star gazing. Many came away from these special evenings with a positive, and lasting impression of their experience. For this, and other reasons Calvin Milner is fondly remembered. Now he's gone.

The unexpected outpouring of affection at his funeral today is a little surprising for his wife, now widow, Clara, who sits in mournful silence after receiving a long line of those offering their respects. After accepting condolences from so many, most of them strangers, Clara Milner finds herself a little unprepared for the wave of genuine sympathy from dozens of well-wishers and is truly touched by their sincerity. After the last few guests begin leaving, a woman in her mid-40s walks over and presents herself.

"Mrs. Milner."

"Yes?"

"My name is Barbara Turner. I was a student in Mr. Milner's class."

"Oh, really?"

"Yes, in my junior year, I'm sorry he's gone."

"Oh, thank you."

"Your husband was loved by so many."

"Please sit down, Barbara. It's nice of you to come today."

"Thank you, I'm so happy to talk with you today Mrs. Milner. I wanted to tell you something."

"What's that?"

"Your husband profoundly influenced my life. He's the reason I became a teacher."

"Is that right? Where do you teach, Barbara?"

"In Atlanta."

"You came all the way from Atlanta?" Mrs. Milner asks.

"Yes."

"How did you know my husband passed?"

"My parents still live here in Lancaster, and they told me."

"I see. So you're a teacher. Do you like it?"

"Yes, I do."

"Calvin loved teaching."

"He told me something I never forgot."

"What's that?"

"When I told him I wanted to be a teacher, he said, "It's not about teaching. It's about learning and curiosity.""

"Yeah, that was Calvin. He didn't like to be called a teacher. He preferred the term 'learning assistant.'"

"Well, he was my inspiration to become a teacher, and I know he had a positive influence on a lot of other students."

"Thank you, that's kind of you to say that. I know that many people were fond of him, but I must say I'm a little surprised to see so many people here today."

"I hope you don't mind me asking you Mrs. Milner, but was he in the hospital long before he passed? I would've come to see him if I'd known he was ill."

"No, he wasn't. He was doing fine. Monday night he went to bed and had a heart attack in his sleep. So he went peacefully."

"I'm so glad."
"Thank you, thank you"
"If there's anything I can do for you Mrs. Milner."
"I'll be all right. Thank you for coming today."
"It's the least I could do. Thank you again Mrs. Milner."

"You're welcome Barbara. Take care of yourself."

"Thank you, goodbye."
"Goodbye dear."

As the funeral of Calvin Milner comes to a close, Clara Milner sits quietly with her thoughts. She tries to grapple with the realization that all she shared and experienced with her husband in the nearly 50 years of their marriage has now passed into the catalog of memory. A mood of somber reflection comes over her. She knows her time of mourning is just beginning.

Activity diminishes as the doors finally close at the funeral home. Cars are filing out of the parking lot, and people are on their way back home. Activity is stirring in another place as well, but this place is very different than most places we know about. This place can't be found on any map. This place exists in a realm beyond the linear time bound reality of human experience. It lies beyond the veil of temporal life, and it waits for all.

As if waking from a dream, Calvin Milner's conscious mind once again feels the pulse of life's coursing energy through his being. He opens his eyes to find himself in his boyhood home. He's flooded with a deep sense of contentment and belonging. As he walks into the kitchen, he hears a conversation between two women. One voice is familiar, and one is not. A moment later he's greeted by his mother as he had been so many times before when he was a boy.

"Hi Cal, are you hungry?"

"Hi Mom, I'm okay," he automatically replies.

"This is Brianna. She's here to show you all those places you once told me about."

"What do you mean?"

Calvin's mother moves toward her son to bestow a kiss, and tells him,

"We'll all be here any time you want to come see us, Cal."

At that moment Calvin sees his father outside brushing the dog he grew up with when he was a boy. Max, a beautiful golden retriever was only five months old when he came into the Milner household. He quickly became Calvin's closest companion, forming a bond that remained for 14 years. Max had died of natural causes two weeks after Calvin went off to college, as if the animal sensed his master would not be returning, and so lost the will to live. As Calvin looks out the window of his boyhood home, he wonders how all of this is happening. He hears his mother's voice again.

"Why don't you go see Max? He's there with your father."

Without making the effort or choice to walk out of the house, Calvin instantly finds himself outside. As he sees his father's reassuring smile, and is quickly greeted by his dog Max, a powerful sense of benevolent and protective love comes over him. Reaching down to eagerly pet his beloved animal companion, he feels the

dog's warm coat of inviting fur through his fingers and the tactile reassurance of his living presence. Then Calvin looks at his father and sees the same expression of ingratiating love he warmly remembers as a boy. An overwhelming sense of belonging comes over him, as he stands to greet him with the strange woman named Brianna looking on from no more than ten feet away.

As a growing child, Calvin was amply cared for, basking in the secure, loving fold of a harmonious family. His father was protective and reassuring, and raised his son with an imperturbable gentleness that never wavered in its constancy.

His memories of that happy childhood now flood his mind with a serene and reassuring contentment and he feels utterly immersed in an all-enveloping embrace of absolute love and acceptance. A mother's nurturing support, a father's protective care, and the devoted loyalty of his dog, make for a potent symbolic trio, as if some ineffable source of transcendent universal love was being expressed through them. Calvin senses something powerful and unseen is at work. All the familial support, protection and love that he knew as a growing child are now all around him. What could it mean? Everything here is comforting, reassuring, and familiar. Only one thing is out of place. Who is the woman standing beside him called Brianna? A woman who speaks with Calvin's parents as if they were old friends. Though unfamiliar, her presence feels natural, and in a strange way somehow necessary.

Calvin hears his father's voice. "It's good to see you Cal."

"I'm glad to be here with you Dad."

As if in a dream, Calvin speaks to his father with the same casual ease of his childhood. It's almost as if he never left this place. Everything here is so natural, familiar and completely understood, that familiar words seem almost unnecessary

He hears his father's voice again. "I have to wash up for dinner Calvin. Why don't you show Brianna your telescope? Don't be too late. We'll be eating later."

Calvin instantly finds himself in the back yard of his boyhood home standing in front of the reflector telescope he had built in his early teens. Brianna is beside him.

"Was this your first telescope Calvin?" she asks.

"Yes, it is. I remember I worked all summer to pay for it."

Moving over to the telescope he carefully built and so often used, Calvin is flooded with rich memories of the many hours he spent observing the night sky. Alone, with only his dog Max for companionship, he would sometimes stay out under the stars all night taking in the wonders of the universe. Now he has somehow returned to the place where those experiences were formed. How is this possible? As he touches the telescope he lovingly crafted as a boy he hears Brianna's voice again.

"What did you see with your telescope Calvin?"

"A lot. I could see mountains on the moon with this telescope, Jupiter's moons, the rings of Saturn, star clusters, galaxies."

"Wow, that's pretty amazing."

"It certainly was for a 14 year old boy."

"Astronomy is a journey of imagination, isn't it, Calvin?"

"That's right. It is. Why do you seem so familiar to me?" Calvin asks.

"I attended one of your star parties about two years ago."

"Oh, really? Well I hope you enjoyed it, but how do you know me, and how is all of this happening?"

"My work allows me to get to know a lot of people, and what you're now experiencing is created and sustained by the radiantly energetic power of absolute love, and its unfathomable mystery. A mystery you are now part of, Calvin. You belong here."

"I feel like I'm home.""You are Calvin, and we're happy you're here. We have work for you."

"What kind of work?"

"You've been chosen to be a guide Calvin, to do what I'm now doing, helping people along in their journey and directing them on to their next destination. That's the work we have for you, but that's something you've been doing all your life, isn't it?"

"It's the only thing that ever made me feel truly alive."

"You didn't realize it at the time, but you made the choice to be here a long time ago."

"How will I know what I'm supposed to do?"

"You'll know. I'll help you learn."

"That makes me your apprentice."

"We're both apprentices here, but that work is for later. First, we want to celebrate your arrival. It's time to visit those places you dreamed about as a boy," Brianna says as she points to the sky.

"... Is that possible?"

"Of course, conventional notions of what is possible don't apply here Calvin. Look," Brianna points to the sky.

As Calvin looks upward, it quickly becomes darker, and stars become visible. The moon in its first quarter shines as it did so many nights before when he was a boy observing it with his telescope.

"Do you remember the first time you saw the moon in your telescope?"

"How could I forget? I was 12 years old. It was amazing, seeing craters and mountains."

"Let's go there Calvin. That's what you wished for many years ago. Now it's granted. Are you ready?"

"But, what about Max?"

"We couldn't leave him behind. He comes with us, of course."

Calvin suddenly sees a section of the ground he is standing on pull away rapidly from the surrounding landscape. He finds himself standing on a portion of ground about 100 feet wide, and circular in shape. Calvin, with his dog, and his mysterious companion Brianna, find themselves riding together as if on a magic carpet, up through the atmosphere, and beyond, as if mother earth herself was furnishing a private speck of her own substance to serve as a customized travel platform in their journey. He looks at the white roses a few yards away, and sees their healthy blooms unaffected by what's happening. Then he sees the sky get much brighter, and suddenly the moon and its incredibly detailed landscape fill the entire sky.

"What do think, Calvin?"

Astounded by the remarkable view he's taking in, Calvin is completely awestruck. "Wow!, with a capital W. I'd say we've arrived."

Curiosity turns to wonder as the lunar landscape Calvin once viewed through his telescope as a boy appears in spectacular abundance before him. Mountains, plains and craters, close enough to reveal individual rocks and boulders, pass before his eager gaze as he silently takes in the strange incredible scenery.

"I doubt if you've ever seen the moon like this through your telescope," says Brianna.

"Unbelievable, I don't believe I'm actually seeing this."

"This place will someday see sustained human activity, but for now it's a silent, uninviting world. Let's go to another place you once observed as a boy. Do you remember seeing Jupiter's moons through your telescope Calvin?"

"Yes, yes I do."

"That's our next destination, the outer planets, then the Orion nebula."

"The Orion nebula, are you kidding? How close can we get?"

"We'll pass right through it."

"Wow, the Orion nebula is hundreds of light years away. How far can we go?"

"As far as curiosity and imagination takes us."

Calvin Milner thinks to himself, How can this be happening? Seeing my parents again, being here with Max, and all of this. Is this a dream? It has to be.

He looks at his mysterious companion Brianna, and though her lips are mute and motionless he hears her voice saying,

"No Calvin, it's not a dream. The dream is what you've just awakened from."

Calvin looks once more at the view passing before him. The other-worldly appearance of chalky gray lunar mountains etched in absolute stillness against a black lunar sky is visually arresting. In marveled astonishment, he gropes for words.

"This is amazing. It's, it's incredible. How am I here? No dream could be this vivid. That must mean that I'm dead, but I don't remember dying."

Looking at Brianna, Calvin asks, "Am I dead?"

"Do you feel dead Calvin?"

"No I, I feel intensely alive, actually."

"And so you are."

"I'm trying to make sense of all this," Calvin says.

"Just enjoy the ride Calvin. It's more fun to marvel at the wonder, than to wonder at the marvel. Don't you think?"

"Uh, yes, yes I do."

"Do you remember seeing Jupiter's moons for the first time through your telescope Calvin?"

"I do. I remember it very well. It was a cold night in December."

A moment later their magic flying platform is moving through space again, and just as quickly, Calvin sees the planet Jupiter looming closer and closer, until the enormous gas giant dominates the entire field of view. The colored bands of turbulent gas streaking across the planet are mesmerizing in their appearance as the entire surface of this world seems to be in constant movement. The 'Great Red Spot', seen only as a small featureless oval through his boyhood telescope, now reveals itself to be the raging monster it is, and the churning fury of its irresistible vortex seems almost threatening in its relentless intensity. "Behold Calvin, a celestial titan. This world has saved your home planet many times. Thousands of comets and asteroids that would've crashed into Earth have been pulled away by this enormous cosmic protector, the planet Jupiter. Earth would never have spawned vertebrate life without the protection of this colossal orb."

With his dog Max still lying patiently only a few feet away, Calvin looks in deferential silence at the world he could only imagine as a young amateur astronomer. "Look Calvin we're coming up on Europa, one of Jupiter's four large moons. Let's have a closer look."

An instant later they're gently sailing over the frozen ice fields of Europa's frigid surface. The singular and utter strangeness of the alien world he sees is spellbinding. With the gigantic image of Jupiter's roiling surface serving as a colossal backdrop, Calvin looks on a frozen wasteland illuminated in the ghostly twilight of this distant world. Unending expanses of ice that extend in every direction appear to go on for countless miles, interrupted only by deep crevasses that seem to have no starting or end point. Flying

over the surface of this Jovian moon, Calvin observes a terrain that no human eyes have ever seen. This cold, forbidding, ice covered world was never more than a small white dot orbiting Jupiter when he observed it as a boy through his telescope in Pennsylvania, but it seems Pennsylvania is now 700 million miles away. Calvin is beside himself with amazement.

"You can guess what's beneath all this ice Calvin."

"Yes, an ocean of water."

"An ocean of water, that's also an ocean of life. Humans will eventually explore the subsurface ocean of Europa, and catalog its many life forms, but for us, that's another time, and another journey. Let's continue."

As Calvin hears these words, he tries to comprehend what he's experiencing. How can this be real? Is it possible that his consciousness is really traveling through the solar system? Calvin remembers often telling his friends that when he died he'd like a private tour of those cosmic wonders he'd observed with his telescope so many times in his life.

That wish has now apparently been granted, and granted spectacularly. Calvin looks down and sees his dog Max lying quietly a few feet away, just as he had so many years ago when he was a boy. He then looks back toward earth. He sees the sun and marvels at being able to look directly into its shrunken circumference. Its markedly diminished brightness and smaller size presents a pale comparison to the blinding intensity of a hot Pennsylvania sun in July, but evidently that was a very different time and a very different place. He's enthralled by the incredible view and as he watches the sun grow dimmer, he simultaneously senses a source of light coming from somewhere in the sky behind him.

"Would you like to see something interesting Calvin?"

Calvin turns to look behind him and is promptly astounded by what he sees. The enormous, point-blank image of the planet

Saturn presents itself in stunningly dramatic fashion. The sudden and unexpected sight of this gigantic planet of swirling gas, encircled by the majestic splendor of its elaborate system of rings, leaves him in startled amazement.

"I don't think you've ever seen Saturn like this through your telescope," Brianna says.

"We won't stop, but since we're in the neighborhood, I thought you'd like to have a look. What do you think?"

"It's, it's beyond thinking. I'm speechless."

As they get closer, the rings resolve into a countless multitude of individual chunks of ice stretching out before them. The endless movement of their slow shifting tumble has an almost hypnotic attraction for Calvin as he silently takes in the remarkable view. When they quickly pass through the rings, he's surprised to see how thin they are relative to their enormous width. Stunned by the visual impact of seeing Saturn at close range, and its magnificent ring system, Calvin is beside himself in silent wonder. "One more destination Calvin, and certainly the most dramatic."

"What's that?"

"It's out there," Brianna says, pointing to the stars.

As they quickly pull away from Saturn and its rings, Calvin sees the sun shrink in brightness and become just another star among the millions that comprise the Milky Way galaxy. He sees a richly populated band of distant stars that completely encircle him. Stars are everywhere. The panoramic view of the galactic plane that surrounds him is overwhelming in its visual grandeur.

"Look Calvin," Brianna says as she points to one side. "The center of the galaxy."

Turning to look, Calvin sees the added concentration of stars and what looks to be enormous clouds of dust occupying

the central hub of the Milky Way. No view or photograph taken through any telescope could ever rival the spectacular sight Calvin is now taking in with his unaided eyesight. The irresistible sense of miraculously rapid interstellar travel is persuasively confirmed as individual stars swiftly pass by.

Then, with unexpected suddenness, their destination looms gigantically in front of them. The giant star forming Orion nebula seems to swallow the entire sky as Calvin finds himself entering its tremendously vast interior, a stellar nursery so large that hundreds of solar systems have been born here. He sees four dazzling stars in the distance, and hears Brianna's voice as they quickly close in on them.

"Look Calvin, the Trapezium cluster, new stars and planetary worlds, new platforms for life and consciousness."

In shocked silence Calvin sees a sky vaulted with rich hues of red, blue, orange, and green, blended together in countless variations. Wispy, billowing swirls of thick cloud-like vapor streak the entire sky with intense colors in every direction. A gaseous shell of stupendous dimensions illuminated from within by the brilliant hot new stars of the Trapezium cluster seem to exist in this moment for Calvin Milner only. This is the Orion nebula. The staggering scale of its immensity leaves him in stupefied amazement.

"What do you think Calvin?"

"I can't think at all, at the moment. It's, it's almost too much. How can I be standing here with you and Max seeing this? My heart is beating. I'm breathing air, but there is no air here. How can this be happening? If I'm dead why do I still have a body?"

"It happens this way for everyone. It's reassuring, and makes the journey more familiar for those in transit."

"In transit to where? Why is all this happening?"

"In transit to their next incarnation; human bodies physically expire, but the soul moves continually onward. Passing through the mirage of death, its journey is endless."

"How does it find its direction?"

"It's guided by and from the daily habit of our own lives. That's the paradox of it, Calvin."

"I still don't understand. Can you explain it for me?"

"Mundane things like the words we use each day, how we look at a stranger, what we say to a request for help, may seem insignificant at the time, but over time these seemingly small things trace out a cameo profile of our soul's image to God, and infallibly reveal who and what we are. That's what determines our destiny. As the ephemeral and the eternal are woven from the same reality, each person weaves out of their own life the inescapable consequent reality of their afterlife. Our inclination becomes our destiny."

Calvin's mind and senses are reeling. What he's experiencing is beyond reason or human understanding. In silence, he looks skyward again at the over-arching canopy of cosmic wonder surrounding him.

"It's quite a sight isn't it?" Brianna says.

"I'm overwhelmed. This place is almost forbidding in a strange way. It makes me appreciate the good, green, earth even more, if you know what I mean."

"I do, Calvin. Long journeys make home a welcome sight. It's time for you to get back. Your parents would like to spend some time with you."

"How is that possible? My parents died years ago."

"There is no death Calvin, only life, and its relentless continuance. We have no choice in this mystery but to go onward."

"Why am I here?" Calvin asks. "For the same reason. The choices you made throughout your life have brought you here. In your case, you made a commitment long ago to serve. Life is calling us to something beyond ourselves and you answered that call. Do you remember what happened to you when you were seventeen?"

"You mean the car accident. I could never forget it." "It changed your life, didn't it?"

"Yes, very much."

"What nearly killed you became the catalyst that spurred you to a life of service."

"Yes, but, what an ordeal."

"It takes the furnace and the anvil to make a sword."

"It was a horrible experience. I was trapped in that car for two hours. I was the only one alive. I begged God to let me live.

That's the last thing I remembered until I woke up in the hospital three days later."

"I know. I was at your bedside."

"What do you mean?"

"I was one of the nurses that took care of you as you recovered."

"How can that be?"

"It's part of my work. I've been in and out of your world many times through the centuries Calvin, as you will be."

"Who are you?"

"I'm just a servant, the same as you."

"How can you be just like me if you can do all this?"

"I'm not causing all this to happen. This is the product of a supremely transcendent universal energy, an energy that's lucid enough to know the thoughts and actions of all of us and powerful enough to grant what each of us desire most. That's the good news, and the bad news, Calvin. It's the same news. We can't escape what we've freely chosen to become."

"I'm glad we got to spend this time together Calvin."

"So am I. Thank you."

"Your parents would like to see you. We have to get back, but before we do, I want to show you something."

Extending her arm and looking skyward, Calvin is reminded of the colossal magnitude of his surroundings. As he takes it in, Brianna says,

"Look Calvin, you have a privileged view of the majestic expanse of creation. What you'll see now is the dramatic intensity of its generative power."

"I think I can guess what that is."

"I'm sure you can. We're inside the Orion nebula and we know what happens here."

"Stars are born."

"That's right. This is a stellar nursery, and I think we're right on time to see a new arrival."

Suddenly Calvin Milner and company pull away from the illuminating light of the bright Trapezium star cluster and rapidly travel to a dark obscure region of the giant nebula, where Calvin sees a source of light that looks unusual. As he gets closer, he observes a huge flattened disk of dark dusty material. In its center, a gigantic ball of super-heated gas is spiraling in on itself. Its distinctly orange glow indicates high temperature and high density. "Do you know what it is, Calvin?" "Yes, it's a proto-star."

"We're about to witness the seminal power of primal creation. Let's have a closer look."

Pulling in closer, Calvin anticipates the momentous event he senses is imminent. "We're now about 90 million miles away, roughly the same distance of earth to the sun. This flattened disc of swirling gas has been spinning in on itself for 10 million years, getting hotter and hotter. The temperature is now over 27 million degrees, hot enough for something to happen, Calvin."

"Nuclear fusion."

"That's right." After a pause, Brianna says, "It's almost time. Behold Calvin, a star is born."

With no prior sign or indication, Calvin sees the nebulous mass instantly turn from a dusty orange to a white hot sphere of brilliant light, its brightness increasing by many orders of magnitude. The threshold moment when nuclear fusion begins has been reached. A titanic high speed blast wave of unimaginable force rushing outward in all directions begins to rapidly push away the enormous ring of gas and dust encircling the new star. The scale of explosive energy released from this event is beyond the descriptive power of human language to convey. As the blast wave expands outward, it reveals a number of much smaller rocky objects of varying size.

"Look Calvin, building blocks for future planets, no human eyes will ever see what you have just witnessed."

Calvin is at once bewildered, mystified, and enthralled by what he's seeing. Groping for words he simply says,

"This is astounding. I'm overwhelmed."

"All that you've seen, Calvin, astonishing as it is, has been created by a force that originates, contains, and governs all existent reality."

Calvin Milner's sense and understanding of that reality is suspended as his mind reels in baffling disbelief at what he's experiencing. A muted, almost incoherent stupefaction comes over him leaving him in stunned silence. "You've seen a lot Calvin. It's time to get back. Your parents want to see you."

As suddenly as they came, the trio pull away and soon the image of the huge Orion nebula, over 40 light years wide, shrinks into the retreating distance. Calvin once again sees stars passing by at an impossible speed, and in only a moment one particular star quickly gets brighter. As they get closer, the reassuring sight of earth comes into view and within seconds Calvin finds himself once again in the backyard of his boyhood home, the starting point for his incredible odyssey. It looks and feels as if he never left. Max, still lying faithfully on the ground a few feet away, is calm and relaxed as if all was normal. Calvin looks up near zenith to see the moon in its first quarter, and has trouble believing that an hour ago he flew just above its mountain tops. Perplexed and silent, he hears Brianna's voice break the spell of his distracted thoughts.

"I hope you enjoyed the tour, Calvin."

"Wow, I'm stunned. I don't know what to say, and now you say I'm going to see my parents," Calvin says as he sees the lights shimmering in the home where he grew up.

"I have to leave you now. I really enjoyed this time with you Calvin," replies Brianna.

"Where are you going?"

"I have to meet someone. I'll be back in a while. When I see you again, I'll show you what you'll be doing here as a new apprentice, but for now, goodbye."

Calvin looks at the house he grew up in as a boy and has difficulty comprehending the thought that his parents are inside, and in only moments he'll be with them again. Seeing the kitchen light on, with the window shutter closed exactly as he remembers it, triggers memories of when he was a boy using his telescope at night and how his mother would never forget to close the shutter to keep the outside area as dark as possible for his stargazing. Calvin Milner asks himself again if this is really happening. He has just been given a private tour of the moon and planets, gone beyond the solar system through deep space, witnessed the unbelievable power of star birth hundreds of light years away, and after all that he has been serenely returned to his boyhood home for an unexpected reunion with parents. How can all of this be happening? He looks back at Brianna but sees only his dog Max sitting looking back at him in steadfast loyalty.

Then the scene around Calvin abruptly changes, and he finds himself seated in his mother's kitchen as she washes dishes a few feet away. Her relaxed and casual demeanor is as reassuringly familiar as when he was a growing boy. Flooded with deep feelings of love and belonging, Calvin surrenders himself to the blissful contentment he's experiencing and without feeling the need to ask or answer any questions, he sits watching his mother as he had so many times before as a child. As Calvin's mother turns to face him, he sees a face that has lovingly nurtured him for so many years. Her radiant smile seems to personify all human benevolence. Calvin intuitively senses that this is not the time or place for questions. The absolute love and complete acceptance he feels somehow goes beyond the need for spoken words. Blissfully silent, he hears the soft sweet voice of his mother.

"Looks like a good night for star gazing. Did you see anything interesting?

Chapter Two: The Uncaring Father

In a suburb of Chicago, a man sits alone in his living room. His name is Shane Keller and today is the first day of a two week vacation he's been happily anticipating. He sits, relaxed and comfortable, in his easy chair waiting for a cable TV technician to arrive and restore service that's been interrupted. Though Shane Keller has been looking forward to this vacation for some time, he has no plans to do anything but stay home and enjoy his leisurely respite. Shane Keller is married, and the father of an only child. Through his daughter Linda he has two grandchildren, but because he and his daughter have been estranged for nearly two years, he has no contact with them. Making no effort to begin healing the sorely strained relations with his daughter, Mr. Keller has convinced himself that it's not his responsibility to initiate the process of reconciliation. Shane Keller is a man who has difficulty admitting he could be wrong about certain things.

His daughter Linda hasn't called or visited her parents' home since this family feud reached its boiling point almost two years ago, when Linda's youngest son was hospitalized with leukemia. The life-threatening illness nearly killed Shane Keller's grandson and his struggle with the disease required a lengthy stay in the hospital, but for some reason Mr. Keller never took the time to visit the boy even though it was a mere 20 minute drive away. In Shane Keller's mind his self-excused reasoning always seemed plausible; he was too tired after work; there was an important ball game on

TV he wanted to watch, or something around the house needed to be done. After repeated requests by his daughter Linda to visit his grandson, it eventually became clear to her that her father was simply not interested. With remission of her son's disease and the return of his health came something else: an adamant refusal on Linda's part to forgive her father for what she regards as callous treatment of her son and her family. Most damning of all, from her point of view, is the fact that after her son returned home from his medical ordeal, not a single phone call came from his grandfather to inquire about his health. For these reasons, Linda's feelings are bitter and intractable. Her enmity, however implacable to her father, does not extend to her mother, who does her best while being in the middle of this simmering stand-off.

Shane Keller's wife, Diane, tries her best to maintain a semblance of normalcy with her family, even though that means doing without the pleasure of having her daughter and grandchildren visit her at home. The dysfunctional arrangement seems abnormal in the extreme for Diane, and has put a considerable strain on her marriage. She's always known of her husband's inveterate habit of not being involved in the lives and interests of others, but she never thought it would so negatively affect her home and family life. Knowing that this disheartening family dilemma she finds herself in is completely unnecessary makes her predicament seem even more galling and utterly pointless.

Adding to her frustration today is the fact that she's just learned an old high school girlfriend of hers was in town last weekend and called to see when she could come to visit, but because Diane's husband failed to relay the message, she never got to see that old friend. She finds it difficult to understand how her husband could fail to convey this simple message. Her grumbling aggravation grows into general resentment as she walks into the living room to ask him about it.

"Why didn't you tell me Sue Beckman called last Saturday?"

"Oh yeah, I forgot."

"She was my best friend all through high school. She lives in Seattle. She doesn't come here that often. I wanted to see her."

"I'm sorry. What do you want me to do?" he asks as he reaches for a stale slice of pizza left over from the night before.

"I don't understand, all you had to do was let me know she called."

"I said I forgot, okay?"

Resigned to her frustration, Diane suppresses her anger and tries to elicit a different response to a different subject.

"I'm driving over to see Linda and the kids. You remember her. She's our daughter. Is there anything you want me to tell her?"

"Nope," he says curtly.

"That's what I thought. I should've known better to ask."

"Come on, it's a big deal over nothin'. I don't know what she's so angry about."

With this rude rebuff still fresh in her ears, Diane simply walks from the room, and out of the front door. After lighting a cigarette, Shane Keller looks at his watch to check the time. Seconds later the doorbell rings, signaling the expected arrival of the cable repair man.

"Mr. Keller?"

"Yeah, that's me."

"Hi, I'm Robert with Constellation Cable. My work order says you have intermittent signal loss."

"I was watchin' the game yesterday and it just went blank."

"You mean it went static, no signal at all?"

"That's right, nothin'."

"Okay, let me check a few things out, and make sure you're getting a strong signal."

"Yeah, do whatever you have to. The game's comin' on later tonight, first game o' the playoffs. I don't wanna miss it."

"I know. I'll be watching it too. Cubs have a good team this year."

"Well, they finally got some pitchin'. If a team doesn't have good pitchin', they don't have anything."

As the repair man begins his work, Mr. Keller hears his phone ring.

"Hello, hey Steve, How's it goin'? Uh yeah, I'm due back on the 23rd. What? He wants to know if I can come in on the 22nd? No, can't do it. Well, so what? His daughter's gettin' married. That doesn't mean anything to me. Listen, Steve, it's my vacation, and I want every day of it. I don't care if it is the last day. I'm not comin' back to work a day early so he can over-eat at his daughter's wedding. It won't happen. Okay Steve, you too, go Cubs."

Hanging up the phone, Mr. Keller voices his annoyance.

"Hmm, somebody callin' for his friend who needs a day off, you're barkin' up the wrong tree pal."

"Who's that, a coworker?" the repairman asks.

"Another driver wants me to cut my vacation a day early so he can go to his daughter's wedding. That's not my responsibility. They should've worked that out beforehand."

Looking intently at the repair man Mr. Keller says, "Don't ever get involved in someone else's problems. All it does is drag you down."

Pointing to a frame mounted on the wall of his living room with an image of three over-sized capital letters printed in black with a white background for emphasis, Mr. Keller drives his point home.

"You see those letters on that wall: D, G, I? I put that up there as a little reminder. You know what they stand for?"

"What's that?" the repairman asks.

"Don't get involved. D, G, I, don't get involved, that's what, and that's the way I choose to live my life," Keller says emphatically. "I mean, don't get involved period, ever, at all, because when you do it's gonna cost ya. It'll cost ya money, time, aggravation, something. It's not worth it. Then if ya do help somebody, you know they're gonna ask you again."

"Yeah, sometimes that happens," the repair man says.

"Not sometimes, it's always that way. You're young. Take some good advice from someone much older. You'll save yourself a lot o' heartache. Take care of number one, and only number one. This sappy nonsense about helping your fellow man is a bunch o' shit as far as I'm concerned."

"I don't know," the repair man says defensively.

"I do. Every year at Christmas the Salvation Army sets up their sympathy bucket in front o' the grocery store I go to. The same guy is there year after year. When he sees me comin' he looks the other way. That's the way I like it, and if you're smart that's the way you'll like it too. People don't like me for it, but I don't care. My daughter hasn't spoken to me now for two years, doesn't bother me in the least."

"Well, she'll probably change her mind," the repair man says.

"She'll have to, cause I'm not changin' mine."

Refocusing on his work, the repair man says,

"I found your problem. You had a frayed wire that was shorting out your connection. Let's see if we have a picture."

After turning on the TV, and seeing all program channels restored, the repair man quickly gathers his tools to leave.

"Good job, that didn't take long," Mr. Keller says.

"It was a simple fix. Okay, I'll leave my card with you Mr. Keller in case you have any problems. You're under our maintenance plan so there's no charge today."

"Great, so that's it?"

"That's it." the repair man says.

"I appreciate you comin' over."

"Well, we appreciate your business. Enjoy the game."

"I will, and remember what I said, D, G, I, don't get involved."

"Have a good day Mr. Keller."

As Shane Keller walks back to his easy chair, he has no idea he's experiencing the last few moments of his earthly life. After sitting down, Mr. Keller reaches for another cigarette and suddenly feels a sharp stabbing pain in his chest and a tingling numbness in his right hand and arm. As he quietly sits back, a terrible apprehension comes over him. Shane Keller is having a heart attack. Trying to be absolutely still doesn't help, and as the pain increases it feels like the weight of a car being placed on his chest. Now only moments remain. Through his agony he hears a preview of tonight's play-off game from the TV announcer. It seems as if he's hearing and seeing it from hundreds of feet away. As his head slowly rolls back to its rest, he sees the framed picture on the wall. Shane Keller takes in the last scene his eyes will ever see of this world, the framed image of three capital letters D, G, and I. A slowly enveloping darkness settles in as the life of Shane Keller comes to its close.

Then, as if waking within a dream, he sees himself reliving a scene from his childhood when he nearly drowned while swimming in a river near his parents' home. The desperately frantic struggle of the 11 year old boy is as fresh and vivid for Shane Keller as the day he experienced it. Seeing the image of panic stricken fright on the boy's face as he gulps in mouthfuls of river water is a shuddering apparition. He also sees the strong arm of the stranger who pulled him to safety that day so many years ago, a stranger who chose to get involved. The scene fades again to darkness. Shane Keller then finds himself walking down a long sidewalk. In the distance he can see a long row of houses on each side of an unfamiliar street.

Mr. Keller wonders where and what this place is. He remembers being home and the terrible chest pain he experienced. Whatever this place is, at least that horrific pain hasn't followed him here. He wonders if he's dead, but how can he be? He's walking forward, feeling the wind in his face, hearing the normal sounds of daily life, seeing what looks like a world very similar to the one he's always known.

If he's not dead, then where exactly is he? This must be a dream, or is it? As he continues walking, he sees a figure ahead coming toward him. He can just barely determine that it's a woman. Within a few minutes the woman approaches him and, by her greeting, seems to know him.

"Hello, Mr. Keller."

"Who are you?"

"My name is Brianna."

"What do you want?"

"Very little, I'm here to welcome you to this place, and help you get to your destination."

"What destination? I have no destination."

"We all have destinations waiting for us, Mr. Keller. You're no exception."

"What place is this?"

"This place is the sum total of personal choices and preferences made over a lifetime, the distilled essence, and logical outcome of those choices, your choices, Mr. Keller. You might think of it as an inheritance, a self-bequeathed inheritance, and it's time for you to collect what's rightfully yours."

"I don't know what you're talkin' about."

"I know you don't, not yet," Brianna says.

"Yeah, well, I don't know where this place is, but I don't plan on stayin'. You do what you want lady. I'm walkin' up to that town and find out how to get back home. I don't believe anything you say. How do ya like that?"

"Oh, I have no preference in the matter, Mr. Keller."

"Yeah right, adios lady."

"Hasta la vista, Mr. Keller."

With this, Shane Keller turns away from the strange woman named Brianna and begins walking toward the small town ahead of him.

It seems like just another day, in any residential section of any town or city across the country. Commonly familiar things in their usual place project an air of normalcy. A sidewalk leading him on, punctuated with driveway entrances every forty feet or so, looks no different than any in his memory. As he walks forward, he sees an endless row of houses, all with porches, only a few feet from the sidewalk. There are bicycles and children's toys in the yards of many of the homes reassuring him that nothing is amiss in this urban landscape. Looking into the distance ahead, he sees no one. It seems he has this world to himself, and so he continues. He walks on and notices a school bus parked on the other side of the street in the distance ahead. As he gets closer, he can see there are children inside and his forward gait finally brings him to the point where the crowded school bus is directly across the road from where he's standing. The children in the bus are all very young. Hearing their noisy gaggle spurs a cluster of memories from his own childhood. Shane Keller almost forgets the sobering words he heard from the mysterious woman called Brianna. In his mind he tries to make sense of where he is, and what's happening around him. He thinks to himself, there's nothing to worry about. This place seems okay. What could happen?

Everything around him is normal, and predictably typical of any neighborhood street he's ever seen. All is as it should be. The sight of a school bus filled with happy children confirms in him a general sense that this is a benevolent place. What and where ever this new world is, it seems not very different from the one Shane Keller was born into, and lived all his life. As he stands there motionless, several children see him and begin waving at him. Their friendly smiles evoke no response on his part and he simply stands there, looking back at them. Then he unexpectedly notices a strong odor. The unmistakable smell of gasoline is in the air around him. Looking beneath the school bus, he sees a steady trickle of fuel coming from the gas tank, and flowing all the way into the gutter, and down the street. Moments later, a passing car goes by and Shane Keller sees the hand from the passenger side carelessly flick the lit cigarette into the gutter where it ignites the trickled stream of gasoline.

Time slows, and apprehension quickens as he sees the flame gradually make its way toward the parked school bus. Instantly perceiving the danger, he looks to warn the driver, but for some reason the driver is absent. These children are alone. He knows what he has to do, but when he tries to move his feet, they are completely unresponsive. An inexplicable paralysis makes it impossible to move his body from the waist down. He sees the approaching flame getting closer to the bus 60 feet away. In an attempt to warn the unsuspecting children he tries to speak but his voice is slow, garbled, and unintelligible. Unable to express himself, his frantic arm waving draws only curiosity and laughter from the children looking at him. The advancing flames continue, following the trickle of gasoline back to its source now less than 40 feet away. Shane Keller tries again to move his legs and feet, but finds he is no longer ambulant. Dumbfounded over his inability to move or speak, complete psychological panic seizes his thoughts.

Time slows even further, as he thinks, is this nightmare really going to happen?He looks on fearfully as the flame continues its progress. Trying to point at the imminent danger isn't any more successful. The children mistake his muddled incoherence for a happy game of pantomime and begin mimicking his unintelligible gestures. The moving flame is now only a few yards away from the dripping fuel tank and a frightful realization comes over him. He'll be able to do nothing but watch the horrible event unfold in front of him. He sees the smiling innocence of faces looking back at him, completely oblivious to what's about to happen. The face of one child in particular holds his attention. He fixes his gaze on the beautiful young girl who looks to be no older than ten. With her well-groomed straight black hair, and oriental face, her diffident smile, and angelic expression, she seems to say 'I'm sorry', as if she was silently apologizing to the man she sees across the street waving his arms incomprehensibly, as if she is ashamed for the other children not showing respectful deference to an elder.

As linear time comes to a slow crawl for Shane Keller, he sees the flame is now directly under the fuel tank. His anguished gaze is transfixed on the beautiful young face looking back at him, a face he'll remember for a very long time. From the periphery of his view he sees the flame rise from the asphalt to the leaking fuel tank. The explosion that follows is instantaneous as fire engulfs the interior of the school bus, and the noisy banter of happy youngsters is suddenly replaced by the shrieking fright of children about to be burned to death. Seeing their terrified struggle as they pound on the windows to escape, their agonizing ordeal is unbearable to witness, yet he finds it impossible to turn away. He looks again and sees the girl in a panic of absolute fear. She manages to look back at the man who appears to be passively witnessing the terrible event from across the street, admonishing him with an expression that seems to say, 'why didn't you warn us?' As their eyes lock, her hair and clothing erupt in flame. One last paroxysm of screaming agony and the pathetic cries of the innocent fall silent. The inferno becomes so hot, the metal roof of the bus melts away. A pall of chemically laden black smoke rises, and with it, the ghastly smell of burning human flesh.

Psychologically traumatized, Shane Keller still finds it impossible to move his legs. Then he hears a siren wailing, then another. Two fire trucks quickly appear, and a frenzy of activity ensues. Time resumes its normal pace, and Shane Keller feels his temporary paralysis suddenly lift. Coherent speech returns with all his prior faculties, and he finds himself in the immediacy of the present moment. He hears the jarring clamor of men with axes cutting open the side of the school bus that is now only a charred ruin. With every sharply pounding stroke the terrible realization of what just happened is driven deeper into his psyche. Flashing lights and sirens signal the arrival of emergency medical teams and their shouting voices heighten the frantic intensity of the moment. Within seconds, they're ready for action and wait only for the fire to be extinguished, but all effort is useless. It's too late. The burned off roof allows bright sunlight to reveal a horrific scene. The bus's interior had become so hot that most of the seats were burned down to their frames, but worst of all, the blackened wreck shows the desperate struggle of the young children who perished, all 29 of them. The sizzling low intensity hiss of skin and muscle tissue being cooked is heard by those first entering the wreck, and the haunting nemesis that every fireman finds impossible to forget, the unmistakable smell of burned human flesh, hangs dreadfully in the air. Hopes of saving anyone from this tragedy are instantly dispelled. There is nothing that can be saved here. Medical teams poised in scrambled readiness have their worst fears confirmed when a fireman walks toward them shaking his head. The two words he utters are hopeless.

"No survivors."

"God in heaven."

The frantic urgency of a rescue effort is instantly transformed into the grim resignation of a recovery operation to identify the dead. As members of the medical team enter the bus, a news van suddenly arrives. A camera man and a female reporter quickly start filming the awful scene and interviewing by-standers. A small

crowd of on-lookers has gathered and are learning about what just occurred.

Shane Keller, still standing in the same spot, is shocked by the appalling scene he wanted so much to prevent. The news woman and her camera man walk toward him, along with many others. Before he has time to consider what he'll say, a microphone is held only inches away from him, and the all-seeing circular eye of a camera lens is staring at him.

Before he can think, he's abruptly asked a question by the news reporter.

"Sir, did you see what happened here?"

"Well yes, I was walking, and uh—"

Before finishing his answer, a voice is loudly heard from the growing number of onlookers gathering around him and, in bitter indignation, a woman points at Shane Keller.

"That man, that man right there, he saw it all. He watched the whole thing happen. I saw him from my window. He stood there for five minutes before that bus caught on fire. He didn't make a move to warn those poor kids. I watched him, no good bastard."

"Is that true sir?" the reporter asks.

"Well, I tried but—"

"He didn't try to do anything. I saw him. I don't know how you can live with yourself, mister."

"No, I wanted to help those kids. I did, but—"

"But what?" the reporter asks.

"I tried to move my legs but, I couldn't. For some reason, I just couldn't."

"You say you couldn't move your legs. Why didn't you yell, or say something to warn them?"

"I wanted to, but I couldn't speak. I tried. I did." "There's nothing wrong with your voice now though. Is there?"

"No, there isn't."

Again, the woman's bitter reproach is loudly heard.

"He's a liar. I watched that man with my own eyes walk down the street no more than 20 minutes ago. There's nothing wrong with his legs. You expect us to believe that?"

"No, it's true. I couldn't. I couldn't move my legs."

"You say you couldn't move your legs or speak but you can do both now?" the reporter asks.

"I know it's hard to believe, but it's true. I wanted to help. I really did."

"And you expect us to believe that?"

As the burned-out shell of what used to be a school bus filled with children is thoroughly drenched with water, word spreads to rescue personnel about the man across the street being questioned about passively watching the tragedy unfold. Suddenly a woman runs up to the fire truck and frantically confronts the crew chief.

"Where's my daughter? Where's my daughter? Her name is Lauren Scott. Where is she? Please tell me where my daughter is."

"Please ma'am, we don't have that information yet."

"I wanna see my daughter. Just tell me where she is," she desperately asks before falling to her knees. After she's helped away, the fire crew chief looks over to where Shane Keller is standing and walks toward him. Seeing his approach, the news team shift their attention to him, hoping to get all the information they can, but he says nothing as he walks past them. Still carrying the axe he used to enter the school bus, he ignores the reporters' questions and instead walks directly up to Shane Keller.

"Come here. I wanna show you something," he says.

The restrained but intimidating demeanor of the stout fireman is enough to convince Shane Keller to follow and after being led up to entrance of the bus, he is told to enter. Upon making his way into the scorched ruin a grisly image immediately presents itself. The visceral impact of seeing piles of charred corpses where children clung together in a hopeless attempt to protect themselves is almost unbearable. As Shane Keller stands transfixed by the ghastly image before him, he hears the voice of the fireman standing behind him.

"I don't know what you did or didn't do mister, but if you stood by and watched this happen when you could've done something to prevent it, then I hope this haunts you forever. Have a good look."

Having made his point, the fireman leaves Shane Keller standing alone in the steamy, water-soaked death trap. The intense urge to get away from this terrible place is overwhelming, and as he hastily turns to exit, he slips on the wet floor of the school bus. To break his fall, he reaches for something to support him and mistakenly grabs the charred shoulder of one of the dead children. Startled by the frightening mishap, he lurches back and bumps into another corpse. Then, wiping the sweat from his face, he inadvertently smears it with the blackened ash of what was once living human flesh. Beside himself in panicked confusion, he exits the school bus as fast as he can, quickly walks past the gaggle of onlookers, and finally retreats from the awful scene.

Unsure of where to go, he retraces his steps the way he came. This time however, those same houses and porches that were so empty an hour ago when Shane Keller walked into this neighborhood, are now filled with the icy stares of countless faces who coldly watch his every step. As he walks on, he sees people pointing at him and hears them whispering. His face, still smeared with black ash, marks him as the one who watched as the terrible school bus fire killed so many children. A feeling of intense discomfort impels him to quicken his pace but instead his gait becomes slower as if his legs are weighed down by some invisible force. Each step becomes labored and deliberate as he trudges onward. Occasionally looking back at the unfriendly

expressions of censuring disapproval, Shane Keller feels the eyes watching him as if they are needles piercing his flesh, and wonders when this nightmare will end. After what seems like an interminable length of time walking block after block, house after house, and porch after porch, he finally reaches the last house.

As he passes, he looks over to see the face of an oriental woman that bears the unmistakable resemblance of the young girl on the school bus who'd caught his attention before it erupted in flames. Was this her mother? Looking at her face, he thinks, how could it not be? Her eyes seem to plead more bitterly than any words ever could, and in their unspoken anguish he could hear one word uttered plaintively: "why?"

Shane Keller looks into the caustic stare of the newly bereaved mother and tries to speak, but before he does she dismissively turns away as if saying, "there's nothing you can say to justify yourself. Your words are not worth hearing." The poignant intensity of the moment is more than he can bear, and he feels an irrepressible urge to escape from this place as quickly as possible. He continues walking and finally reaches the open highway, leaving behind the town's residents and the gauntlet of their incessant stares.

Relieved to have such a terrible experience behind him, Shane Keller keeps walking as he tries to make sense of what just happened. He thinks this must be a nightmarish dream he's going through. It can't possibly continue. How can it? Everything about this place defies logic and rational explanation. It can't be real, and yet at the same time it feels intensely real. What could it possibly mean? Whatever it is, Shane Keller senses he has no choice in being part of what's happening around him. An unsettling intuition seeps into his mind that this reality, and his reality are now the same reality. As a somber fatalism takes hold of his thoughts, he continues onward and, in the distance, he sees a figure walking toward him. As he gets closer the discernible image of the woman he'd encountered earlier becomes clear, the same woman who had welcomed him to this strange, unfriendly world. Moments later she re-greets him.

"Hello Mr. Keller."

"I remember you. You were the first person I saw when I came to this place. You were the one who said you wanted to help me get to my destination. That was you. 'We all have destinations.' You said that. Remember?"

"Of course."

"Well lemme tell you somethin' lady. You didn't do anything to 'help me with my destination' as you put it. Instead you welcomed me into a nightmare. That's what you did."

"What happened, Mr. Keller?"

"I'll tell ya what happened. I watched a bus load o' kids get burned to death, and though I had nothing to do with it, I was blamed. That's what happened."

"Well, at least you didn't have to get involved Mr. Keller."

"What?"

"I said at least you didn't have to get involved."

"What's that supposed to mean?"

"No more or less than what it implies."

"If you're talking about what happened back there with that fire, I wanted to warn those kids. No, I wanted to help. I did. I didn't choose this place. You did. You created this place and whatever it is, it's worse than bein' in hell."

"I didn't create or choose this place Mr. Keller. You did."

"Are you crazy?"

"No, but sometimes I think it might help."

"What are you talkin' about? How did I create this place? That's ridiculous."

"There are an infinity of worlds, Mr. Keller, realms known and unknown, visible and invisible. There's always one to perfectly match every personality and this one matches yours."

"I have no idea what you're talking about."

"You will."

"Lady, you must be insane. How does this place match my personality?"

"It's very simple. You wanted to live in a world where you didn't have to get involved. This is that world Mr. Keller, but a world where people don't get involved is a world prone to calamity, like the calamity you witnessed back there."

"I don't belong here and I'm not staying here."

"I'm afraid you have no power to leave this place, Mr. Keller. Look on the bright side: you'll never have to get involved."

"You keep saying that. That's not who I am."

"You are Shane Keller, aren't you?"

"Yes."

"D. G. I., Don't Get Involved, that was your credo. Do you remember the last person you spoke with before you came here, when you were at home in Chicago?"

"You mean my wife Diane?""No, after that."

"I don't know. I was ... you mean the cable guy?"

"Yes."

"What about him?"

"Do you remember the advice you gave him? D.G.I., don't get involved is what you said, and it's also what you lived Mr. Keller. How revealing it is that the last thing you would leave to the world is advice to a stranger counseling him to close his mind and heart to pity and empathy. That's really what D.G.I. implies, isn't it Mr. Keller?"

"Come on. I said a lot o' things."

"You sure did. You sure did."

"What about my wife? I can't stay here. She needs me."

"Yes, your wife Diane, that good woman. You don't have to worry about her. She'll be fine. She'll mourn your passing, more from her integrity than your deserving. She doesn't need you as much as you think, more likely the contrary. You treated her more like an attachment to your life than your partner. For 28 years she stood beside you in silent patience. How many of her happy hours, rightfully hers, has she traded for your inconsiderate stubbornness?"

"I worked hard for my family for those 28 years, almost never missed a day o' work. Who do you think I did that for?"

"Mostly yourself; but yes, you paid your bills on time, didn't you Mr. Keller?"

"That's right, all of them."

"But even if you were a bachelor, you would've had to work and pay bills like anyone else."

"I did my part."

"What part is that Mr. Keller?"

"Are you saying I didn't provide for my family?"

"You provided shelter, but little comfort. You provided food and clothing, but not much love. You did what was required, and very little that wasn't."

"So what happens now?"

"You'll continue on your journey, Mr. Keller. Right now, for you that means just keep walking. The next town is only a few miles away, and then after that the next, and the next, and the next."

"And what if I refuse to go?"

"How long do you think you can stand here, Mr. Keller? A day, a year, a million years? Your destination will always be waiting, for as long as it takes. You will move on. You have no choice."

Silent and crestfallen, Shane Keller stares blankly at his counterpart as she bids him goodbye.

"Well, I have to go. I have to see my new apprentice."

"Wait, I'll, go with you."

"That's impossible. We must wear those garments that we've woven from the fabric of our lives, you yours, and me mine."

Perplexed, Shane Keller turns his back on the woman named Brianna as if turning his back on all he's heard. When he turns again to look at her, she's gone. He calls out, but to no avail. After several minutes Shane Keller begins walking again.

Chapter Three: The Sex Addict

On a gray Tuesday morning, a woman is walking down a side street in one of the outskirts of Atlanta, Georgia and she's doing so for a reason. Her slow pace and alluring appearance signal to those who drive by what her intent is. She doesn't want to do what she's doing, and she never made a conscious decision to earn money this way, but she lives in a world where economic opportunities are scarce to nonexistent, and where the raw edge of economic need is a daily experience. With a four year old daughter, and very little financial help from others, she feels very much on her own. She doesn't think of herself as a prostitute, but as a person who's just struggling to keep her life together, and she tells herself this is only temporary until things are more secure. As she walks onward, she regularly looks in both directions and is always wary of the police. Her furtive world is very stressful and can sometimes be dangerous. In this illicit game she frequently finds herself riding in a stranger's car with only the hope that he'll bring her back unharmed. She wears a cross on her necklace and trusts in providence.

Glancing ahead, she sees a man turn into the parking lot in front of her. With the car waiting in place and the engine running the driver sends an unspoken signal, and when he rolls down the window and looks directly at her, he makes his intent clear. Seconds later she gets in the man's car and looks at the face of her day's first customer. His name is Keith Chandler, and he's a compulsive sex addict.

Mr. Chandler is a man who has succumbed to a personal weakness that's become a serious fault and is now a crippling vice. For Mr. Chandler, sex has nothing to do with the joyful affection shared between two people physically expressing their love for each other. For him the act is nothing more than a form of self-gratification. The overwhelming sensation of pleasure he experiences when he copulates with a woman blinds him to the fact that he's essentially doing nothing more than masturbating with a human prop, an experience completely devoid of any emotional intimacy. Though married, he prefers prostitutes to his wife, and is uncomfortable with the genuinely honest affection she offers. After inheriting his father's real estate business and rental properties, the added income provided the time, money and cover needed to lead the double life he lives. The plausible rationale of needing to meet clients and tenants effectively screens his clandestine involvement in the illicit world of sex for money that he inhabits. Maintaining an apartment kept secret from his wife gives him the privacy to indulge his powerful habit, and minimizes the risk of being discovered.

Keith Chandler has copulated with hundreds of women since he took his marriage vows. Once the visual trigger of seeing a woman's healthy body claims his attention, an irresistible pull that always ends in sexual gratification seizes him. It's an urge as difficult to resist as any heroin or cocaine addiction and for some, like Keith Chandler, resistance is next to impossible. That ultimate throb of orgasmic delight that floods his brain with the chemistry of intense pleasure is now its master.

For the past three years it has driven him to act out his sexual urges at least several times a week, but in the last few months he's increased the frequency of his encounters. Another aspect of his escalating compulsive behavior has dramatically augmented the health risk of his reckless promiscuity. To heighten the erotic intensity of sexual intercourse, he has stopped using condoms. Abandoning even a semblance of restraint, his life has essentially become an extension of his neurotic fixation on sexual pleasure, and now he's sitting in his car, alone with a willing female. She tries to feel him out and begins with the same question she asks every man she encounters.

"You ain't a cop are you?"

"No, don't worry."

With this terse reply he drives away, and they disappear into the common flow of traffic.

Meanwhile, twelve miles away, Mrs. Keith Chandler - who believes her husband is showing a property this morning - is feeling uneasy about things in general, and her husband in particular. She's known for some time that her marriage is in serious decline. The near complete absence of intimacy with her husband she naively ascribes to what she believes is the demanding work he's engaged in. Dealing with so many people in managing a real estate business and its properties she assumes must be physically and emotionally taxing. This could be why he's so inattentive, but this reasoning is not as plausible as it once seemed. Her husband's behavior has, in recent months, become even more cold and unresponsive, and she's reached a point where she can no longer ignore the crisis that now threatens her marriage.

Laura Chandler is not an unhappy person by temperament, and she will not allow herself to be made unhappy by the actions of another, including her husband. She is wise enough to know that the beautiful home she lives in can never be a substitute for a stable, happy marriage. She earnestly wants to save her marriage and is resolved to find the reason why her husband is so aloof and uncaring. Her suspicions center on one hunch: there must be another woman. With these thoughts occupying her mind,

Laura Chandler is beside herself as she walks into her kitchen this morning. After pouring a cup of coffee she sits down and reaches for something in her pocket. It's a key, inadvertently left by her husband in his jeans that she washed earlier.

Not thinking much of it at first, a thought suddenly crosses her mind. Could this be the key to the room in the back of the garage that's always locked? Told by her

husband that it contains expensive tools and must be kept locked for security, she never had a reason or the means to open the door. She looks at the key and sees no connection to anything that might cause her marital problems. As she sits thinking about her situation, she feels the key touching her fingers. The subtle, tactile quality of it is an almost imperceptible presence in the background of her agitated thoughts.

While sipping her coffee, she wonders how she will broach this subject with her husband when he returns home later in the evening. If she could only find an answer to this problem, her life could resume its normal course. Laura Chandler's intuition informs her that her husband has a secret he's concealing from her. What could it be? she asks herself as she looks again at the key in her hand. She examines it more intently and thinks, if I could open my husband's heart and mind as easily as this key opens a door, I would know this hidden secret, if it were only that easy. After a final sip of coffee she looks at the wall clock and casually slips the key into her pocket. Despite being preoccupied with her marital problems, daily obligations must be met, and a trip to the grocery store is certainly one of them. As she prepares to leave, she thinks tonight will be the time to fully air her feelings to her husband. After a candle lit dinner of his favorite meal to set the mood, she'll gently but firmly tell her husband what's been bothering her. Laura Chandler is optimistic that things will somehow work out.

Within minutes she enters the garage, gets into her car, and reaches for the car keys. The feel of her keys reminds her of the single key she put in her pocket earlier. Instead of starting the car, she pauses and looks over at the locked door in the corner of the garage, and wonders if that key will open it. Curiosity builds as she sits motionless. This is silly, she thinks to herself, and inserts the ignition key, but before starting the car she pauses again, and glances once more at the locked door only 20 feet away from her. It somehow seems to beckon her, as if it has a dark secret to tell. She slowly gets out of the car and walks to the strong metal door and tries to open it. She finds it locked as expected. Then she reaches into her pocket and pulls out the key she found while washing her husband's jeans earlier.

Slowly unlocking the door, she expects to see a nondescript collection of tools and equipment common to any workshop, but after entering and turning on the bright florescent ceiling light, Laura Chandler is presented with a sight that's totally unexpected. Dozens of pictures with graphic images of women engaging in every conceivable sex act adorn the walls. A few feet away on a small table lay scads of adult magazines. After picking one up, Laura Chandler gets a close up look at the world of hard core pornography, but even this will seem tame compared to what she's about to discover. Mrs. Chandler is shocked by the volume of the material she's seeing, hundreds of DVDs on the shelf, dozens of magazines, sex toys, vibrators, and all the acquired paraphernalia of a full blown male sex addict. After taking several DVDs from the shelf, a cursory look at their titles is blunt and immediately revealing. 'Teen Sluts Get Rammed', 'Slow Suck Masters', and 'Tag Teaming Tanya,' are just a few of the hundreds on the shelf. Then Laura Chandler sees twenty or thirty DVDs that look different. She notices they have no commercial jacket and appear to be privately recorded. As she picks one up, she sees the name 'Julie,' written with a magic marker on the front. The presence of a TV and DVD player spurs her curiosity and impels her to see for herself what's been recorded. Turning on the DVD player, and opening the disc tray, Laura Chandler is apprehensive and more than a little uneasy about what she's about to see.

The first image she sees is her husband's face looking into what appears to be a wall mounted camera as he slightly adjusts its viewing angle. After he pulls away, Mrs. Chandler sees a room with a large centrally placed couch. After going blank momentarily, she sees a young woman enter the scene accompanied by her husband Keith Chandler. She looks no more than 20 years old and her suggestive style of dress strongly hint that she's a prostitute. By all indications, she seems unaware of the camera recording her activity. A hidden microphone also records their conversation, a conversation that doesn't last very long, as Mrs. Chandler hears her husband say to the young woman, "Okay Julie, you know the routine. It's time to earn your 200 bucks."

With these words the young woman undresses Laura Chandler's husband and within minutes is performing oral sex on him. Mrs. Chandler watches in shock as he completely gives himself over to the carnal intensity of addictive sexual pleasure. After a few minutes, Laura Chandler notices a change in her husband's behavior. His expression becomes cold, and contemptuous; the same expression that Mrs. Chandler has been seeing more frequently on the face of her husband in the last few months. She sees him become more aggressive and demanding with the woman. The words Laura Chandler hears her husband speak are deeply disturbing.

"Oh yeah, suck it hot bitch. Suck it bitch. Take it all, you fuckin' whore."

With her eyes and ears thoroughly scalded by what she's seeing and hearing, Laura Chandler stops the DVD, fast forwarding it for eight or ten seconds, and is then presented with the jarring sight of her husband engaging in anal sex with the young woman named Julie. With every vigorous thrust Keith Chandler loudly verbalizes his deviant pleasure. His coarse, aggressive language seems calculated to degrade and intimidate the young woman who, judging by her expression, was experiencing a considerable measure of physical pain. With this, Laura Chandler can watch no more. Quickly turning the TV off, she stands in silence, her mouth agape and in a complete state of emotional shock. Now she knows why her husband is estranged. Now she knows why there is no intimacy, joy or even mutual respect in her marriage. Now she knows.

As she regains some measure of composure, she retrieves the DVD and puts it back on the shelf. She then looks at dozens of other privately recorded discs and sees name after name written with a magic marker: Carol, Linda, Susan, Pamela, Ashley, etc. etc. etc. Laura Chandler has just learned that she's married to someone who's not only addicted to sex and pornography, but has an added vice grafted to his compulsive perversion: he feels a sick desire to record his encounters so he can revel in watching them again later. Trying to intellectually and emotionally digest what she's just witnessed, Laura Chandler is shocked and psychologically overwhelmed. In silence, she slowly puts everything back in its place, turns off the light and walks out of the room closing and re-locking the door behind her. She doesn't know it yet, but a door is also closing on a chapter of her own life, one that she will eventually be grateful to leave behind.

Meanwhile, 12 miles away across town, the subject of her thoughts has just concluded another illicit episode with the woman he picked up from the street several hours before. Having served her use, she's been paid and returned to the same street she was walking on earlier. Now that his habit has been gratified, Keith Chandler is in a hurry to get back to his office, but as he's driving, he sees a woman walking in the opposite direction on the other side of the street. He knows he's driving through a part of town where prostitutes frequently walk, and all the unspoken hints in her demeanor suggest she is just that. Her short dress and appealing figure immediately pique his interest, and even though he just had his way with a different woman less than an hour ago, he feels the irresistible urge to double back and pick her up. His brain, like that of every compulsive neurotic, is governed by impulse, and once it's triggered, acting on that impulse is nearly always a foregone conclusion. With a quick U-turn, Keith Chandler will start that compulsive sequence all over again.

He checks his rear-view mirror, and though he knows it's an incautious move, he suddenly turns his steering wheel to cut across the other lanes of traffic. The glare of reflected sunlight that flashes in his eyes for a split second blinds him to the fast approaching tractor-trailer that's bearing down on him. The impact is sudden, powerful, and deadly. Striking the car at an oblique angle, damage to the truck is minimal. The collision's full impact is directed to the driver's side of Keith Chandler's car, and the resulting blunt force trauma instantly kills him.

By the time the first medical team arrives to assist with any possible survivors, it's clear that the only thing to be done is remove the lifeless body of Keith Chandler from the mangled wreckage. Several blocks away the woman walking down the street has heard the crash and looks back from a distance at the fatal accident scene. After pausing for a few minutes, she casually starts walking again as if nothing happened.

Keith Chandler doesn't remember the crushing impact of steel and glass that ended his earthly life. All he recalls of the event is the glaring flash of sunlight that dazzled his eyes and then being immersed in a strange shroud of darkness that enveloped him. Then, as if in a dream, he finds himself walking down a forest pathway in a setting that's totally unfamiliar. As he walks onward, he's completely baffled by what's happening. Looking at his hands and arms, it appears that nothing is wrong with him. In fact, he feels healthy, strong, and confident. He wonders what will happen next. He won't have to wait very long to find out.

Chapter Four: A Violent Encounter

In a place no map can locate, and in a time not marked by any clock or calendar, the dreaming soul of Calvin Milner remains blissfully enthralled. Still reeling from the strange, alien images of those other-worldly places shown to him on his tour through the galaxy, Calvin Milner is still rapt in silent amazement. Was it a dream? If it was, it's not over yet. Still in his boyhood home, surrounded by the reassuring familiarity of what was a very happy time for him, he sits in the comfortable living room he knew so well as a boy. Calvin looks over to see his father reading as he did so often many years ago. He sees his mother in the kitchen doing the dishes. All is happy, normal, and reassuring.

Calvin Milner is beyond the need or desire to rationally understand what he's experiencing. As he looks at his mother and father it occurs to him that the benevolent faces of his parents represent something much deeper, a love that transcends all temporal reality, as if the power and intensity of that love was so extreme it could only be experienced vicariously in the attenuated form of devoted familial affection. Looking at his parents, he feels the overpowering presence of something mysterious and unseen, but undeniably real. A deep sense of acceptance and profound gratitude seems to flood outward from the core of his being. Calvin Milner feels the mystical, silent, all-encompassing presence of absolute love.

In a moment of serenely blissful perfection he hears his mother say,

"Calvin, Brianna's here for you."

Calvin responds with the casual ease of one expecting an old friend.

"Thanks Mom, I'll see you later."

"Okay."

A moment later, without rising from his chair, or leaving his parents' home, Calvin Milner somehow instantly finds himself outside, walking down a country road with the woman named Brianna. The mystery of what's happening around him is tempered by a calm, reassuring sense that he's exactly where he should be and needs to be. It somehow feels right and natural that he's once again with this mysterious woman, and for some reason they are going somewhere together. Calvin smiles and looks at Brianna, who smiles back.

"I'm sure you enjoyed seeing your parents."

"I don't know what to say. It was incredibly joyful."

"I'm glad."

"Where are we?" Calvin asks.

"That's a hard question to answer. We're in a place that has no address, occupying a space that has no dimensions, existing in a realm where linear time has no meaning, but to answer your question more directly, we're going to work. You're an apprentice, Calvin. Don't you remember?"

"Yes, I remember. I'm an apprentice."

"Well, that's why we're here. We're about to meet our first arrival."

"If I'm an apprentice, what exactly is my craft? What is my role in all of this?"

"Your role, Calvin, is to see all those you encounter on to what's waiting for them. It's not unlike the role you once played as counselor to your high school students back in Lancaster."

"This is very different from my days with high school students. I don't know what exactly is expected from me."

"That's why for now you need to just observe and learn."

"What if they ask me a question?"

"No one will ask anything of you. They won't even know that you're here with me. Your presence is concealed for now. When you're ready, you'll interact with your charges."

As they continue walking, they come to a side path leading into a wooded area.

Brianna leads.

"This way Calvin, there's something I want you to see."

After a few minutes walking the forest path they see a man approaching and, within seconds, he's standing in front of them. It's Keith Chandler.

"Hello, Mr. Chandler," Brianna says.

"Who are you?"

"Just someone who's here to help you find what you want."

"How do you know what I want?"

"That's not hard to guess. Is it?"

"Why don't you come with me? We'll find it together," Keith Chandler says.

"Would you like that?"

"Since you asked, yes, I would. You're beautiful. I'd love to spend some time with you."

"Do you mean spend time with me or on me?"

"I don't know, maybe both. You're a lovely woman."

"I'm not available, Mr. Chandler. What you're looking for is right over there waiting for you. She's more than ready."

Pointing to an open area of the forest, Brianna directs his attention to a very attractive woman lying in the shade. Slender, healthy and erotically alluring, her eyes lock on him as her head nods unmistakably signaling her invitation. Keith hears Brianna's voice quietly whispering in his ear.

"Go ahead, Mr. Chandler. That lubricious delight that you made your life a slave to is waiting for you."

Keith Chandler begins walking toward her and she begins touching herself in suggestive ways, enticing him to a temptation he cannot resist. As he gets closer, she starts audibly moaning. Her body is wet with perspiration and pulsing with sexual tension. This is what Keith Chandler knows. This is where he feels in control. This is where he wants to be. Standing over her, he hears her teasingly sultry voice.

"Give it to me, Keith. I'm ready. Put it in me deep. Come on Keith. You know I need it."

Free will is vanquished by his compulsive neurosis and within seconds he's undressed and ready to mount. She quickly gets into position and tells him, "You're new here. I'll have to break you in myself," and then says very aggressively, "and this won't be the last time fucker boy."

Compelled to take his unexpected prize, he's completely distracted and doesn't see something very dangerous charging in from the side until it's too late.

Before his first coital thrust he feels the violent motion of a strong hand ripping off part of his left ear as a vicious attack begins. Keith Chandler turns toward his assailant. It's another male, large, strong, and very aggressive. Within seconds he's fighting for his life as he frantically tries to fend off the unprovoked attack. His opponent seems to fight with an almost crazed ferocity, as if he were a wild animal. The sheer brutality of the attack is overwhelming in its sudden intensity, and completely unexpected. Blood soon flows from open wounds as Keith Chandler summons the strength to defend himself in what has become a fight for his life. He looks into the face of his attacker and sees what looks more like a snarling beast than a human being. Whoever or whatever this creature is, it's clear he's not letting up any time soon. This fight is to the death. Another surge of hormone driven aggression comes over the fiend and Keith Chandler struggles desperately to resist. Mustering all his physical strength he's finally able to achieve something of a stalemate with force enough to hold back his attacker, but not enough to secure his retreat. As they're both locked in a deadly contest of brute force, he looks over and sees the female he was ready to mount only seconds before, vigorously copulating with a third male. When his attacker also looks over and sees the female with another male, he instantly jumps up and runs over to attack the new male. Shaken, bloodied, and exhausted, Keith Chandler watches as the two males ferociously attack each other. Seeing his chance to flee, he staggers to his feet and runs as fast as he can from the violent mayhem.

As he runs, he hears the female screaming at him, "Hey fucker boy, we'll meet again. You hear me fucker boy? We'll meet again. I like you fucker boy. I'll find ya."

Running as fast as he can, while at the same time staunching the blood from the side of his head with his open hand, he eventually finds his way back into the forest. After a few minutes he catches his breath and slows his pace a little. As he follows the path before him, he hears a commotion some 30 or 40 feet away in the undergrowth. Still naked, bleeding, and exhausted, he knows he can't risk another encounter like the one he just survived. He slowly and silently approaches to see the disturbance and soon comes upon a scene so gruesome he's instantly repulsed by its shocking intensity. He sees a man lying on top of what looks like a female, but a clearer view shows the man copulating with the blackened corpse of a dead woman. Self-possessed, he eagerly pursues his hideous pleasure, and as Keith Chandler looks closer at the dead woman's face, he clearly sees maggots dripping from the rotten flesh of her open mouth. Shaking with fear at what he's witnessing, he becomes absolutely still and silent, hoping to withdraw unnoticed from the lurid scene, but as he does the fiendish degenerate looks back at him and their eyes lock. With a malevolent smile, and not missing a stroke in his copulative rhythm, he speaks. "After I'm done, it's your turn, Keith. Then we'll both do her. She's hot. Isn't she?"

When the man shows his black teeth in sick laughter, a lightning bolt of fear and panic seizes Keith Chandler. He runs as fast as he can from the awful sight. With his heart pounding and his face still bloodied he keeps running until exhaustion finally overtakes him. Panting heavily, and at the end of his strength, he staggers to the side of the footpath, finding a spot in the dappled shade of the forest to rest. Trying to catch his breath he looks from side to side and wonders where and what this terrible place is.

Meanwhile, observing him at every point, Brianna and her new apprentice Calvin Milner quietly walk the same footpath. Seeing everything that Keith Chandler has just experienced, Calvin is aghast at what he's witnessed. As they walk together in silence, Calvin is troubled and emotionally subdued, prompting Brianna to ask, "Are you shocked by what you saw, Calvin?"

"Yes, very, I don't understand. What I experienced was so beautiful. You took me on a tour through the galaxy. It was wonderful, but what he just went through was a nightmare."

"You mean Mr. Chandler?"

"Yes, why is he so different?"

"Because he chose to be."

"What do you mean?"

"One life was given to service; one was given to abuse and self-indulgence. One life was given to imagination and appreciating the wonders of creation; one was given to callously using others for self-gratification. Is it a surprise to see those two very different lives leading to two very different outcomes?"

"I suppose not."

"Differences in human tendencies are magnified over time."

"But both of us are still human."

"That means you both had the same starting point."

"I don't understand."

"Two parallel lines can run close to each other forever, but if one angles away even slightly, in time they'll be miles apart. Your life took a very different course than Mr Chandler's. That's why your experience was so different from his."

"Do many come to a place like this?"

"Only those who warrant entry."

"This place is extreme."

"Every destination is tailored in exact accordance with the Karmic profile of those destined to arrive there. Every journey matches the traveler who makes it."

"So all you do is see them along their way."

"Yes."

"Why can't they make the journey themselves?"

"It makes it easier for them if we help them along their way, and it lets them know they're not alone. Despite anything they've done, there's usually always a way back."

"And this will be my job, you say."

"That's right."

"I'm not sure I can do this. How will I know what to say to them?"

"You'll be fine, Calvin. You wouldn't be here if you couldn't do this."

"What's the most important thing I need to know?"

"Every sojourner who passes through this realm is uniquely individual. Every life is a story, and every story produces its own ending and also the beginning of another story, and then the next and the next. The human soul incrementally pulses through incarnations as our own heart beats on and off to sustain our daily lives. There's no other way. Forward progress is gradual and constant, with no ending. Destiny is mandatory, Calvin, and everything unfolds according to what precedes it. That's all you need to know about this place. Don't worry about what to say or do. Everything here is instantly known by its intrinsic quality. There is no camouflage or concealment, no artful deception to hide who and what we are. This is not a world where falsehood thrives. Don't worry. The most important thing for you now is to be a silent, patient observer."

As they continue walking, the haggard sight of a man sitting alongside the pathway comes into view. It's Keith Chandler, his naked figure still bloody from the wounds he received earlier. As they approach, he recognizes Brianna as being the woman he spoke with before his ordeal began. Looking at the man sitting on the ground with his body covered with dirt and blood she tells him, "Mr. Chandler, it doesn't look like you're having fun yet."

"You, I remember you. I remember. You were the one who set me up. It was you who sent me over to that woman, and I nearly got killed."

"I didn't send you to her. You made that choice through your own volition."

"I didn't choose to be viciously attacked."

"That's right, you didn't. What you chose was to mount another female, to live for the perpetual gratification of your sex organs, to trade the tempered restraint of self-governed behavior for the raw animal drive of the perennial rut, to surrender the emancipating freedom of disciplined self-control for the crippling neurosis of a compulsive sex addict. That's what you chose. You made that choice, Mr. Chandler, not me. That's why you're here, but you should know that in this world you're not the only breeding male with an excess of testosterone, and as you found out they get very aggressive over females. Maybe your next encounter won't be as violent, if you're lucky, and you'll be happy to know every female here has a voracious sexual appetite, just like yours. Isn't that what you always wanted?"

Speechless, Keith Chandler stares back at Brianna in disbelief.

"Just remember to be careful Keith. Males outnumber females ten to one here."

Looking to the ground momentarily, Keith Chandler tries to digest what he's just heard. When he looks back at Brianna, he sees only the open space where she was standing. After getting up to see where she went, he sees nothing. A gripping sense of panicked disbelief comes over him as he thinks about having to remain in this awful place. This must be some kind of strange living nightmare. It has to end. What can he do to escape this horror? As his thoughts grapple with the questions and implications of what he faces, he hears the slow labored approach of someone coming his way along the path. She came back. It must be the mysterious woman named Brianna, he thinks. This time he'll press her for answers. She must tell him how to get out of this place, but when he turns and realizes who's approaching, his heart sinks and fearful dread seizes him. It's the degenerate fiend, carrying the rotting corpse of his dead sex partner. His demonic red eyes and malevolent smile send Keith Chandler once more into a fearful panic and he runs again, as fast as he can. As he does, he hears a woman's voice calling from a distance.

"Hey fucker boy, I'm lookin' for you. You ain't done with me fucker boy."

He keeps running as darkness slowly descends around him. The night is coming, a long, dark and violent night.

Chapter Five: The Politician

On a warm Saturday morning, a few miles north of Kingman, Arizona, a woman is getting ready for a day trip. Later this afternoon she'll be attending a political rally near

Nogales, close to the Mexican border. Her name is Natalie Burke, a conservative state senator who's been in the Arizona state legislature for the past 14 years. Though her political views are seen as extreme by many, she still managed to win her seat with 60% pluralities in her last two elections. The rally she's attending today is being organized and sponsored by Ken Boorman, a friend and campaign contributor. An ardent anti-immigration activist, Ken Boorman has been deeply involved in a conservative push to severely restrict the freedom of undocumented workers. Today's rally will focus on this effort and will be held on Ken Boorman's 1,200 acre ranch near the southern border. At his personal request, Senator Burke has agreed to travel the considerable distance and speak at the event. In appreciation, Ken Boorman, a licensed pilot, has offered to fly her personally from Kingman to his ranch near Nogales in his private plane. Senator Burke has been asked numerous times to speak at such gatherings and does so gladly.

The anti-immigrant faction of the Arizona Republican Party has, under her leadership, been able to sponsor a successful bill that makes it easier to arrest and detain any worker suspected of being undocumented. The close vote was seen as a decisive win for radically conservative elements, both in and out of government. Ken Boorman was foursquare in his enthusiastic support for the bill and, as a gesture of appreciation, has asked Natalie Burke to make a guest appearance today. Though she is more than happy to do so, something else is on Natalie Burke's mind and has been for some time.

Colin Burke, her 24 year old son, has recently gone through the physical and psychological ordeal of life saving heart transplant surgery. Born with a fatal congenitally defective heart, Colin was facing a hopeless outcome. It was understood by all that, without some intervening miracle, Colin Burke would never survive the wait time in finding a suitable donor, yet that's exactly what happened. On a stretch of road nine miles south of Winslow, Arizona, a young man of the same age was killed in an accident while riding his motorcycle. Being an organ donor, his heart was rushed to Phoenix for immediate placement and Colin Burke was the recipient. Now at home recuperating, he and his mother State Senator Natalie Burke are increasingly optimistic about his recovery. He sits watching the news as his mother comes to check on him.

"How are you feeling today, Colin?"

"Good, actually very good," he says as he turns off the TV.

"I'm glad to hear it. You know I have to go in a few minutes. I'll be back tonight, but your dad's coming home in an hour or so."

"I'll be okay, Mom. When's Mr. Boorman picking you up?"

"I'll meet him at the airport at nine."

"How long will it take to get there?"

"About two hours."

"That's pretty quick to travel almost the length of the state."

"It's a lot faster than driving," she says.

"When are you supposed to speak?"

"Probably around four, but you never know. Schedules get changed a lot."

"Maybe I'll see you on the evening news."

"Who knows? I spoke with you doctor yesterday. He's very pleased with your progress."

"That's good to hear."

"Very good to hear. You've been given a new lease on life Colin, and I couldn't be happier."

"Thanks Mom, me too."

"Okay, I need to get going. I don't want to have Mr. Boorman waiting on me. Remember Colin, no stressful activity. You need to build your strength back up again."

"I understand."

"I'll be okay."

As Natalie Burke leans over to kiss her son goodbye, she tells him,

"I might be late tonight, so don't wait up for me. Get to sleep early."

"I will Mom, thanks."

After exiting, Natalie Burke glances at her watch, checks the time, and within minutes begins the drive to the airport. In less than an hour she and Ken Boorman are airborne flying to his ranch in southern Arizona. As they traverse the nearly 350 miles from Kingman to their destination, the conversation doesn't stray far from the well-worn themes that dominate their political thinking. Their agreeable talk makes the trip seem much shorter than expected and they are soon within ten miles of Ken Boorman's ranch and private landing strip. Mr. Boorman is grateful for Senator Burke's participation in today's rally and takes the opportunity to let her know.

"Senator Burke, I wanna thank you for doin' this for us today. We really appreciate it."

"It's my pleasure Ken. I'm happy to oblige."

"After we land you can come up to the house and freshen up, meet my wife and have some lunch."

"Sounds great."

"The rally starts at two, so we have an hour to spare. I think we're right on schedule."

"Perfect, who else is gonna be at the rally?" she asks.

"Uh, Bob Kidman, John Cabot and his wife, Rick Phillips. He's with the minute men. Tom Schofield and his militia buddies, probably have a lot of NRA people there."

"Yeah, I know Tom Schofield and his wife. Well that's good. We'll have a good crowd."

"I got the word out early on this rally, so I think we'll see a hefty turnout."

"I think we will. People are fired up about this," says Senator Burke.

"Sure, they're finally wakin' up to the fact that the government isn't gonna do anything about it."

"You mean the federal government."

"That's right," Mr. Boorman says.

"Washington is useless. If anything, they make the problem worse."

"They created the problem to begin with if you ask me."

"I completely agree."

"That's why we appreciate your efforts in the legislature on this. You're standin' up. Other politicians are too spineless to do anything."

"Well they're too worried about losin' the Hispanic vote."

"Yeah, more worried about losin' votes than losin' their own country."

Minutes later the single engine aircraft lands on the private air strip at Ken Boorman's ranch, 20 miles west of Nogales. Greeted by Ken Boorman's wife and several friends, Senator Burke is welcomed and ushered into the Boorman residence for lunch before going to the rally.

Meanwhile, back in Kingman, Senator Burke's son Colin is still resting at home. His daily regimen of physical therapy, and post-operative rehabilitation amply affords him leisure time for reading, watching movies or using the internet. Colin looks at the widescreen TV his mother recently had installed to help him through his recovery, and picks up the remote. As he turns the TV on, the phone simultaneously rings. After muting the TV, he answers the phone and hears his mother's voice. Colin is accustomed to having his mother call to see how he's doing.

As they talk, the local TV station breaks in, warning of an approaching system of severe weather expected to pass through later tonight, but because of the muted sound and Colin's distracting phone conversation with his mother, the weather bulletin goes unnoticed. Turning the TV off, he continues talking with her until she tells him she has to go. After saying goodbye, he sits back and picks up the half-finished cross word puzzle he began earlier, while 340 miles to the south his mother prepares herself for another public speech.

From Ken Boorman's point of view, the rally is off to a good start. The wooden stage he had built to accommodate the speakers is more than large enough for the four piece Country and Western band he's engaged to perform at the intermissions. As they close another set, Mr. Boorman mounts the stage and moves over to the microphone.

"How about our musicians today? All the way from Tucson Arizona, the 'Hair Trigger Band' ladies and gentlemen, let's give

these boys a big round of applause. You're soundin' great boys. Okay friends, we have a special guest here today who came all the way from Kingman to be with us, and before I have her come up and say a few words, I need to remind everybody about the recent victory we had in passing HR 1206 a few months ago. This bill finally puts some teeth in the law and makes it possible to get these illegals off our streets and behind bars where they belong."

Interrupted by applause, Mr. Boorman pauses.

"Ladies and gentlemen. Ladies and gentlemen, that victory would not have been possible without the hard work of our next speaker. As a matter of fact, the new law I'm talkin' about was originally drafted in her office in Phoenix. I've known her for almost seven years, and I can tell you she's been with us on this issue every step of the way. So, I think it's time for me to shut my mouth so we can hear from the lady herself. Ladies and gentlemen, all the way from Kingman Arizona, State Senator Natalie Burke, let's give her a big hand."

Loud applause fills the air from the five or six hundred strong audience gathered in front of the stage, and within seconds Natalie Burke is behind the microphone. After adjusting it slightly, she's ready to begin.

"Can you hear me? Good, good, wow what a fine group of American patriots, I always know I'm with the right people when

I look out into the crowd and see at least half of our good citizens packin', if you know what I mean. Yeah, that's right. First, I want to say thank you to Ken Boorman for hosting this rally. Thank you Ken, you're a great American. You know when I look out and see so many people showing support for their second amendment rights, it reminds me of where the real political power is supposed to reside in this country. That's right. That's right, and I know a lot of you helped us pass HR1206. It was your grass roots support that helped turn the tide in the state house. I can tell you that for a fact. I was there. When it comes to this issue, we have politicians runnin' scared up in Phoenix. Now they know, now they know that if they don't act, we will, and we'll remember on election day who was with us and who wasn't. That's right. It's a real simple proposition, we don't want illegal aliens in this country. What part of that don't you understand, Phoenix? What part of that don't you understand, Washington? Apparently they don't hear too well in Phoenix and Washington, but you know somethin'; when we passed HR1206 we turned their hearing aids up a couple o' notches. Didn't we? That's right. That's right! They can hear us loud and clear now. You know, after that bill was passed, I was asked by a liberal reporter whether or not, get this now, whether or not it bothered me to sponsor a bill that would have the effect of breaking families up. You know what I told her? I said listen honey, if it doesn't bother you to stand by and watch your country being mongrelized, then it doesn't bother me to do everything I can to stop it. Yeah, that's what I told her. I said it doesn't bother me at all."

Senator Burke's inflamed rhetoric provokes a thunderous applause.

"That's right. It doesn't bother me at all to stand up for my country. It doesn't bother me at all to make sure our children don't have to speak English as a second language. It doesn't bother me at all to see people arrested who broke the law. No, it doesn't bother me to say, arrest all illegals. Illegal aliens need to be rounded up and deported now. That's my position, and I'm ready and willing to take that fight to the state house and anywhere else I have to. That's right, and remember, we can't do it without your support. Thank you, thank you ladies and gentlemen, and thank you Ken Boorman for being an ally. Keep up the fight. Thank you."

Sustained applause fills the air and Natalie Burke moves away from the microphone as Ken Boorman briefly speaks.

"Ladies and gentlemen, State Senator Natalie Burke, let's give her a big hand."

As the music resumes, and the speakers descend from the stage, Ken Boorman expresses his pleasure to Senator Burke for her presentation.

"That was real good Natalie. I'm so glad you came."

"I'm glad to be here Ken."

As sandwiches and beverages are freely dispensed, a carnival-like mood is in the air and the crowd becomes festive. Though food and music make for a convivial atmosphere, Natalie Burke is thinking about her son back in Kingman. It was understood that Senator Burke could stay only long enough to speak and immediately afterwards fly back to Kingman. Ken Boorman knows she's eager to return home and would also like to get underway as soon as possible. By the time he flies her back to Kingman and makes his return flight home, he will have put in a very long and eventful day, so they're both ready to start the final part of their journey. The time is almost 6pm, and within twenty minutes they're in the air again heading back to Kingman. In his haste to take his guest back home and distracted by the day's events Ken Boorman neglects the first rule of every pilot or mariner: always be aware of impending weather conditions you are traveling toward. The first leg of their trip is routine as they talk about the rally they left. All seems ordinary.

"I'm really pleased with how it went," Ken Boorman says.

"I think it went very well. I enjoyed it. Thanks, Ken, for taking me back so soon."

"That's quite all right. I know you're concerned about your son. How's he doin'?"

"He's doin' a lot better now. A couple of months ago we thought we might lose him."

"But he's doin' much better you say."

"Thankfully. His doctors are very optimistic."

"That's great. How old is he?"

"He's 24."

"That's a lot for a 24 year old to go through."

"It was a miracle we found a donor heart when we did. He didn't have much time left."

"Do you know where it came from, his new heart?"

"All I was told was that a young man, also 24 years old, was killed in a motorcycle accident a few miles south of Winslow. They immediately asked his parents if they could harvest his organs and they said yes. So, that's all I know."

"Wow, well they must've been good people. I mean to be told your son is dead, then at the same time to be asked if his organs can be collected for someone else. I can't imagine that."

"I was told they didn't hesitate. His parents, whoever they were, said if their son's death could help someone else live, that would bring them a measure of comfort."

"That takes special kind a people to say that. We need more people like that in this country."

"Absolutely."

As they continue onward, they notice what looks like a fast-moving storm system coming in from the west. With 34 years of piloting experience, Ken Boorman is confident that this flight, like so many others, will be routinely uneventful. After they touch down in Kingman, he'll check weather conditions before his return flight home. Nothing out of the ordinary is expected.

Meantime, for Colin Burke back in Kingman, the passing hours of evening bring the usual tedium he's grown accustomed to in coping with his physical condition. After watching another feature length movie and receiving a phone call from his dad telling him he'll be late coming home, Colin Burke rests on the couch, gently drifting into a quiet sleep, and though the TV is still on with its background noise, it doesn't prevent him from dozing off.

Several hours pass and he remains oblivious to the intermittent weather bulletins that are being aired on the widescreen TV less than 15 feet away from him. Still sleeping, Colin Burke doesn't hear the announcer's voice break in with the news that a single engine plane has gone down about 60 miles south of Kingman because of the severe weather. It will be another four or five hours before authorities learn the identities of the two crash victims. One of the last things Colin Burke told his mother was that he would look for her on the evening news. Little did he know how tragically ironic those words would be. Though he won't receive the terrible news until the next morning, Colin Burke's mother is now dead.

As Natalie Burke wakes to find herself in a very different place, she remembers nothing about the violent impact that ended her mortal life. It's late at night. She's driving her car through a strong thunderstorm and she's in a hurry. She's trying to get back home to check on her son. Flashing emergency lights ahead of her indicate that driving conditions are hazardous. She's feeling anxious about her son, so she continues onward, despite the risks.

She comes to a partially flooded section of the road. After slowing down and proceeding with caution, what looked like a few inches of surface water quickly builds to something unmanageable. A strange sense of déjà vu comes over her, a vague recollection of trying to get home through a storm, as if she was reliving an experience from a thousand years before in some distant prior lifetime.

When Natalie Burke feels the car start to float, she knows she's in serious trouble. As the current gets stronger it carries her in its unrelenting grip. Sensing there is no escape from her fate, she suddenly feels her car lodge itself against a large tree. When water starts rapidly rising inside her vehicle, the panic of imminently drowning seizes her mind. Then, at her most desperate moment, she sees a young man struggling to open the door from the outside. After they both manage to get it open, Natalie Burke sees the rope tied around his waist and knows it leads to safety. She thinks of her son Colin and summons all her strength to save herself. After an initial struggle, the young man ties himself to the struggling woman, thereby sealing his fate with hers. As they make their way through the threatening tumult, Natalie Burke sees that without his labored effort, she would've been swept away. There's a strange, surrealistic quality to what she's experiencing, as if she is present and somehow not present in the chaotic events surrounding her. She feels the presence of something profoundly mysterious and, even with the torrent swirling all around her, it evokes a primal human memory.

This experience is strange and yet somehow deeply familiar for Natalie Burke. She asks herself, where am I, and who is this young man? Then, unexpectedly, a calming reassurance comes over her, dispelling any fear or confusion. In the slow, deliberate, protective strength of this man's dedicated effort, she senses something more than the selfless action of another human being, something else seems to be revealing itself, something profound, something powerfully expressed through the intimate presence of her rescuer's benevolent strength and compassion. The moment seems completely surreal and an unexpected thought enters her mind. Seeing the faithful constancy of this young man's continual effort against the water is very much like the soul's journey through this world, she thinks, and the rushing water with its danger very much like the streaming unpredictable swirl of our own lives. These thoughts are atypical for Natalie Burke. Though she regards herself as a believer, belief in God for her is little more than an intellectual acknowledgment that he exists, not a relevant, living presence in her daily life.

These are the thoughts of Natalie Burke as she feels the welcoming relief of solid ground under her feet, and as the two pull away from the danger, she turns to thank her rescuer.

"You saved me. Thank you. Thank you, the water came so fast. How did you know I was there?"

"I saw your car get swept away."

"Well, thank you. I don't know what I would've done."

"I'm just glad I saw you."

Natalie Burke sees a young man who appears to be in his mid-20s. His dark hair and eyes suggest a mix of Anglo and Hispanic heritage. His voice is calm and reassuring. His friendly smile and courteous demeanor immediately put her at ease.

"You're soaking wet, ma'am. I live with my grandmother very close to here. You're welcome to come and dry your clothes if you want."

Exhausted and shivering, Natalie Burke is quick to accept the invitation. After taking off his jacket to keep her warm, they both walk the short distance to the young man's modest home and are welcomed by an elderly woman whose immediate concern is getting Natalie Burke warm and comfortable. Her benignant manner and gentle bearing speak a perfect vocabulary of kindness that her broken English scarcely conveys. After gesturing something in Spanish to her grandson, she gently touches the hand of her guest, who is still soaked and shaken from her ordeal. She leads Natalie to a private room and takes from a small closet one of her own dresses. After offering the dress and a warm dry towel, she leaves the room closing the door quietly behind her.

As Natalie Burke dries herself and puts on fresh attire, she looks at the mirror on the wall. Seeing her own image awakens memories of when she would check her appearance before making a speech or public meeting, and it calls her back to that frame of mind.

Wait a minute, am I really here? What is this place? I remember. I was in a plane flying home and something happened. I know who I am. I'm Senator Natalie Burke. I'm a member of the Arizona state legislature. I've received telephone calls at my home from the governor. How many people can say that? This must be a dream. By tomorrow morning the storm will be over and I'll be on my way home again. After putting on the warm dry clothes provided by her host, she moves closer to the mirror and checks the fit of the tri-colored dress she's now wearing. As she adjusts the collar and buttons the front, its snug fit feels warm and reassuringly comfortable. It's not immediately obvious to Natalie Burke that the green, red, and white garment she's just donned bears the same colors as the Mexican flag. When she emerges from the small side room back into the living area, she sees a table with a bowl of hot soup waiting for her. Seated a few feet away are the young man and his grandmother. She walks over to the elderly woman and reaches for her hand.

"Thank you. Thank you," she says with sincere gratitude.

"Yes, okay. It's okay." the elderly woman says, and with a warm expression of genuine kindness points with an open hand to the bowl of soup on the table. Before sitting, Natalie Burke steps over to the young man and offers her thanks to him as well.

"I want to thank you again for what you did for me." "It's my pleasure ma'am. I'm glad I was there." Sitting at the table Natalie Burke begins her simple meal. "This is very good. Thank you," she says.

As her curiosity rises, she asks the young man,

"How far is Kingman from here? Can you tell me the best way to get there?"

"No, I can't tell you how to get there from here ma'am. I'm sorry."

"I have to get back to check on my son. He just had a heart transplant. I have to make sure he's all right. What's the name of this place?"

"It has no name."

"Well, how did you get here? Where are you from?"

"I used to live in Winslow."

"Are you going back?"

"I can never go back. I wish I could go back to help my mother, but I'm happy to be here with my grandmother. This is where I need to be," he says.

"Well, I need to get back to Kingman to be with my son. Do you know how serious heart transplant surgery is?"

"I can imagine. I hope your son will be okay, with all my heart."

"So do I. Why did you leave Winslow?"

"I left Winslow by accident."

"I don't understand. Did you say you have family there?"

"My mother is still there."

"Why did you leave?"

"My father is undocumented. After the law changed in Arizona, he was arrested and taken to a detention center. I was on my way to visit him, riding my motorcycle south of Winslow when it happened."

"Wait a minute. You said you were on a motorcycle south of Winslow?"

"Yes ma'am."

"What happened?"

"The accident."

"What kind of accident?" she asks tentatively.

"I was hit sideways by a pickup truck that ran a red light."

Stunned at what she's hearing, Natalie Burke wonders how this could be? Is this where Colin got his new heart?

Knowing the donor's age was the same as her son, she asks the young man hesitantly, "How old are you?"

"I'm 24."

"... Are you an organ donor?" she asks.

"Yes, it's on my driver's license."

Stupefied, Natalie Burke looks away in bewilderment and asks, "Where am I? What is this place?"

She looks over at the elderly woman. The warm light of burning candles illuminates a face that seems to exude an angelic aura of good will. Then she hears a knock on the door, and moments later sees a middle-aged woman with a dark complexion and shoulder length hair enter the room. After the newcomer is welcomed by the old woman, they embrace and greet each other in fluent Spanish. Their familiar and affectionate exchange convinces Natalie Burke that the woman must be a relative. After their greeting, the newcomer moves toward the young man who stands to offer his respects. The woman then turns to Natalie Burke. She walks over and sits at the small table across from her.

"Hello Senator Burke."

"How do you know who I am?"

"That's not a surprise. Is it? Senator Natalie Burke is well known. Your public appearances and speeches have been seen and heard by many. You command a following."

"Who are you?"

"My name is Brianna."

"How do you know about me?"

"Are you not a public figure?"

"I'm just a citizen like anybody else."

"You're being much too modest, Senator Burke. Your name is known in the halls of the state capitol."

Before Natalie Burke can respond, their elderly host brings two cups of tea and places them before her guests.

"Thank you, Maria," Brianna says.

As the old woman moves back to her chair and sits, Brianna looks at Natalie Burke.

"Isn't she kind?"

"Yes, she is."

"I'm so glad Antonio is here with her. He's a fine young man. He came to your aid earlier."

"That's right. Who are you?"

"I told you. My name is Brianna."

"How do you know these things? Why are you here?"

"I'm here to help you get to your destination."

"Do you have a car?"

"No."

"Well, how did you get here?"

"I walked."

"How is a woman walking around in the dark alone going to help me? It sounds like you need the help."

"I'm not alone. My apprentice is with me."

"Your apprentice; who's that?"

"His name is Calvin."

"Well does Calvin have a car? Because I need a ride to Kingman. Tell him I'll pay him to take me there. Where is he?"

"He's here beside me."After pausing a moment, Natalie Burke asks,

"If he's here beside you, how come I don't see him?"

"He's not part of your journey. Your destiny and his are immiscible."

"What's that mean?"

"It means this place is for you and only you."

"This is ridiculous. What are you talking about? I have to get back to Kingman to check on my son."

"There's no need to worry. Colin will be all right."

"How do you know about my son?"

"I know a lot about you, Senator Burke, and your work."

"If you know so much about me, then you know my son needs my help."

"You care deeply for your son. Don't you?"

"Yes, of course, doesn't every mother? How can you say you know my work? You don't know me."

Pointing to the elderly Hispanic woman patiently seated across the room, Brianna says,

"Maria has a son too, Antonio's father. He was a hard worker who paid his taxes and took care of his family - until Arizona's new law HR1206 was passed. He was arrested and placed in a detention center in Nogales. One morning, Antonio set out from Winslow on his motorcycle to visit his father, and through no fault of his own was killed in an accident on the highway. Your son now has Antonio's heart beating in his chest. So your work product, HR1206, had an unexpected benefit for you, but not very beneficial for others. In one sense you could say your son had a change of heart while you didn't. So, you see, I do know your work Senator Burke. I know it very well."

"Well I- ... That law was passed by a majority of the state senate. I was just one member."

"Yes, but you worked especially hard to get it passed, so your newfound modesty is a little unconvincing, Senator."

A state of general disbelief comes over Natalie Burke. If what this woman is saying is true, then she must be dead. How can this be? She doesn't remember any particular moment when her life ended. Can any of this be real? It's impossible. Reasserting her identity, Natalie Burke convinces herself that what she's experiencing is not to be taken for reality. She knows who she is. She remembers being on stage and hearing hundreds cheer as she spoke. She silently tells herself, That was real. That's who I am. At that moment she looks across the table and into the piercing gaze of the woman named Brianna and, without seeing her lips move, hears her voice saying, "No Natalie, that's not who you are."

Despite this, Natalie Burke feels the pull of that worldly identity with its meretricious lure of title and status. She wants that life back, and she wants it badly. She feels an immediate urge to get out of this strange, disturbing place.

"I need to go," she says.

"Where will you go?" Brianna asks.

"I need to find a hotel for the night and head back to Kingman in the morning."

"You don't have any money or credit cards and even if you did, those things have no value here, but you don't have to worry. You are in the home of Maria Victoria Sanchez. With traditional Mexican hospitality she'll see to all of your needs, and besides, if Maria knew you wanted to spend the night in a hotel, her feelings would be hurt. Mexicans are always ready to welcome a guest into their homes. Maria and Antonio will treat you like a family member while you're here, which might be for a very long time."

"I can't stay here."

Ignoring her words, Brianna continues. "Oh, you'll be here for some time Senator Burke, but you'll have very good company. In Maria you'll find a well of kindness as reliable as sunrise. Her quiet dignity will rouse humility in you, and from that you'll grow to become an awakened being.

In Antonio you'll find a brother and a son. What he did for you earlier tonight, he would do a thousand times over on your behalf. The life he gave your son, that life he lost that terrible morning on his motorcycle, he would gladly offer many times over in your defense. You're in very good hands, Senator Burke. Don't worry."

"What are you saying?"

"I'm just trying to help you through this."

"I don't intend on staying here. I'm grateful for what these people did for me, but I have to get back on the road. I have to get back to Kingman."

"There is no road back to Kingman."

"No, I have people who depend on me."

"They'll learn to depend on other things."

The sobering words leave Natalie Burke dumbstruck. This can't be possible.

"I forgot to tell you, Natalie, how nice you look in Maria's dress. I love the colors. Don't you?"

"Well I ... Yes I, I do."

"I wish I could stay longer, but my apprentice and I have an appointment to keep."

As she hears the strange woman named Brianna say goodbye to Antonio and sees her being walked to the door by Maria, her mind is reeling in perplexed confusion. Seeing Brianna leave, Natalie Burke sits for a moment in silence, then feels the impulse to follow her. After standing and walking to the door, she looks over at Maria, then opens the door and goes outside. She sees the woman named Brianna walking in the distance with a man beside her, then they disappear. Though the storm is over, the road in both directions is completely dark with no sign of any hotel or gas station. The breezy late evening air is chilly as Natalie Burke stands there looking into the night. A moment later Antonio comes out with a sweater and tells Natalie that her room is ready when she wants to rest. Resigning herself to the moment and her condition, she follows Antonio back inside.

As Brianna and Calvin leave, they reflect on the episode.

"Any thoughts about what you saw, Calvin?"

"I don't think Senator Burke was ready to leave the world she knew."

"Very few are ever completely ready."

"What will happen to her?"

"She'll stay with Maria and Antonio until she's ready to leave."

"When will that be?"

"When she becomes Natalie again instead of Senator Burke. Those who bear titles live in danger of being seduced by them."

"I wish her well."

"So do I Calvin. So do I."

Chapter Six: The Child

On a rainy Sunday morning in Portland Oregon at Wellcrest Regional Care Center, a residential facility for terminally ill children, another day has started. Nearly all the children living here are afflicted with a condition for which there is no known cure. Those with chronically debilitating diseases like Multiple Sclerosis, Muscular Dystrophy and Motor Neuron Disease are housed here and cared for by a medical staff that does its best for the 31 resident patients who are mostly under 16 years of age. Despite their hopeless prognosis, the caregivers who work here try to maintain a positive attitude both for themselves and those unfortunate souls in their charge. Visitors are always welcome, and encouraged to return, but the sad truth is many of the children are seen by their relatives either infrequently, or not at all.

One such case that's particularly sad, is nine year old Caitlin Pierce. Caitlin came here two years ago suffering from Tay Sach's Disease, a hereditary condition that slowly kills its victims through a gradual, wasting paralysis. She was brought to Wellcrest by Child Protective Services, and has no relatives or family that show any interest in her. Caitlin Pierce is a child seemingly forsaken by all but those few who administer her care and monitor her condition. She has been here for 25 months and in that time has never received a visitor. State officials tried to track down her parents, grandparents, or any other relatives, but were unsuccessful, and have given up the effort.

It was eventually learned that Caitlin's

father is dead and her mother has left the state with no interest in being contacted with information about her daughter. Caitlin Pierce's parents were methamphetamine addicts, and could barely cope with the confusion in their own lives. The added burden of caring for a severely handicapped child proved to be far too daunting for them, so they simply walked away. Most who are familiar with Caitlin's case agree that it's better for her to remain in the sheltered care that only a medical facility can provide. The progressively degenerative effects of her condition has robbed her of the ability to swallow and, as a result, Caitlin Pierce receives nourishment through a feeding tube. All know it's only a matter of time before she's gone.

Tay Sach's Disease is always fatal, and puts its sufferers through a slow agonizing death spiral before finally extinguishing its host. All involved with Caitlin's care agree that to put her through the wasting agony of letting Tay Sach's Disease run its full course is unthinkable. Tomorrow morning a judge will be asked to rule on whether the state has jurisdiction in this case. The matter is complicated further because no parent or relative shows any inclination to get involved, and so the fate of Caitlin Pierce will be determined in a courtroom, by people who have never seen her. The fear shared by many of those who are trying to find a humane solution to this tragic dilemma is that this case will become a rallying call for others who would use it to advance a political agenda. Though state law in Oregon is more thoughtfully formulated than most other states, the question of how the court will resolve this difficult issue is likely to be fraught with controversy. Advocates on both sides of this question preparing their arguments for the scheduled court hearing don't know it yet, but their work on this case will soon be rendered moot and irrelevant. The center of this heated controversy, a frail, helpless nine year old girl, tenuously clinging to life in a hospital bed a few miles away, will save them all the trouble. When one of the staff nurses comes to check on Caitlin later tonight, she'll find the short painful life of Caitlin Pierce has come to an end.

In that realm where journeying souls pass through to their eventual destinations, where past, present and future flow in and out of each other, two spirits stand together on the crest of a high hill overlooking an enormous ocean. It's Brianna, and her apprentice Calvin Milner. They stand together looking out on the beautiful scene of an ocean front paradise. Ahead are the clear pristine waters of an emerald blue sea, behind them a long grassy hill with a steeply pitched upward path leading to where they're standing. A cloudless canopy of deep blue sky towers above them and the warming rays of gentle sunlight illuminate everything around them. Calvin takes in the scenic vista in silence before curiosity prompts him.

"Why are we here, Brianna?"

"We're here to meet our new arrival Calvin, a creature pure and innocent."

"Is our new arrival a child?"

"Yes, she is. She's been suffering from a terrible disease. Now she's free."

"Is she on her way here now?" Calvin asks.

"Yes."

"What are we going to do with her when she gets here?"

"Have fun, that's what a child does best. Look who's coming up the path, Calvin."

Pointing to a child in the distance running up the path, Brianna says, "Here comes our new arrival."

Straining to see the distant figure, Calvin asks, "Where?"

"There, can you see her?"

"Yes, now I see her. She's so far away. Can she make it up here?"

"Just watch her and see, Calvin."

Calvin sees a child running up the steep grade with what seems to be boundless, inexhaustible energy.

"Look how fast she's running! Who is she?"

"Her name is Caitlin Pierce, and she's just broken free of her bondage."

"I've never seen a child with so much energy," Calvin says.

As Caitlin gets closer Brianna calls to her. "Come on Caitlin. You're so fast and strong."

Calvin sees Caitlin running swiftly to the crest of the hill where they're standing and looks behind at the water below. He thinks for a moment that if she doesn't slow down she might overshoot the edge of the precipice and tumble below. Seeing her swift approach Brianna cheers her on.

"Come on Caitlin. Let's fly. Let's fly, Caitlin."

Now close enough to see the eager smile on Caitlin's face, Calvin stands aside and watches as Brianna waits to take the child's hand and greet her momentum as they run together to the edge of the cliff and leap over its threshold. Calvin watches as they soar without effort through the open air and across the water. An ecstatically jubilant expression of sheer delight comes over the child as she triumphantly exults in her newfound freedom. Calvin observes with a smile as Brianna and Caitlin soar over the magnificent expanse of water and shoreline. Turning through the air at will, their exhilarating flight is tantalizingly inviting. Minutes pass as they continue their airborne frolic. Then, they make one final pass overhead and gently land back on the crest of the hill where they began. Calvin looks at Caitlin and sees a healthy nine year old girl brimming with life and energy. Brianna kneels to embrace her new young friend.

"Oh Caitlin, that was incredible. You can run. You can fly. You can swim. You can do anything you want, just like anyone else."

"I can run like other kids now."

"Yes you can, Caitlin. Yes you can!"

"That was fun!"

"It was fun Caitlin. It will always be fun. I'm so happy you're here."

"Me too."

Brianna looks into Caitlin's face, and sees the ingenuous, frail innocence of a young child, and in her, every child. She knows she must send her back, back to a normal life, back to a home with loving parents, back to where life can start again on its natural course, back to something that was meant to be.

"Caitlin, I have a surprise for you."

"For me?"

"Yes, would you like to see your mom?"

"I would like to see her, but she went away somewhere."

"Well, she came back, and she misses you very much. Sometimes she cries because she wants to see you. She has a special name for you. She calls you her Kimberly angel, because that was her mom's name. Do you like that name?"

"Yes, I like it."

"Can I call you that name too?"

"Yes."

"Thank you, Kimberly."

"You're welcome."

"Would you like to see your mom?"

"Yes."

"Come. Let's walk down this path and I'll take you to her."

Hand in hand, Brianna and her young friend set off down the path, with Calvin observing in silence as he follows.

On a warm Saturday morning in South Australia, Paul and Kathleen O'Neil are making their weekly trip to Royal Children's Hospital in Melbourne to visit their daughter. The four hour drive has become a familiar routine for them. An auto accident 17 months ago has left their child in a prolonged coma, and though the resulting head trauma from the accident was not extreme, the injury has left their daughter unconscious ever since. Paul and Kathleen O'Neil have been making the drive from their home near Swan Hill to the Royal Children's Hospital in Melbourne for almost a year and a half and it's always a somber trip. The couple's anguish is made more poignant because Kathleen O'Neil believes she is responsible for her daughter's condition. On the day of the accident she forgot to make sure she was wearing a seat belt. The force of the collision was not great, but because the child was not strapped in, she was knocked unconscious by the impact of her head striking the door window. Since the day it happened, Paul and Kathleen O'Neil have lived under a pall of sadness. Making the trip to Melbourne each week is difficult, especially for Paul, who sees his wife increasingly preoccupied with self-recrimination. He notices a heaviness about her lately that seems to be getting worse, and he's genuinely concerned about his wife's emotional wellbeing. As they turn onto Flemington Road, a few miles from the hospital, he broaches the subject to his wife.

"Kathy, I'm worried about you, and I think you know why."

"I can't get it out of my head. How could I be so stupid?"

"Come on Kathy. How could you possibly know there would be an accident? You're killing yourself with this."

"It might've been better if I had."

"Please don't say that. We have to go on with our lives."

"Yeah, sure."

Minutes later they drive into the hospital parking lot and are soon entering the main lobby. Royal Children's Hospital is a new, state-of-the-art facility, impressive in all respects. From its distinctive modern architecture to its innovative and enlightened approach in offering the most effective care to children receiving treatment, Royal Children's Hospital is second to none. A dedicated staff is particularly sensitive to the concerns of family members, and make every effort to keep them informed and involved in their child's care. Paul and Kathleen O'Neil know their daughter is in very good hands. Because of their regular visits to the hospital, they are on familiar terms with many of the staff and today is no exception. As they pass by the exotic aquarium in the main lobby they are recognized and greeted by Dr. Mark Emerson.

"Mr. and Mrs. O'Neil, nice to see you again."

"Hi, Doctor Emerson, any news?"

"No, no changes, but her vital signs are strong, and stable. That hasn't changed. Her heartbeat and breathing are normal."

"Then why doesn't she wake up?" Mrs. O'Neil asks.

"Well, we don't know she won't. Trauma induced coma is unpredictable in its duration, but in your daughter's case we think there's every reason to be optimistic. Aside from her coma she's in relatively good health. I'm sure part of the reason for that is because you come to visit her every week. I have no doubt that she's aware of it."

"I think so too," she says.

"So, we have to be patient for now. Okay?"

"Thank you Doctor Emerson," Paul says. "Can we see her now?" asks Kathleen.

"Of course."

"Thank you doctor."

Minutes later Paul and Kathleen O'Neil enter their daughter's room and see their child as they saw her last week and the week before. Despite Doctor Emerson's hopeful words, the sobering image of a young girl in a perpetually unresponsive sleep, a somnolent, wakeless captivity, that is at once both dead and alive and yet neither, is instantly disheartening. An emotional numbness he finds hard to resist comes over Paul when he sees his daughter in this helpless condition. After both give their daughter a kiss, it's Kathleen that stays with her constantly through the five hour visit as Paul sits passively most of the time.

Meanwhile, an ocean away at Wellcrest Regional Care Center in Portland Oregon, the death certificate and formal report on the passing of Caitlin Pierce is being prepared. Caitlin's death comes with a mixture of sadness and relief for those who cared for her. Most are relieved to know her suffering is finally over. On hearing of her death several of her caregivers remarked, "She's in a better place." That prescient hope is far more intuitive than they can guess.

The tender spirit of the departed subject they speak of is free and thriving already. The spirit of the child once called Caitlin Pierce is emancipated, as if waking from a captive dream of endless pain into a liberating reality of physical joy, a transformation that is literally and factually a second birth. Her buoyantly eager spirit is impelled to find and express itself in and through a physical human body. Brianna knows this as she leads her down the pathway and with her apprentice Calvin silently observing behind them, she says to the child, "I can hear your mother."

"What is she saying?"

"She misses her angel, her Kimberly angel. Would you like to see her?"

"Yes."

"Come this way then."

Brianna leads the child to where the path divides in separate directions and then kneels to embrace her young friend. Pointing to the separate path she tells her, "Your mother and father are waiting for you down this path. They've been calling for you."

Looking at her intently she tells the child, "It's time for you to take a new name. You were Caitlin. Now you are Kimberly. You will breathe again, measuring the pulse and cycles of life."

Then Brianna whispers in her ear.

"You will remember this perfect moment Kimberly, and in your coming life it will make you fearless against time and death."

Brianna then bestows a silent kiss on the child, and the changeling walks alone on her path. As Brianna and Calvin watch her depart Calvin asks,

"Why did she choose to go back? She was so happy here. Was it just to see her mother?"

"It's more than that, Calvin. Her spirit needs the adversity of human experience to grow and thrive. She must live that struggle before she can transcend it. It's true for all of us."

"Will she be all right?"

"Yes, she'll do better than most."

Meantime another struggle continues for Paul and Kathleen O'Neil visiting their coma stricken daughter in Royal Children's

Hospital in Melbourne Australia. The heavy moments of seeing their nine year old daughter in her helpless condition is a taxing vigil that drains them both of emotional and physical energy. Since the accident that caused their daughter's coma they've made the drive from their home every Sunday to see her. After more than seventy consecutive trips, their steadfast dedication to their child's welfare and strong resolve to support her in whatever way they can is apparent to all.

Kathleen O'Neil remembers watching a news report on TV some years ago that was based on the true story of a South Korean mother who had two sons who fought in the Korean War. When the conflict had ended, they had remained captive as prisoners of war. After pleading unsuccessfully to the North Korean government, the mother of the two men began praying for their return. As an added measure of devotion, she would get up in the middle of the night at 3am to voice her prayer request.

She did this night after night, without missing a single night, for 43 years. Her story was told and eventually retold on nationwide television. Public pressure finally persuaded the North Korean government to relent, and the two men were released. A mother's quiet resolve and unwavering faith proved stronger than the stern decrees of a totalitarian government. This news story stuck with Kathleen O'Neil, and she remembers it until this day. She also remembers how the story ended. The notoriety ensured that when the Korean mother's two sons returned home to her, film crews were there to record the event. As the two men approached their mother's house, they paused several hundred feet from her home and fell to their hands and knees to crawl the rest of the way, publicly showing their profound filial respect for their mother's tireless devotion. Kathleen remembers the expression of quiet strength and dignity on the woman's face as her two sons approached her. The image of that face has remained with her through the intervening years, with an uncanny sense she would somehow need it someday to deal with her own struggle. Since her daughter's brain injury, she thinks more often about that woman and identifies with her remarkable story of faith and patience.

The emotional ordeal that Kathleen O'Neil is going through is similar, but in one critical respect, very different. Kathleen O'Neil carries an added burden of self-blame. In her one-sided conversations with her daughter when she's visiting, her tone is defensive and apologetic, so much so that Paul is concerned about his wife's psychological and emotional health. Kathleen makes it a point to talk to her daughter when they visit and read to her from books that Kimberly was familiar with before the accident. As Paul sits passively, he winces to hear the title of the book his wife has brought to read to their daughter.

"I brought your favorite book today Kimberly. It's called 'The Lost Princess'. We used to read this book together. Do you remember?"

Paul pulls away and moves toward the window as Kathleen reads to their daughter. Looking out of the window affords at least a partial distraction from his despondent mood. As he hears his wife's obsequious voice read the simple strain of words, he surrenders to the perfect sadness of the moment. Then he hears something strange, or is he imagining it? He hears a faint second voice in parallel with his wife.

"Once there was a princess who went walking in the forest one day, and ..."

A sudden apprehension comes over Kathleen as she hears a faint but audible voice in sync with her own.

Paul rushes forward and asks, "Did you hear that? Keep reading. Keep reading."

Flustered, Kathleen finds her place and begins again, this time more loudly.

"'She went ... she went into the forest.'"

"Not so fast honey, slow down a little," Paul says.

"'She went into the forest and started picking berries.'"

Again their daughter's voice begins, this time clearer and stronger.

"She was having so much fun - Yes, yes that's it. That's it, Kimberly! - She was having so much fun, that she spent the whole afternoon with her basket picking-"

Kathleen breaks off in her nervous excitement.

"She's talking, Paul! She's talking! Honey can you hear me? Kimberly I'm here. I'm here angel. We're both here. Please come home. We're waiting for you."

Then, with no prior hint, Paul and Kathleen see their daughter do something she hasn't done in nearly a year and a half. She opens her eyes. Startled, Paul looks on in muted amazement, but Kathleen cannot contain her emotions.

"Kimberly! Oh God, oh God, Kimberly you're back. You're back. Oh honey, we love you."

Kathleen sees her daughter looking back at her and hears the words she's waited so long to hear.

"Hi Mum."

When Kathleen hears her daughter say these words, a mother's fervent hope instantly becomes an assured reality, triggering the release of a torrent of pent up emotions and she breaks down in tears.

"Oh Kimberly, Kimberly I'm sorry. I'm sorry angel."

"It's okay, Mum."

Leaning to kiss her daughter's face, Kathleen drinks in through tear-soaked eyes the joyful sight of her daughter's animated countenance. As his wife tries to cope with the flood of emotion she's experiencing, Paul tentatively moves toward his daughter, almost afraid that she will slip again into oblivion. He moves closer, and as she looks back at him, he too is greeted by her.

"Hi Daddy."

"Hello sweetheart."

His daughter's words are emotionally wrenching, and he too succumbs to the tearfully joyous moment. As tears flow copiously from Paul and Kathleen, Kimberly is comparatively calm and

relaxed. Then a knock on the door signals the entry of a nurse making her daily rounds, who is alarmed by the commotion.

"What's wrong?" she asks.

"She's back. Our angel is back," Kathleen says.

"What?"

"Our angel is back. She's finally back."

"What do you mean she's back?"

As the nurse moves over to see for herself, she too is startled to see young Kimberly looking back at her.

"I have to get Doctor Emerson up here. Don't do anything until Doctor Emerson gets here."

As Paul and Kathleen watch the staff nurse quickly leave, they pay little heed to her words. As far as they're concerned, they need not be told what they already know. Their daughter is back. Kathleen struggles to express herself.

"We've missed you, Kimberly. We missed you so much!"

"I was flying, Mummy."

"You were flying? Oh honey, that's just your imagination. That's okay."

"How do you feel Kimberly? Are you okay?" Paul asks.

"Yes, I'm okay. ... What is this place?"

"It's a hospital darling. You've been here a while."

"Why?"

"Well, we wanted to make sure you were all right."

"I was in a hospital before I was flying. Can we go home now Mummy?"

"Oh Kimberly, we'll take you home as soon as we can." "God in heaven thank you, thank you," Paul says, still rapt in amazement.

Suddenly, the door opens. Two doctors and a nurse enter and quickly move to Kimberly's bedside. Doctor Emerson and one of his colleagues move closer and see Kimberly O'Neil awake, animated, and lucid. His medical training prompts him to do the obvious. He checks the child's vital signs and, as Paul and Kathleen pull back, they are aware that an extensive battery of tests will most likely follow. That is of little consequence to them, however. They are now both of one mind. They will stay in the hospital or nearby for as long as it takes, and when they drive back home, they'll be taking their daughter with them. Kathleen is still weeping when Doctor Emerson tells her, "Mr. and Mrs. O'Neil, I know you want to be with your daughter, but it's vitally important that we run some more tests on her, just to be safe."

"We understand Doctor. We understand perfectly," Paul says.

"It might be best if you could wait downstairs, and I'll talk with you as soon as I can. I promise you."

"Sure, that's what we'll do," Paul says.

"I need to tell her where we're going," says Kathleen.

"Absolutely," says Doctor Emerson.

Paul and Kathleen return to their daughter and again see her keenly alert. Her face brightens as they approach, and the heart-warming moment is joyfully palpable, as Kathleen tells her, "Kimberly, the doctors want to make sure you're okay, so we have to let them do their work. We'll be back as soon as they get done, okay?"

"Okay, can we go home then Mummy?"

"We're not leaving here without you angel. I promise."

"We'll be back soon Kimberly," Paul says as they kiss their daughter through a flood of emotion. After leaving the room they

stand together in the hallway for a moment and Paul comforts his wife, who is still emotionally overwhelmed. Moments later, Paul and Kathleen O'Neil are walking down the hallway, beside themselves in an almost dream-like ecstasy of renewed happiness. As they walk down the hallway, they have no way of seeing or knowing of the presence of the two souls who are observing them. Brianna and her apprentice Calvin are present and have seen all.

As Paul and Kathleen O'Neil walk past them Calvin says, "They look so happy."

"The best is still ahead for them. Caitlin is now Kimberly."

"What about the original Kimberly?" Calvin asks. "She began her new journey months ago. She's doing fine."

"That's wonderful."

Calvin pauses for a moment. "But I get the feeling our next arrival is very different."

"Your intuition is correct, Calvin. Yes, our next arrival is very different, and to take his measure we have to descend into a dark place. It's time to look into the face of the beast."

Chapter Seven: The Serial Killer

When 34 year old Spencer Phillips reaches over to mute his alarm clock beside his bed, it signals the start of a day he's been anticipating for some time. Today is a travel day for Mr. Phillips. The six o'clock alarm means he has three hours to catch his flight to Munich, Germany and then make the connection to Milan, Italy where he'll be staying for at least one week. The purpose of his trip is not to visit family or friends. It's not business related, and it's not a holiday excursion for himself. The reason for this trip, like his last overseas trip, and the 11 he's made prior to that, is to find a victim. Spencer Phillips is a serial killer.

It's been over six weeks since his last 'encounter' as he calls them, and he had found it not particularly satisfying. The more time he spends with a victim before he murders them, the more sated he feels afterward. His last encounter was a target of opportunity that presented itself when he was driving through Montana several months ago, and though it was only partially gratifying, he relives it over and over again in his memory. He recalls every detail as if he was reliving it in the present moment. Always alert for a vehicle on the side of the road, he vividly remembers seeing the truck parked off to the side with a man fixing a flat tire. Like a predator looking for a weakness he instantly notices the flat tire is on the passenger side of the man's truck and hidden from the view of anyone driving by, and he notices something else. The man is alone. Spencer Phillips has mastered the art of the friendly approach since, and can wear it like a mask to suit his purpose. Once he saw the man kneeling to loosen the lug nuts to change his tire, a murderous, predatory impulse with an almost erotic lure surged within him, as if his consciousness was amplified, taking in every detail with magnified intensity. Spencer Phillips can recall perfectly every word spoken that day.

"Hi there," he says as he approaches.

"Hi."

"What can I do to help?"

"I think I'm all right. I must've picked up a nail or something."

"I have a can of Fix a Flat."

"That's okay. I'll just change the tire and be done with it."

"No, take it with you. You might need it."

Quickly moving to his car, Spencer Phillips opens his glove compartment, but not for a can of Fix A Flat. The 9mm Glock he carries with him is always fully loaded. Walking back to the man still kneeling beside his truck, and with no approaching traffic, Spencer Phillips saw his chance and took it. He gets excited when he relives the moment of the kill and clearly recalls the moment he approached and what he said.

"Maybe this'll help," he said, firing three times into the man's back. As he slumped forward motionless, Spencer Phillips became incensed.

"Maybe this'll help dumb ass," he repeats with another three shots. The sharp staccato sound of each pistol shot seemed to heighten the sick intensity of the moment.

"Maybe this'll help, you dumb son of a bitch!"

Working himself into a frenzy, Spencer Phillips emptied his clip into his helpless victim that day, then casually pulled away as if all was normal. One day later he had four used tires put on his car and paid for them with cash. Mr. Phillips is meticulous in leaving the scene of his encounters with as little incriminatory evidence as possible.

Recalling in vivid detail each of his killings is the closest Spencer Phillips can come to reliving the actual experience. Of his numerous murder victims, one in particular stands out in his memory. It was a year ago in Thailand when circumstances allowed him to spend over two hours with his victim. In that time, the native 15 year old girl had begged him to spare her before he strangled her to death. That experience changed Spencer Phillips forever and added a sadistic quality to his homicidal psychopathy. Since that experience, he has returned three times to Southeast Asia, each time killing at least once.

Spencer Phillips is a successful serial killer for several reasons; foremost among them is his habit of carefully considering the risks he exposes himself to in each of his encounters. He avoids as far as possible any physical struggle with his victims to prevent inadvertent DNA contamination. Mr. Phillips can still check his psychotic urge to kill if the perceived risk is too great. Highly intelligent and personable, he's confident in his ability to extricate himself verbally from almost any situation.

Another reason he's never been caught is more basic. Five years ago, Spencer Phillips won almost $860,000 in lottery money. This boon allows him to travel overseas to places that are less likely to investigate any crime scene with the modern array of forensic technology available to other governments. The money also enables him to travel the highways of America hoping for a chance encounter. He likes fast, powerful cars and can easily drive over 100,000 miles in one year.

Spencer Phillips has killed 26 times since committing his first murder when he was 22. Twelve of those 26 have been outside the U.S., 19 of his 26 victims were women or girls and, of the total number, eight were children.

His preference is to spend time with a victim before murdering them, so he can watch the paralyzing fear of a human being seconds before they die. Hearing some of them beg for their life is for Spencer Phillips an experience of complete omnipotence. He often travels with a small hand wound cooking timer, ostensibly to wake him from a short nap after jet lag. His real use for it is something very different. Mr. Phillips likes to pull the timer out of his pocket and tell his victim he has only ten minutes to live. Then he coldly stares into the pleading face of terrified desperation. These are the moments Spencer Phillips lives for.

To increase his victim's terror, when only a few minutes remain, he slowly puts on his leather gloves and wraps the cord around his hands. When the timer rings he moves closer to his victim who is bound and gagged, and with one final taunt whispers, "You're not gonna like this, but I'm gonna love it."

The moment of strangulation is supremely thrilling for Spencer Phillips. He becomes very excited when his victim breaks down in absolute panic as many do, sometimes calling like a child for their mommies and daddies. In his mind, nothing compares to the eyeball to eyeball contact of absolute power staring into the helpless gaze of doomed innocence.

All the pain and abusive humiliation once forced on him is suddenly his to wield, like someone whipped every day of their lives now finding the whip in his own hands. Spencer Phillips calls it payback time.

Most people who see Mr. Phillips in a normal setting see a man whose calm exterior conceals the seething anger that rules his tormented inner life. The product of a broken home, he never knew his father and his mother was an alcoholic. Her erratic behavior included selling herself to make ends meet, and the abuse was more than psychological for Spencer Phillips. His mother would often slap or kick him because he was a living reminder of his father, the man who raped her and left her pregnant. Forcing him to watch as she performed oral sex on men was her way of saying, "if I have be a whore, then so do you."

The twisted logic that Spencer Phillips learned when young, through the grim example of direct experience, was that abuse is a normal part of life. Now, as an adult acting it out on others, he finds that killing helps to disgorge some of the toxic rage he lives with day to day. His longest held job before winning the Illinois State Lottery was at a slaughter house, an occupation he found very much to his liking. After leaving his mother's home at 17, stable employment enabled him to find a cheap apartment where he lived for eight years. A loner who never made friends, he secluded himself from human contact as much as possible. His personality by this time had been profoundly damaged, resulting from years of psychological trauma.

The freedom and privacy of living alone provided the time and place where he could indulge his fantasies. Realistic portrayal of sadistic violence was the recurrent theme in movies he watched repeatedly, and he soon began dreaming about killing people. His most disturbing dream is one where he finds himself teaching in a first grade classroom. He must punish the children for not doing their homework and does so by slowly and methodically walking from desk to desk, and one by one strangles each child to death. Spencer Phillips has had this dream over 100 times since he was 15. Psychotic, homicidal impulses became increasingly prevalent in the waking thoughts of this deeply disturbed young man.

After winning the lottery when he was 29, he bought a house in the suburbs of Chicago and does his best to blend in with his neighbors. Today he's flying to Munich, Germany, and from there on to Milan, Italy hoping to find his next victim. His last nine trips abroad have been to Southeast Asia, and to break the pattern he chose Italy this time, trying to appear as just another tourist.

Spencer enjoys the anticipation of killing someone almost as much as the act of murder itself. The moment he bought his airline ticket to Italy, he tacitly promised himself another victim, and he intends to keep that promise.

While Spencer Phillips readies himself for his flight, eight time zones away in a small mountain village near Varenna, Italy, 23 year old Maria Theresa Polomo is doing what she does most every afternoon: sitting before a canvas sketching out another landscape painting to be sold at her parents' Bed and Breakfast Inn, or at a nearby tourist shop on Lake Como. Maria's parents own a small hotel a few miles from Lake Como and cater to tourists who walk the hiking trails of Italy's northern mountains. The Polomo family has made a good living through the years on tourism and employ all their children in the family business. Maria's three brothers are all hiking guides and by day spend their time leading visitors on the many walking trails in the surrounding countryside. Because of Maria's love for painting, and since her paintings consistently sell, she uses the afternoons to walk the beautiful mountain paths in search of a compelling view to render on canvas. Maria began painting when she was 12 years old and, though she has undeniable difficulty drawing the human form, she excels at rendering images of the beautiful mountain scenery in her native Lombardy. Her parents hang her paintings prominently on the walls of their inn with their attached price tags. When several sold within three weeks for over $2,000, the economic value of Maria's artistic talent became apparent. Her creative skill and youthful beauty make her the darling of the Polomo family.

Today she'll return to the secluded spot she's visited daily for the last few weeks. She's trying to capture certain highlights of light and shade the afternoon sun casts on her subject, a flower laden meadow with a distant background of snow-capped mountain tops etched against a deep blue sky. This particular work has extra meaning for Maria. The moment she first walked into the sunlit meadow three weeks ago and took in the picturesque view she knew it would be the subject of her next painting. The work has been sketched out completely. What remains is the meticulous process of coloring the image. Landscapes, particularly mountains, are very difficult to replicate on canvas with oil based pigments. Maria knows it would be easier to use water colors to render her landscape images, but she's keenly aware of the enormous reputation and prestige associated with the history of Italian painting and so chooses the traditional medium of oil. Her resulting images are crisp, well delineated paintings that are visually appealing.

In this particular work Maria has omitted one specific detail she can't quite put out of her mind. The original view of the meadow and the mountains behind it clearly shows the image of a cross cut into an outcropping of rock on one of the mountain-sides in the distance. The choice to leave it out of the painting seems sensible. Religious imagery dominates classical Italian painting and for many this is enough reason to keep landscape images free of any association with religion. One of the tourist shop owners who purchased several of Maria's paintings recently expressed this opinion, telling her the tourist market for art is now much more diverse and includes a sizable non-Christian component. Though this rationale seems logical, Maria is ambivalent about the omission. An accurate and faithful depiction of that particular view would have included the image of the cross carved into the exposed rock clearly visible to any observer, but the safe choice would be to leave it out. Omitting the icon would preclude any possibility of alienating the sensibilities of a potential buyer. This would be the safe choice. That the work is sketched out completely makes it even more practical to just leave it as it is. The decision is for Maria, and only Maria to make. The easiest and simplest choice is to just move on to her next painting.

Back in Chicago Illinois, Spencer Phillips has boarded the flight that is now taking him to Munich, Germany. With a connecting flight to Milan, Italy he will arrive sometime this evening. After renting a car, tomorrow morning he'll drive to his intended destination near Varenna beside Lake Como for a putative hiking trip in the mountains.

Meanwhile, Brianna and her apprentice Calvin, in their timeless otherworldly realm, where only departed souls inhabit, walk down a country path. A beautiful sunny sky hangs over them as they unhurriedly make their way. Calvin knows they will soon receive another arrival and this one is from a dark malefic world of human cruelty. He walks on in silence until his curiosity prompts him.

"Brianna?"

"Yes, Calvin?"

"When is our next arrival coming?"

"Soon."

"Has he done terrible things?"

"Yes, he has, unspeakably terrible, he's taken innocent life to gratify a psychotic addiction to killing. Children have fallen under his hand."

"What will happen?"

"He, like all others, will be given what he wants."

"Where are we?"

"You might also ask, when are we?"

"What do you mean?"

"We're in Italy, in the time of the Roman Empire."

"How is this possible?"

"After all you've seen Calvin, how can you think it's not possible? We're in a realm that's not bound by linear time."

"Why are we in Roman times?"

"We are to witness an execution, and I must offer in person testimony. The intended victim is a woman of Italian descent.

It's fitting that the fiend be condemned by Roman law. In their jurisdiction the crime was planned, and so by their authority, it will be answered. The symbolism is apt. Roman law, the mother of civilizations, lawfully sanctions this action and warrants the fall of Spencer Phillips."

"I thought nobody could die in this place since they're already dead to their earthly body."

"That's right. The execution we will witness is symbolic, and spiritual, but the results for Mr Phillips will be frightfully real."

"What do you mean?"

"Observe Calvin. Observe in silence and surmise."

Calvin takes his cue to be patient and walks on in silence with Brianna.

Back in the temporal world of life and the living, another busy day of tourist activity is underway in Varenna, Italy. A beautiful afternoon of sunshine and blue sky finds Maria Theresa Polomo again walking the hiking trails near her home searching for another inspiring view. She always carries a sketch pad and a digital camera with her to capture any interesting scenes she might want to render later on canvas. As she walks, Maria occasionally passes others hiking the same trail, and always offers a cordial greeting. In groups, pairs or singly, people come from a number of countries to experience the historical charm and natural beauty of Northern Italy, and now is the peak season for it. Hikers are a common sight in the mountains at this time of the year. Solitary hikers are also not an uncommon sight, like the one Maria saw earlier from a distance, walking the same trail she's on.

All seems normal as Maria continues her deliberate pace along the trail. She's going back to a secluded meadow to take a picture of the scene she's just finished painting. After thinking it over, Maria has decided to include the image of the cross in her painting, just as it appears, and so she's returning to the secluded meadow this morning for a quick photo of the terrain. She'll use this for reference when she adds the cross to her finished canvas later tonight. The path to get there lies off the main walking trail and is seldom found by any who trek that way.

As Maria walks on she sees a solitary hiker in the distance walking her way. As they pass, a terse hello is exchanged, and they continue in different directions. Seconds later they're yards apart, but the man slows down and looks back at the young woman moving away from him. He advances a little further and again turns to see the woman's receding figure. This hiker looks like any other with his backpack, binoculars, and hiking shoes. He carries with him items common to most trail hikers and also something very uncommon, something that most would consider strangely out of place. It's a baker's oven timer. Spencer Phillips has arrived at his destination, and he believes he's just found what he's looking for. He stoops and pretends to tie his shoes as he watches Maria. After he's convinced she suspects nothing, he follows her, and sees her veer off the main path and make her way up a rocky slope strewn with boulders. He watches furtively as she finally passes over the ridge and disappears from view.

Spencer Phillips immediately, and correctly, senses she knows where she's going, and when she gets there she'll most likely be alone and isolated. He feels a surge of anticipatory excitement, and carefully begins stalking Maria from a distance, taking care to remain unnoticed. After reaching the crest of the ridge, he sees her enter a narrow passage through what looks like two large rock walls. The pathway leading to the passage comes very close to a steeply graded, downward sloping section of the mountain that requires cautious footing. One misplaced step could result in a dangerous fall. After carefully negotiating the hazardous section of the path. He comes to the narrow passage-way that Maria passed through minutes before. Then, after passing through himself, he sees something very enticing.

The young woman he has followed is seated on a portable folding chair with her back turned to him. His pulse quickens as he sees her preoccupied with her camera. It's a perfect opportunity to kill. Watching her in silence, he knows he'll be able to spend time with her. This is why he came to Italy. This secluded meadow seems tailored exactly for his purpose. Spencer Phillips is sure this encounter will be thrilling. All he has to do now is make a casual approach. As he observes his next victim, she suddenly looks to the side for some reason, and Spencer Phillips quickly conceals himself behind a large rock. With his attention focused still on his unsuspecting victim, he doesn't see the well camouflaged viper sunning himself on the sun-warmed rock only inches away. As he stretches his head forward to view his victim again, he places his hand on the animal and the poisonous snake instantly strikes, and strikes in the worst possible place, very close to the carotid artery in the right side of his neck.

Mr. Phillips looks over to see his nemesis, and gets an 'up-close and personal' look at 'Vipera Ammodytes', commonly called the Horn Nosed Viper, who has just discharged a full dose of his venom. Any hope that he might have received a dry bite is dispelled as he feels the hemotoxic poison entering his bloodstream. Trying to reason through his panicked thoughts, he knows he must get to a hospital as soon as possible, and makes his way back the way he came. He knows a racing heart will only spread the poison through his body more quickly. When he touches his neck, he feels the swelling has already started. He must hurry.

After negotiating the narrow passageway, he quickens his gait, and makes a fatal mistake. He loses his footing at the very point on the path overlooking the steeply graded downward slope and falls. After blindly tumbling several times he feels a crushing pain in his back, and after another jarring impact he loses consciousness. When his dangerous fall finally ends, his body is lying precariously inverted with his feet higher than his head. His foot is lodged between two rocks, and that has prevented him from falling to his death. The empty backpack he is still wearing was scant protection from the fall. Besides having the venom of a poisonous viper in his blood stream, his back is now broken. Sealing his fate is the fact that Maria is still unaware of his presence. Unconscious, with life threatening injuries, the life of Spencer hangs in the balance. His doom is sealed with fitting irony. If Maria, the person he had intended to kill, knew he was there, she would immediately get help, and even more ironic is the fact that she always carries an antivenin kit in her backpack.

The bite from a Horned Nosed Viper isn't usually fatal, and a broken back can heal, but only if aid and medical care are quickly given. That will not happen for Spencer Phillips. One hour later Maria starts hiking back home. Preoccupied with her own careful descent, she doesn't notice the human figure still lying silently over a hundred feet away on the slope below her. All seems normal as she returns home, and several hours later she's back with her family eating dinner. She'll spend the evening retouching the painting she thought was completed. Using the photo she's taken, Maria will repaint her work, adding the image of the cross, and as the sun goes down, she retires to her room and prepares. After positioning the canvas, and setting up her paints and brushes, she begins.

At the same moment when Maria's brush touches the canvas, Spencer Phillips opens his eyes. The swollen mass on his neck is extremely painful, and his breathing is slow and labored. The blood poisoning effect of hemotoxic snake venom has done its damage, but what frightens him even more is that he finds it impossible to move his legs. His excruciating back pain is unmistakable. Spencer Phillips knows his back is broken and in knowing that, he also knows he's going to die tonight. Apart from each other, neither the fall nor the snake bite would've been enough to kill him, but together they insure a slow, agonizingly painful ordeal that will last nearly eight hours before it ends.

Meanwhile, a few miles away, Maria is still working alone in her room. She feels a mild chill in the air and gets up to close the window. As she does, she sees the approaching thunderstorm that's been predicted to move through the area tonight. After stretching for a few minutes, she sits down to continue her work. She intends to finish retouching the painting tonight, even though it could mean another six hours of work. She starts again and hears thunder in the distance. Minutes later the rain begins and, as she works on, she says to herself, "It's a good night for painting."

It might be a good night for painting, but it's not a good night to be stranded on a mountain, paralyzed, snake bitten, and waiting to die. Now cold and shivering from the soaking storm, Spencer Phillips is enduring the last few painful hours of his life. The slow agony of his ordeal is intensely painful. Minutes later the rain stops and the skies clear. A full moon illuminates the surrounding landscape. Spencer Phillips, still hanging with his feet above his head, sees an inverted image of the surrounding mountains, and because of the moon's radiance, he sees something else: the unmistakable image of a cross carved into the side of an adjacent mountain, but from his perspective the cross is upside down. As minutes pass, he stares at the cross and thinks about his life and the people he's harmed. One by one he remembers each of his 26 victims. He remembers the eight children he murdered. He remembers the pregnant woman he strangled in the outskirts of Manila three years ago. One by one in sequence they appear in his memory. As it gets darker, the bright moonlight illuminates the cross in the distance even more clearly. It seems to beckon the tortured soul of Spencer Phillips. In his mind he sees a single collective image of all the 26 faces of his victims. With their unblinking eyes staring back at him, they seem like witnesses in a jury trial patiently waiting to give their damning testimony. Moment by moment his agony continues.

Several miles away, Maria has worked for nearly six hours on her painting. All that remains is the final insertion of the cross, and it will be complete. As she touches the canvas for the last series of brush strokes, Spencer Phillips feels a spasm of intense pain. It's been almost 11 hours since he broke his back, and for the last six hours he's been fully conscious. The excruciating ordeal is about to end. He looks again at the upside down cross, and in the brilliant light of the full moon it appears almost luminous in its intensity.

Spencer Phillips senses the end is near. He pauses for a moment and looks once more at the cross, and in a weak fading voice asks a question.

"Do you want me to say I'm sorry? Well I'm not. I'm not sorry."

Back in her room, Maria is about to complete her work. Both Maria Theresa Polomo and Spencer Phillips are only a moment away from delivering a last finishing touch; one to a painted canvas and the other to a corrupted earthly life. Maria touches the painting for the last time with a final detail to the image of the cross she had decided to include in her painting and, as she does, Spencer Phillips looks one last time at the inverted cross in the distance and spitefully utters his blasphemy.

"You think I'm sorry? I'm not sorry. Fuck you God! Fuck you."

Spencer Phillips curses God for the third time, but as Maria lifts the very tip of the brush from the canvas, he's consumed by an agonizing spasm of convulsive pain. A moment later he expels his last living breath. All motion is stilled and then, oblivion.

Spencer Phillips wakes within his soul's journey and discovers himself walking down a road in an unfamiliar landscape. He remembers his earthly life as if it were a dream, but this place where he now finds himself seems far more real than the world he just exited. He walks along and observes his surroundings. It's a sunny day in the country. The road stretching on before him contains no signs of human activity, with no buildings or streets to be seen.

The landscape Spencer Phillips sees is rustic and, except for the dirt road he's walking on, devoid of any trace of human activity. As he progresses on, vague memories of a painful death seep into his thoughts, but they seem more like a distant unpleasant memory. Continuing onward, he feels more relaxed and confident. After passing a row of hedges he sees a young woman with her back turned to him, picking apples. With her attention focused on what she's doing, a deadly impulse echoes through his mind, and a latent instinct to kill rises to the surface.

He's irresistibly drawn closer and thinks to himself, I have unfinished business to take care of.As he lunges forward to surprise her from behind, she screams and tries to run. After quickly overtaking the woman, he gets on top of her and starts choking his victim. Suddenly, from out of nowhere, four men appear and violently pull him off his quarry. Spencer Phillips is manhandled by several men who appear in every detail to be ancient Roman soldiers. Surrounded, he looks up to see another woman looking back at him. Her voice is clear and direct.

"We've been expecting you, Mr. Phillips."

"Who are you?"

"My name is Brianna," she says, and then turns to one of the soldiers.

"As I said it would be Commander, you saw it with your own eyes."

"We all saw what happened. This case is capitol. Caesar must hear it." Turning to Brianna, he continues. "My lady, you're a witness to this and must give your statement."

"All in accordance with Roman law," Brianna agrees.

"Must I go as well?" asks the assailed woman.. "No, his guilt is plain. You can go."

"I want to go home," she says.

"Lucius," says the commander.

"Yes sir."

"You and Trebonius escort this woman home, with all courtesies."

"Yes, Commander."

"The rest of you follow me."

"Wait a minute. Who are you people? If you think I'll just march off with you, you're mistaken. I'm not going anywhere," declares Spencer Phillips.

With no signal of his intention, the Roman officer walks over to Spencer Phillips and with a full, swinging blow, slaps his face. The stinging surprise of the unexpected assault is immediate and very painful.

"Oh, you'll go, either on your legs or I'll have my horse drag you. Wretch, I saw you try to kill a woman. You're under arrest."

This sharply unpleasant experience and being physically manhandled earlier convince Mr. Phillips this place is not imaginary, and that it's just turned very unfriendly toward him. As all parties walk away, two soldiers escort the woman home with her apples, while Spencer Phillips is led away. Accompanying them is Brianna and her still unseen apprentice Calvin Milner who, as before, is anonymously observing everything in silence. Passing along the same road that Spencer Phillips traveled earlier, they come to a turn and, as they make their way around it, something amazing comes into view. Stretching out across a huge field, he sees an entire Roman legion of over 5,000 men bivouacked on the open ground. Hundreds and hundreds of men, many dressed exactly like those escorting him, along with many horses, seeming to cover the ground in every direction. Spencer Phillips has never been a student of history, but everything he sees suggests they have arrived at an ancient Roman military camp. As the party of five enter the encampment, they pass dozens of men, some peering out through their tents as they pass, and even though a woman in this place is very unusual, no ill-tempered remark is heard. The disciplined restraint characteristic of a Roman soldier is expected from every man and, without exception, is shown by every man.

Curious glances are directed not at Brianna, but at the strangely dressed man being led under guard. They soon come to a large tent and are directed by the commander to wait as he approaches the soldier posted outside its entrance. Spencer Phillips looks around him and feels very apprehensive about what will happen. He sees men staring back at him, men who appear tough, masculine and, above all, disciplined. He rightly senses he's about to encounter the person whose authority rules here.

As they wait, Brianna hears a question whispered in her ear. Her unseen apprentice Calvin asks, "Are we really here?"

"We're only visiting, Calvin," she says quietly.

"But how?"

Brianna stops as all direct their attention toward a man emerging from the tent. The demeanor of those accompanying him immediately conveys without words that he and he alone is in command. He radiates confidence. A certain air surrounds him that seems to exude total authority, and for good reason. Spencer Phillips has no idea that the man standing before him is none other than the emperor Marcus Aurelius, absolute ruler of the Roman Empire in the year 168 A.D.. One of Rome's greatest emperors, Marcus Aurelius exemplifies the wisdom, virtue and restraint of Roman law and civility. In hearing the many cases brought before him his judgments are uniformly condign and, if possible, always reflect a penchant for mercy. Seeing the strangely dressed man before him he begins his inquiry.

"What man is this, Commander?"

"Caesar, we caught this man strangling a woman, and in my judgment trying to kill her."

"I am loathe to condemn any man, but if you prove to be so heinous as charged, the scales of justice must weigh against you."

Turning to the Roman officer Caesar asks, "Are there witnesses to this?"

"Four other soldiers, and this woman, Caesar, we all saw it happen."

"What is your name, woman?"

"My name is Brianna."

"Are you here to give honest testimony?"

"I am, Caesar."

Turning to Spencer Phillips, the emperor asks him,

"I'm curious. What drives a man to commit such an outrage?"

After a lengthy and what all see as a disrespectful pause, Caesar demands an answer.

"Speak!"

"I don't have to answer anyone's questions here. I don't know who you people are. I want a lawyer."

"It's very telling you offer no defense, and very damning. Look around you. Every man you see here is a Roman soldier who's risked his life many times. Tomorrow we face the Parthians. Some of the men you see here will have to swallow their own blood in the next battle. Do you know why? To defend civilization and the rule of law, law that protects the weak and the innocent, protecting them from criminals like you. You're not worth the slightest of their wounds. Vile, wicked man to come here with a fast intent to harm one of our own, a harmless woman picking apples."

"Worse than that Caesar, and much worse. I know this man's work."

"Speak then Brianna. I know your oath is holy."

"Caesar, this man has killed to satisfy his lust for murder. Twenty six times he has taken an innocent life. Eight of those were children, and one was a pregnant woman. Their promise cut short by the malignant hand of this murderer."

"Oh human viper! Methinks I see some fiend from the underworld before me in human form. What monster from Hades are you, to do these unspeakable things?"

Spencer Phillips hangs his head and comes the closest to uttering an honest statement about the life he's lived.

"I am what I am."

"And what is that but a thing loathsome and contemptible? Every breath you take is an affront to the potency of Roman law. Therefore, by that law, we purge ourselves of you, and your wicked offense. We find your crimes so heinous as to warrant immediate execution."

With a dismissive wave of the emperor's hand, the judgment and sentence is final. Spencer Phillips begins his protest.

"You can't do this to —"

In mid-sentence he feels a hand seize his left shoulder and the sudden thrust of a Roman sword entering cleanly through the soft space between his ribs, and in one push Spencer Phillips sees the tip of the blade exit his chest cavity, with the skill of the swordsman ensuring that the blade passes through his heart. Though he clearly sees the sword point protruding from his chest, for some reason the wound is not as physically painful as it should be. It's a symbolic wound, a wound that condemns, not a wound that kills. However, when the swordsman suddenly pulls the blade out, it's painful enough to bring Spencer Phillips to his hands and knees.

He feels a force pulling him downward as if gravity is somehow magnified beneath him.

Moments later he hears a voice in his ear. He remembers it as being the voice of the woman called Brianna.

"Thus you die a second time, once to the flesh and now to the spirit. Your posture is fitting. Never will you stand again with the erect dignity of the human form. Never again will your tongue sound with the liberating voice of language. Therefore descend. Live henceforth in the blind prison of brute instinct, a slave to the basest drives of fear and aggression. You wanted a world where you can kill. That world is now waiting for you."

Spencer Phillips feels a darkness enshrouding him, as if he were underground or in the deep recesses of a cave with no way out. He struggles to crawl on his hands and knees and somehow keeps moving forward. He feels a numbing heaviness to his labored effort as if he's dragging something behind him. A strange overpowering urge to get to water pushes him onward. After crawling on all fours for what seems like hours, he finally sees a river in the distance ahead. The sight of water has a powerful effect on him, drawing him onward like a magnet. A primitive drive to get as close as he can is irresistible. Finally, crawling to its edge, he looks on its surface and sees the reflected image of a face looking back at him, a non-human face, a face covered with scales instead of skin. He sees an appendage with claws rather than fingers. He sees a long row of teeth, and each one is an incisor for ripping flesh. He looks closer at the eye staring back at him with its vertical pupil, characteristic of reptiles. In his mind, part of him still seems human, but like a glimmering memory of some distant past event, it gently slips away. Thought, recollection and memory of all things human disappear, and then the final descent.

Somewhere in the deep interior of Africa, on the banks of a tributary of the Nile river, a male crocodile silently slips into the water and submerges. Keeping below the water line he turns back

toward the bank and waits, waits for his next victim, waits to kill again.

Seeing the animal glide into its ambush position, two disembodied souls watch from the river bank. It's Brianna, and her apprentice Calvin. Nonplussed for an explanation, Calvin tries to understand what he's witnessed.

"He's actually descended into a sub-human form. That's incredible."

"And rare; only a few of many thousands who arrive are destined for such an end."

"Will this animal ever remember it's former life?"
"No, that life, the life of Spencer Phillips, is gone forever."

"What happens now?"

"This creature will live out its life. Decades from now he'll still be here stalking and killing his victims, even eating its own offspring when it has the chance. This is the world Spencer Phillips lived for, and so now it's his."

"It's a tragedy."

"Yes it is, Calvin, but our next arrival is something very different, a gentle soul, a lady of genuine qualities."

"Are good things waiting for her?"

"Yes, of course. Come, let's go and see her arrival."

Calvin looks one last time at the submerged silhouette of the waiting reptile in the water, and pauses. Brianna looks at her apprentice and tells him, "Come Calvin. It's time to go. This place is fit for mayhem."

Chapter Eight: The Volunteer

In a quiet suburb of Indianapolis, Indiana, a woman is getting ready to leave her home and drive across town as she has three times a week for the last four years. Her name is Louise Robinson, and she's a volunteer. Every Monday, Wednesday and Friday, she works in a soup kitchen for four hours, and even though she's expecting a visit from her sister today who's flying in from New York for the weekend, because it's Friday, she's going to her volunteer job, as usual.

Louise's husband, Joseph, is growing more ambivalent about his wife giving her time as she does. When Louise started volunteering several years ago, he was still working full time, but Joseph retired six months ago and would now prefer to have his wife home with him. Joseph Robinson does not like being alone. He worked in the post office for 25 years and is psychologically unprepared for the leisure time that now fills his life. He knows he has to find a way to occupy his time each day, but nothing seems to spark his interest. Some days a pervading sense of ennui comes over him, and he becomes anxious and fidgety. Mr. Robinson never trained himself to a practiced habit of self-reliance, and so often calls on his wife for things he should do himself. Having Joseph home every day has been an adjustment for Louise, and not an easy one. This is part of the reason she values her time spent volunteering. Besides helping to forge a connection to the larger community, it provides her with a needed respite from domestic obligations.

Today Louise is looking forward to seeing her sister later on this afternoon. As she finishes washing the breakfast dishes her husband asks her, "What time's your sister coming in?"

"She should be here about four or five o'clock."

"Why don't you stay home today?"

"That won't get her here any faster. Her flight doesn't land until 3:30."

"We could meet her at the airport."

"She prefers to rent a car. Her employer pays for it."

"I guess being a corporate attorney has its perks," says Joseph.

"I suppose."

"You and your sister are very different."

"I don't think we are."

"You don't think so?"

"We're actually more alike than different."

"One person is a corporate attorney and the other volunteers in a soup kitchen. They sound like very different people to me."

"Maybe you should listen for other sounds Joe."

Pausing for a moment Louise tells her husband,

"I have to go."

"How long do you intend to volunteer at this food pantry, or whatever it is?"

"I don't know. Why do you ask?"

"I'm just curious. You've been giving your time to this place for four years now. What do you get out of it?"

"I guess it's the satisfaction of helping others." "I hope you don't bring one of these unfortunate souls home with you."

"You never know Joseph. You never know. I have to go."

Getting up and moving toward the door, Louise glances back at her husband. "You should come down some time and volunteer, Joe. You might like it."

As she closes the door behind her he takes another sip of coffee and says, "I don't think so."

As Louise Robinson makes her way across town to start her day, she's thinking about seeing her sister in a few hours. Her mood is upbeat and positive, but for a woman living seven miles to the south in Beech Grove, Indiana, this day is anything but pleasant, and just like the one before, is fraught with worry.

Regina Cooper and her family are facing a serious dilemma. The house she's lived in for the past ten years with her husband and nine year old daughter is being repossessed. Thomas Cooper is a loving husband and father, but after losing his job as an assembly line worker when his employer relocated overseas, his best efforts were not enough to make up for the loss of income. It was an unexpected setback for Mr. Cooper, who was told, along with his co-workers, that the company they worked for had no plans to move off-shore. When that decision was reversed, employees were given 30 days prior notice before their employment was terminated.

The bad news was made worse when, only days before, an unforeseen emergency forced his wife to undergo medical treatment with an extended hospital stay. Though insurance paid for most of the cost of his wife's care, a high deductible, and frequent doctor's appointments, combined with his loss of income, forced him to default on his mortgage payments. Despite his best efforts to work with the bank to try to keep his home, time has run out, and nothing more can be done. Things beyond their control have brought Thomas and Regina Cooper to a realization that they must accept something that now appears inevitable. Though they are mature enough to know they will eventually recover from this experience, their biggest concern is for their daughter Angela, who is still confused about what's happening.

Her mother has told her very little, only hinting at the possibility of moving somewhere else, and remaining silent about why they have to leave their home. Regina is trying to make the change as easy as possible for her daughter, but it's clear that Angela is unhappy with any talk about leaving the only home she's ever known. Sensing her parent's stress and the looming prospect of leaving her school and neighborhood friends is negatively affecting the sensitive child. Regina Cooper knows Angela will be unhappy about leaving, but can only hope that her daughter will adjust to the change as quickly as possible. The entire family is going through a crisis , the outcome of which is still uncertain. It's been less than three weeks since they learned of the bank's intention to foreclose on their home. Regina's mother has offered to take them in until they can find a place of their own, but she lives in an apartment with limited space. A second option would be to refinance and borrow enough from the equity to pay off the existing mortgage. The problem is finding a bank willing to loan the $72,000 needed to achieve that. Although Thomas Cooper is working again, his diminished income and his wife's inability to resume work until she fully recovers has made the likelihood of getting a loan very improbable.

Mr. Cooper and his wife have done everything humanly possible to avoid losing their home but are now resigned to what they both see as inevitable. Most galling of all, the loan manager, Scott Palmer, who's been assigned to see the foreclosure process completed, is the man who's been calling the Cooper home repeatedly for the last several months demanding payment. He has let it be known he intends to show the house whenever any prospective buyer wants to see it, whether the Coopers are home or not. Rather than stay and prolong their exit, Thomas Cooper believes it's better to begin the next chapter of their lives as soon as possible. As they sit having lunch before he leaves for work, Regina tries to be optimistic about the coming days.

"We'll be okay, Tom."

"I hope so ... How's Angela doing?"

"She's okay."

"I know she's confused about all this."

"She doesn't wanna leave," Regina says.

"She'll get over it. I talked to my uncle last night. He said we could live on his farm in Ohio if we wanted."

"In Ohio? That means Angela would have to start over in a new school. If we found a place in this area, she could stay where she is."

"That might not be possible," Tom cautions.

"Your uncle lives pretty far out in the country. What would you do for work?"

"What am I doing now? I'm working second shift in a retail outlet. I think I could do at least that good."

"If we stayed with my mother, we'd still be on familiar ground. I could take Angela to school every day until summer vacation starts. That's only two months away. I think moving all the way to Ohio's a little drastic."

"How can we stay at your mother's house? The place is so small."

"We'll adapt. Let's think about every option before we choose one so drastic."

After finishing his sandwich, Thomas pauses and looks around at the remodeled kitchen he spent so much time on years ago when they were both enthusiastic young home owners.

"I wish we could stay here," he sighs. Then, without hearing a response from his wife, Thomas Cooper stands up and readies himself to leave for work. After a terse goodbye from her husband, Regina sits alone and wonders what the coming days will bring. The thought of living on a farm in rural Ohio is distinctly unappealing, and she has serious doubts if she could ever make such a change. Moving to another state, moving away from everything familiar, and starting over, is not something Regina Cooper is willing to consider, at least not yet. That however doesn't change the fact that a decision has to be made soon and agreed on by both of them.

Regina Cooper is deeply conflicted about what she's facing. A visceral intuition tells her she'd be unhappy living on a farm hundreds of miles away. At the same time, she's aware of the basic obligation that marriage partners have to make sacrifices. Another consideration silently weighs on her thoughts; because of the expense of her prolonged illness, Regina Cooper can't quite escape the feeling she's at least partly responsible for what her family's going through. As she sits, her thoughts are a mixture of jumbled and conflicting emotions that seem to have no apparent resolution.

She looks over at the shelf next to the window and sees a picture of her daughter when she was five years old, dressed up as a miniature Santa Claus. She remembers when it was taken, four years ago in her own home, a home she and her family will soon leave forever. Quietly sitting, alone with her thoughts, an air of sadness comes over Regina Cooper, and is only partly dispelled by the sound of the doorbell. She hesitates before getting up to respond. When she opens the front door, the sight of a deputy sheriff standing in front of her is an unexpected and slightly unnerving surprise.

"Mrs. Regina Cooper?"

"Yes."

"I'm sorry ma'am, but I have to give you this."

After handing her an envelope, he wastes no time in leaving. "Good luck, ma'am."

Returning inside, Regina Cooper opens the letter addressed to Thomas and Regina Cooper. After seeing the county's letterhead and three words in large red type, the purpose of its content is instantly clear. It reads in capital letters, 'Notice of Eviction'.

Regina Cooper feels her heart sink as she absorbs its impact. Reading on, she learns her family has 90 days to vacate the house located at 1262 Parkman Court, an address she recognizes as her own. This is what they feared most and now it's happened. It now falls on her to tell her husband that they have three months to find another place to live. Angela will be home from school in a few hours, and Thomas will be back from work about 10:30 tonight. Regina has a long afternoon to think about what she'll say to her family.

While Regina Cooper ponders her dilemma, 17 miles to the north, in an opulent, lakefront home on Diamond Point Drive, a man is finishing lunch with his wife. His name is Charles Beckler, manager and CEO of Beckler Enterprises, a chain of retail furniture outlets throughout the mid-west. Unassuming, with an air of plain dealing bluntness about him, he's a man who achieved his wealth gradually through many years of hard work. Opening his first furniture store with borrowed money when he was 22, Charles Beckler practiced an austere work ethic, and for years stoically put in 14 hour days, doing everything he could to build a successful business. Now, over five decades later with 37 stores across 14 states, he delegates most of the responsibilities to his daughter and two sons who now manage the enterprise.

Though he no longer runs the day-to-day operations of the company, all major decisions affecting Beckler Enterprises are made by Charles Beckler and only Charles Beckler. His formidable personality and direct personal commitment to socially responsible business practices have been a driving force behind his personal and economic success. Mr. Beckler has for decades made it company policy to hire 20% of his workforce from impoverished backgrounds, including a successful program setting aside half that number for applicants with a criminal record. When asked about the policy, he just shrugged and said, "we all need a second chance sometime in our life."

Charles Beckler has enjoyed as much success as any reasonable man could ever hope to achieve, and developed a reputation for personal integrity both as a corporate and private citizen. His dedicated wife Connie has been with him from the beginning, standing by him when he was an indebted young businessman, and still with him now 51 years later, remaining a faithful and steadfast companion. Their three children are honest, competent, and as professionally committed to the continued success of Beckler Enterprises as their father. Charles Beckler knows he's leaving the company in good hands. He also knows he's now facing a new challenge in his life. Mr. Beckler has recently stopped working and is not accustomed to being home every day. At 74, he's in excellent health. The disciplined regimen of a healthy diet and years of moderate living are now paying back their dividends. Charles Beckler still feels relevant and vital. He must now channel his personal energy in new directions. To ease his transition into retirement he returns to his office in Indianapolis once or twice a week to keep his finger on the pulse of his company's business life. Today he's home. As he sits with his wife Connie enjoying the spacious lakefront view from their breakfast room, their maid Anna, serves coffee.

"Thank you Anna, lunch was delicious," Mr. Beckler says.

"Oh, you're welcome. More coffee ma'am?"

"No, I'm fine Anna, thank you. Oh Anna, that reminds me. Thank you for helping out with the party last week."

"I'm glad to do it ma'am," Anna says as she exits.

"So, tell me Charley. What do you think about going overseas for a month or two? You might enjoy yourself."

"You mean Australia?"

"Yes, and New Zealand."

"We've been there once."

"Yeah, but only for a few days. You said you wanted to go back some time."

"Did I say that?"

"Yes, you did. Remember that restaurant where we ate, with the guitar player who came to our table?"

"I remember. He played classical guitar. It was wonderful."

"Remember the view of the Pacific Ocean from our hotel balcony? It was incredible. I think of all the places we've visited, that was my favorite."

"It was beautiful."

"We should go back there and spend a couple of weeks, Charley. I'd like to hear that guitar player again. Wouldn't you?"

"It's been four years since we were there. He's probably gone."

"I'll bet I can find out."

"How would you do that?"

"I'll call the hotel where we stayed and ask someone to check."

"And if he's still there, what then, dearest?"

"Just something to think about."

"I guess we could get away for a while," Mr. Beckler concedes and, after pausing for a moment he tells his wife, "You know, I really feel good about the kids taking over the company."

"I know it's been hard for you to let go," says Connie.

He shrugs. "Can't hold on forever, I guess. You're right about that."

"It's time to relax, Charley."

"Maybe you're right ... You know what I'm gonna do?"

"What's that?"

"Grow a beard."

"A beard, why?"

"I always wanted to, but felt I couldn't because I'm the face of the company."

"Well, I think you should grow a beard then."

"I could get my hair spiked and dyed purple."

"Mm, I think the beard's enough for now."

Connie Beckler has known her husband for over 50 years. The courtesy and mutual affection they show each other is based on the love, trust, and respect that's been tempered through decades of their marriage. She knows better than anyone that her husband will need time and patience to accept fully the idea of relinquishing control of a business enterprise that represents the sum total of his life's work. Charles Beckler is fortunate to have such a wife as Connie, and he would be the first to say it. Since he's now retired, she would prefer more time with her husband, but knows for now she must be supportive and patient.

She feels a mixture of gratitude and contentment, and also a renewed sense of responsibility to see him through his transition to full retirement. Connie is optimistic about their future. She knows time is on her side. Looking out on another wonderful day from her opulent lakefront home, Connie Beckler finishes her coffee and thinks about the guitar player who played for them at dinner when they vacationed in New Zealand, and her curiosity stirs.

Meanwhile, close to downtown Indianapolis, Louise Robinson is finishing her day of volunteering at the free soup kitchen and

food bank. As she's cleaning off a serving table, she recognizes an elderly man who's a regular at the soup kitchen approaching her.

"Hi Anthony," she says.

"Hello Miss Louise, how are you?"

"I'm doing great. My sister's coming to visit me today."

"Well that's nice. Are you close to your sister?"

"Yes, we've always stayed in touch with each other."

"That's the way it should be," he says.

"How are you doing Anthony?"

"Well, that's what I wanted to talk to you about. I'd like your opinion on something."

"Sure, what's on your mind?"

"My brother called me last weekend from Toledo. His wife died, and he wants me to move in with him."

"Is that something you wanna do, Anthony?"

"I'm not really sure."

"Does your brother have a home?"

"Yes, he does, a nice one. It's just that I haven't spoken to my brother in years. I don't know if we'd get along."

"Well, you don't know that you wouldn't get along. Why don't you go there for a few days and then come back and think about it?"

"I suppose I could do that."

"Who knows? Living with your brother could be what both of you need. If it doesn't work out, at least you gave it a try."

"I knew you'd give good advice Louise. You always do."

After a pause, Louise looks at her watch and says, "are you gonna be alright Anthony?"

"Oh yeah, I'm alright. I'll be seein' ya Louise."

"Bye Anthony."

As Louise Robinson finishes work and prepares to return home, she's thinking about her sister, who's already called her from the car rental desk at the airport, and is now driving to Louise's home. Barbara flies from New York usually two or three times a year and her last visit was only five weeks ago. This visit was unexpected, and it seems a little curious to Louise that she would call only two days before arriving, but this will in no way diminish the enjoyment of spending time with her sister, whose welcome company she always finds pleasant. As she begins the short drive home, the eager anticipation of seeing her sister preoccupies her thoughts.

Meanwhile, Louise's husband Joe is occupying his time with a crossword puzzle when he sees an unfamiliar car pull into the driveway. He instantly recognizes the driver as his sister-in-law Barbara, and moments later opens the front door to greet her.

"Hello Barbara,"

"Hi Joe, good to see you."

"Good to see you Barb. How was the flight?"

"Nice, and smooth, and on time."

"Well that's good. Louise should be home soon. She's probably in traffic. Can I get you something?"

"No thanks Joe, I'll just sit for a while. I've been running all day."

"Yeah, sure have a seat. So you're in town for just a few days."

"Actually I go back tomorrow night. So it's just a quick visit."

"Well that's nice. Louise is looking forward to seeing you."

"How's she doing?"

"Still down at the soup kitchen, I think she's wasting her time."

"Why do you say that?"

"She's there three days a week, five hours each day. That's a lot o' time. It's easy to take advantage of Louise. It's her weakness."

"Do you think that's what's happening?"

"I think so. They know they'd have to pay someone to replace her."

"How about you, Joe? How do you like retirement?"

"To be honest, it's a little different from what I thought it would be, but I'll manage. How about you Barb? What's it like being a corporate attorney?"

"Most of it's pretty mundane actually, a lot of talking on the phone, working out contracts, that type of thing. None of it's very dramatic."

"I'm sure it's important stuff."

"It is for the client. He's paying for it."

"You probably have a lot of responsibility on your shoulders."

"That's true for anybody who works, at least to some degree."

"I don't know how true that is for your sister. She doesn't even get paid."

"Well, she's a volunteer. More people should do that."

"I wish they would. Maybe then she could spend more time at home."

"I'm sure she finds it personally rewarding."

"I guess so, whatever."

The sound of a car pulling into the driveway signals Louise's arrival, and when Louise sees Barbara's rental car already parked, the two sisters happily anticipate seeing each other again.

Suppressing a smile, Barbara says, "That's Louise." Moments later the front door opens.

"Hi Barb."

"Hi Louise, how are you?"

"I'm fine, I had to stay a little longer at the kitchen. So how've you been?"

"I'm doing okay, busy as usual."

The two women embrace in unfeigned mutual affection.

"Good to see you, Sis."

"Good to see you, a little unexpected," says Louise.

"Yeah, I hope you don't mind the short notice."

"It's always good to see my sister, short notice, long notice, or no notice at all."

"You're sweet. I don't know, I just felt an impulse to come see you, so here I am."

"I'm so glad you came. Have you been telling Joe about how much trouble we used to get into as kids?"

"Oh, I think that would bore him."

"Not at all, I'd love to hear all about it," Joe says.

"You look good Louise. You're staying healthy."

"I feel good."

"You were always careful with your diet," says Barbara.

"She's trying to get me to eat healthy too," Joe says.

"Speaking of food, are you hungry?" Louise asks.

"I'm okay. I'll have something later. What about you? You just got home from work."

"I know a good restaurant you'd like," Louise says.

"Which one is that?" asks Joe.

"Antonio's,"

"Oh yeah, excellent."

Barbara hesitates. "Actually, I'd rather just stay here and visit with you."

"Sure we can go out tomorrow if you want. I'll get something started on the stove."

"Why don't we do this," Joe says. "I'll drive down and get some Chinese takeout while you two catch up on things. How's that sound?"

"Chinese okay, Barb?" asks Louise.

"Sure, that sounds great."

"Thanks Joe."

Minutes later Joe exits and Barbara looks at her sister intently without speaking. The moment is instantly perceived by Louise and she asks, "What is it, Barbara?"

"I don't know. I just had a strange thought that you were going somewhere."

"Where would I go?"

"I don't know ... It's nothing. I'm really glad to see you," says Barbara.

"Well, I'm more than happy to see you. So, how's work?"

"Oh, it never changes, tedious and repetitive. Let's not talk about that. Seeing you standing there reminded me of something."

"What's that?"

"When we were kids, you used to stretch your arms out like that. Are you still doing yoga?"

"Yes, every morning, it keeps me limber."

"Are you surprised to see me back so soon?"

"A little, when you called to tell me you were coming I thought it was a bit curious. Is something on your mind?"

"The past few weeks I've been thinking about how we grew up together in that house on Piedmont Avenue back in Muncie."

"I remember. That was nearly 40 years ago. They say time speeds up as you grow older. I believe it."

"So do I ... You know why I came to see you Louise?"

"Why?"

"To say thank you."

"For what?"

"For being a good sister and friend ... I never told you, but when I was in high school, and you were one grade ahead of me, it was a relief to know you were always around. I was pretty shy. high school was kind of intimidating for me. You always made an effort to check on me. It was nice to know that you were there."

Taking her sister's hands into her own, Louise tells her. "Oh Sis, and I thank you, you were there for me as well."

"No, I wasn't, Louise. You were the strong one. You were my protector. I wasn't yours."

"Well, we both got through it Barb, and guess what, we had some fun along the way."

"We did. We sure did... It's always good to see you sister."

"The feeling's mutual Barbara. I assure you. Well, what would you like to do tonight? We can stay here or go out."

"Let's stay home."

"Sure."

"Now, I'll test your memory," Barbara tells her sister. "Okay, I'm ready."

"Do you remember when Dad set up our TV in the attic so we could watch it on weekends?"

"Sure, I think I was about thirteen when we started doing that. It was fun staying up late."

"That's right, because I was eleven. Do you remember the first movie we watched?"

"Uh, no I don't."

"I do."

"What was it?"

"It was this," Barbara says as she reaches for her purse. "Here, this will spark your memory."

"What do you have? Let's see ... Oh wow, 'Teenage Mutant Zombies', and two Woody Allen movies, you do remember. Don't you?"

"Of course. You know what I'd like to do?"

"What?" Louise asks.

"I'd like to watch these again with you. Does that sound silly?"

"Not at all, it sounds like fun."

"We'll have some Chinese food and watch them together."

"You think Joe would like that?"

"I don't think so. He reads in the evening. It'll be just you and me."

"That sounds wonderful," Barbara says.

As Barbara and Louise happily reminisce about their high school years both feel a renewed emotional connection to their past and each other, but for Barbara in particular who felt impelled to make this trip to be with her sister, the experience is especially poignant. This night, giddy with the laughter and savored memories of two sisters, will become for Barbara one of the most cherished memories of her life.

Chapter Nine: A Family Crisis

The following morning in Beech Grove, a suburb of Indianapolis, Tom and Regina Cooper are feeling very uncertain about the future. Last night, after seeing their nine year old daughter

to bed, Regina Cooper had showed her husband the eviction notice that had been delivered by the deputy sheriff. Its impact was immediate, and a tense mood of apprehension has hung uncomfortably in the air since. It seems the Coopers are having difficulty initiating a conversation they both wanted very much to avoid.

As their daughter upstairs gets ready for school, Regina Cooper breaks the silence.

"So what do you think?"

"I hate to say it, but I don't see any solution. We'll have to leave. It's a court order. What can we do?"

"We have three months to find something."

"I don't wanna stay here that long."

"Why not? It'll give us more time to save money. We'll be better off if we wait."

"I can't live with the idea of this guy Palmer coming into our place with a stranger any time he wants, just so he can sell it and get his commission. The man's a vulture. Look Regina, I know you don't wanna go to Ohio. It's tough starting over. I know that."

"Why does that have to be our first option? We have some time to think about this. As far as Scott Palmer's concerned, that's exactly what he wants, to chase us off this property. He works for the bank. That's his angle."

"I don't like that man."

"Neither do I. So are we gonna let this guy chase us off our property? I don't think so."

"I agree with you, but we'll still have to go eventually. What if my uncle changes his mind? I mean living on a farm in Ohio can't be too disagreeable, can it? I understand it's not your first choice Regina, but we have to do something."

"Let's do this, let's wait a few weeks. We just got this notice yesterday. Let's think about it for a while."

"What do we tell Angela?"

"Nothing for now."

"We have to tell her sometime."

"Let me handle it please."

After hearing their daughter descending the stairs, Regina says to her husband in a hushed breath, "She doesn't know about the eviction notice, so don't say anything."

As Tom looks at his wife, he hears his daughter's voice. "I'm ready."

"Did you get enough to eat, Angela?"

"Yes."

"Let's go then. You don't wanna be late for school," Regina urges.

"Oh, I forgot to ask you something," Angela says.

"What's that sweetheart?"

"There having a field trip next month and they're asking us to sign up if we wanna go."

"What kind o' field trip? Where are they taking you?"

"They wanna take us to the zoo. Can I go, Daddy?"

"Uh, we'll see honey."

"I'll see you later," Regina says to her husband, avoiding eye contact as she leaves to take her daughter to school.

The closing door and ensuing silence seem to transform the room instantly, as if his home, the house he lives in, already belongs to someone else. In an almost out of body experience, Tom contemplates the room he's sitting in and now sees only a somber reflection of a past that seems to have already slipped away forever. How can he feel an attachment to a place where he and his family have no future? Losing the only home his family has ever known is the biggest financial and psychological setback Thomas Cooper has experienced in his adult life, and though he did everything he could to avoid it, it still represents a measure of personal failure.

As he sits alone in the silence of his thoughts, he thinks of his daughter Angela and wonders what he'll say when she asks again about her school's field trip to the zoo next month.

Hours later, and less than twenty miles from the Cooper residence, Charles Beckler is finishing lunch with his wife in their magnificent lakefront home on Diamond Point Drive. The affluence and financial security of their lives stand in stark contrast to the pecuniary struggles that Tom and Regina Cooper are experiencing.

Though he's now well beyond any likelihood of material want, Mr. Beckler is a man who understands the nagging exigencies of economic privation. Charles Beckler's father was a railroad worker and supported his family with a modest income, but after he died when Charles was 12, that income disappeared and real hardship ensued for him, his mother and three siblings. This early experience with poverty is something he never forgot. It taught him that circumstances and economic conditions can change without warning, and no one is immune from unforeseen misfortune. Charles Beckler has been tempered by his life experience. As a result, he has acquired wealth without being fundamentally changed by it. Now he's retired and attempting to live a very different life than that of a busy executive, the idea of developing new interests is becoming more appealing.

With support and gentle encouragement from his wife, what seemed only weeks before to be an unlikely and difficult transition into retirement is seeming more tenable with each passing day for Charles Beckler. Connie has noticed the incremental change in her husband's mood and outlook. She sees a man a little more relaxed, a little more carefree, and at times even a little more introspective. Connie Beckler knows the small changes she's seeing in her husband are exactly what he needs, and she's prepared to do everything she can to encourage it.

As they sit together after lunch, Connie comments on her husband's new facial appearance. "Hey, Charley."

"Yes love?"

"Now that you've stopped using a razor, do you intend to trim your beard or let it grow willy-nilly?"

"I don't know. I imagined the freedom to live without a razor was absolute, rather like a statement of uncompromising human freedom. Wouldn't you think?'

"How would it limit your freedom if you trimmed your beard? Come on, and besides, you'll look like a caveman. It might be scary to wake up in the middle of the night and look over at a caveman in bed with me."

"It's funny you should mention that. I had a strange dream last night."

"What was it?"

"I was sitting on a dock by a lake. It was a beautiful, warm day. I was fishing. I had a basket of fish beside me and this woman walked up to me and asked me what I was doing. She asked, "why are you still fishing when your basket's already full? You have too many fish in your basket. You can hardly lift it." I asked her what I should do with

it. She said, "Keep what you need and give the rest away." I tried to lift the basket, but it was too heavy. I told her I couldn't lift it and she said she would send someone to help me. That's all I remember. It was a strange dream. It was so vivid."

"Did you recognize the woman?"

"No, I'd never seen her before. Her name was Brianna. She was very unusual."

"She said she'd send someone to help you?" Connie asks.

"That's what she told me."

"What do you think it means?"

"I don't know. It's hard to say."

"Dreams are hard to decipher."

"This one seemed pretty real ... Oh well, who knows?"

"Oh, I forgot to mention, I have to go into town this afternoon. The garden club is meeting today."

"I thought they met on Wednesdays."

"They usually do, but they moved it up a day so the painters can start working on the building tomorrow."

"I'll have John drive you."

"There's no need. I can drive my car," Connie says.

"Why don't you let John drive you? That's why he's here."

"What will you do if you have go somewhere?"

"Don't worry love. I'm home for the day."

"Are you sure?"

"Yes, of course, I'll be all right. Besides, I'd feel better if John drove you in. He's such a good driver. Here, let me get him."

As Mr. Beckler reaches for the cell phone on the table, he asks Connie, "When do you wanna leave?"

"It starts at two, so I need to leave about 1:30. I'd better go and get changed."

"Hi John, would you get the car ready and take Connie into town today? She'll be ready around 1:30. Uh huh, okay, thanks John."

Putting the cell phone down he tells Connie, "It's all set. John is coming at 1:30."

"Thanks Charley."

"I know you're capable Connie, but I feel better when you ride with John."

"I know you do."

"Besides, he likes driving you."

"He's such a gentleman. How long's he been with us now?" she asks.

"I don't know, at least 12 years or so."

Connie stands to kiss her husband and says, "Thank you for lunch. I could get used to it."

"So could I, Connie. I can't think of anyone I'd rather have lunch with."

"You're sweet. Have a nice afternoon."

"You too, love."

After a parting kiss from his wife, Charles Beckler sits back and thinks for a moment about his new life of retirement, but his thoughts soon turn again to the dream he had last night. What could it mean? Was it significant, or just the random musings of his imagination? This dream was different, not only for its intensity, but in the curious way it abruptly ended. He remembers standing on the dock looking down at a basket of fish he'd just caught and trying to lift it.

He especially recalls the strange woman named Brianna and what she told him. "You have too many fish," she said. "Do something with them or they'll rot, and if they do, part of you will rot with them. Don't let that happen, Charley."

What could she mean by that? The prospect of revisiting this dream is somehow a vaguely comforting notion for him. In its last few moments when he'd strained to lift his basket of fish, Brianna had looked at him intently and, with an expression of friendly encouragement said, "Don't worry. I'll send someone to help you."

The immediate effect of hearing those few words brought a calming sense of peace and well-being to his thoughts. Now, remembering the details of his dream, his thoughts are tinged with an imperceptible desire to return to it, but how does one return to a dream? Then the practical and rational side of his mind asserts itself. He's a realist and accustomed to dealing with matters of choice, necessity and action through logic and objective evaluation. This is the way he's lived his life and successfully forged a long business career.

Divining the portents of a dream, any dream, no matter how compelling it might be, suddenly seems a pointless exercise of idle speculation. Besides, what could be gained from it? Dreams are wispy, insubstantial and fleeting, and are best left to memory. The real world is what matters. As he looks out on the beautiful lakefront view from his wonderful home everything in his life and world seems tranquil and happy. Everything seems perfectly in place.

As the leisurely afternoon hours pass for Charles Beckler in his comfortable home near Indianapolis, in another part of the city a different scene is playing out. Louise Robinson and her sister Barbara are spending the last few minutes of their time together before Barbara leaves to catch a flight back to New York. As they sit together on the couch, Barbara glances at her watch.

"I know you have to go," Louise says. "I still have a few minutes." "I'm so glad you came, what a wonderful surprise."

"Next time I'll let you know I'm coming," Barbara says.

As the two women rise and embrace, they feel that surge of loving mutual affection that the departure of a loved one always brings, and in a soft hush of words intended for the hearer only, Barbara tells her sister,

"I love you."

"I love you too, Sis."

A moment passes, and it's time to leave. A salutary hug from Joseph and Barbara is ready. She tells her sister, "Listen, I'll call you later when I get in."

"Please do. I'll walk you out," says Louise.

After a final goodbye to Joe, Barbara and Louise exit the house and within seconds are standing beside Barbara's rental car.

"Thanks for everything."

"Thank you Barb, for coming, and thank you for bringing the movies. I loved it. Let's do it again."

"We will, goodbye."

"Bye bye,"

After one final, long embrace, Louise walks back to her front door, turns around for one last wave goodbye and then re-enters her home. She glances over to the TV and sees the two DVDs that her sister brought with her. Rushing back out the front door with them, she sees Barbara's car has already pulled away. She closes the door and walks back into the kitchen where she sees Joseph making a cup of tea.

"Want some tea, Louise?"

"Oh, no thanks."

"Well, that was a nice visit," he says.

"Yeah, it was. We had fun."

"Good, that's what visits are for."

"I'm gonna take a nap. I'm tired."

"You should be. You were up with your sister all night."

"Yeah, almost, I'll see you later."

Minutes later Louise is resting in bed and quickly slips into a deep sleep. Several hours pass as she sinks deeper and deeper until the threshold of her dreamscape is reached and she enters. After waking within her dream, Louise Robinson is sitting on the front porch of her parent's home where she grew up as a child, decades earlier.

She looks out at the driveway where the old station wagon that carried her to so many places is parked. All appears as it did when she was a child; the green bicycle she rode so frequently to the local store is still at the end of the porch where she always kept it, the rose hedge she helped her father plant with its beautiful deep red blooms looks the same as it did when she was a girl. All is as she remembers it. Then a familiar voice calls her name, a voice she knows well.

"Louise, supper's almost ready."

The sound of her mother's call to dinner is as routine and familiar as it had always been. As she sits gazing out from the porch of her childhood home, she sees a woman waving back at her from across the street. It's Mrs. Carlysle, a neighbor Louise remembers from her teen years.

"Hi Louise."

"Hi Mrs. Carlysle," Louise hears herself say without hesitation. Everything appears relaxed and casual as if passing time and accumulated age had never happened. All seems routine and unremarkable. A moment passes, and she hears her mother's voice again.

"Louise, can you help me with something?"

As Louise hears her mother's request, she finds herself in the kitchen standing beside her. A pervading sense of love and deep well-being comes over her as she watches her mother a few feet away washing dishes.

"Could you dry these pots off for me honey?" she hears her mother ask. Louise sees no show of surprise or greeting in her mother's face and all seems routine and completely normal. With a profound, almost mystical contentment, Louise finishes drying the last of the cooking pots and hears her mother say, "There, now we're ready for you when you come back for dinner tomorrow. Your father had to work late today but he'll be here tomorrow when we eat together."

Hearing her mother speak these puzzling words leaves Louise momentarily perplexed. Then she hears a soft knock on the kitchen screen door.

"That's our friend Brianna," she hears her mother say.

Louise watches as her mother dries her hands and walks over to open the door.

"Hi Brianna, come in."

"Hi Carol, thank you."

Hearing the woman named Brianna address her mother by name, and seeing her embrace her warmly somehow affirms the presence of something mysterious and benign. The appearance of this dark complected woman is immediately compelling for Louise Robinson. An aura of magnetic benevolence seems to surround her. Who could she be? Her gentle, compassionate smile seems to be for Louise only, as if love and mercy incarnate were looking back at her.

"Hi Louise, your mother and I were expecting you."

Without replying, Louise hears her mother speak.

"Honey, I know you have to work tomorrow at the food pantry, but we'll pick you up afterwards and you'll come back for dinner. Then Brianna needs your help with something."

"We'll be there with you tomorrow Louise, both of us. There's nothing to be afraid of," Brianna says. "When I see you again Louise, we'll have work to do."

Then suddenly the dream ends, and Louise Robinson hears the unpleasant sound of an alarm clock. It's morning again and minutes later she's on her feet and waking to a new day. One hour later Joe rises and enters the kitchen to find Louise alert and ready for her day.

"Morning."

"Morning Joe."

"I bet you're well rested. You went to bed early," he says.

"Yeah, I was exhausted."

"Your sister called last night about 10:30. She got home safe. I told her you were sleeping."

"Oh good, thank you. That's nice to know ... I had the strangest dream last night."

"What kind of dream?"

"I was back in my parents' home where I grew up. It was just as I remembered it. I actually spoke with my mother. Everything was the same, except for a strange woman who was there with my mother. They told me they'd pick me up at work today."

"Is that all?"

"She asked about Barbara."

"Who did?"

"My mother, then she told me I'd be back today to have dinner with her and Dad."

"Your parents have been dead for years. I wouldn't read too much into it. You can drive yourself crazy trying to figure out a dream. Speaking of your sister, if you weren't at the soup kitchen so much, you could visit her more often, spend more time with her, and me for that matter."

"I told you Joe. I like working there."

"I don't know why."

"It gives me a good feeling. I have friends there, people I know."

"Then let them come here and visit you."

"Most of them don't have cars. They don't drive."

"Who are you talking about?"

"People I know at the food pantry."

"You mean homeless people?" Joe asks.

"Yes."

"I thought you were talking about staff and co-workers. Are you kidding? Why would you wanna be friends with people who are essentially destitute? I have nothing against them, but —"

"But what?" Louise asks

"These people go there because they can't even feed themselves. Isn't that right?"

"Of course, you don't show up at a soup kitchen unless you're hungry."

"Well, even if you weren't there, they'd still get fed. Beyond that, what can you possibly do for these people? They live their lives in a permanent state of emergency. Realistically, what can you do for them?"

"I talk to them. I listen to what they have to say. Sometimes they ask for advice."

"Really? So now you're a counselor to the destitute?"

"Sometimes, I'm only gone three days a week for a total of fifteen hours. The rest of the time, I'm usually here. What's the big deal?" Louise asks.

"I'd like you to be here all the time."

"Having friends outside the home is normal, Joe."

"I think most people would say you're wasting your time."

"My sister doesn't think so. She said she might start volunteering somewhere herself."

"Oh, come on Louise. You can't make that comparison. She lives in a different world."

"Really? How so? We were both on planet earth the last time I checked."

"She's a corporate attorney with international clients. She's paid a fortune for her legal advice. I'd say that's a lot different from giving some derelict advice on where he can flop for the night."

Louise pauses before stating, "Actually, they're probably not that different."

"Okay, sure, whatever."

"You don't see the similarities?"

"No, I don't. How are they similar?"

"Well, people who talk to my sister are looking for a solution to a problem. I talk to people with problems all the time who need solutions. People who talk to my sister are trying to avoid being harmed in some way, just like a lot of the people I talk to."

"Here's the difference, the big difference Louise, people who talk to your sister pay for her advice and always take it. The people you talk to don't act on your advice. They just want some attention."

"How do you know that?"

"Come on. Do you really think these people take you seriously?"

"Yes, they do."

"No, they don't. You're dreaming."

"They do listen to me."

"Don't be naïve. I hate to break the news to you, but the only place your advice will ever be taken is in dreamland. In dreamland, okay? I'm gonna take a shower."

With these few curt, ungentle words, Joe gets up and walks out of the kitchen without looking at his wife. He has no idea he'll never see her alive again.

Later that morning as Louise is volunteering at the soup kitchen, Regina Cooper in Beech Grove, south of Indianapolis, is dealing with an immediate problem. She's just received a phone call from Scott Palmer, the loan officer who's handling the foreclosure of her home. He told her he's coming today to show the house to a potential buyer. She sits with her husband, whose slow, simmering anger is palpable, and he asks her, "When did he say he was coming?"

"Some time in the afternoon."

"I need to stay home."

"No Tom, you need to go to work. I'll be fine."

"I don't like the idea of him being here when I'm gone."

"Look, if it makes you feel any better, before he gets here I'll call the sheriff, just to let them know what's happening. So don't worry."

"I really don't like that man. What kind of person would march through someone's home with a stranger while a family's still living there? I couldn't do that."

"Tom, it's not worth getting into an argument over. It'll only make things worse. Look, do me a favor, just go to work. We'll talk about it later. Show some restraint. This is still our home."

"Thank God Angela's in school... Are you sure you'll be all right?"

"I'll be fine."

"Calling the sheriff is a good idea, and when Palmer gets here, let him know that's what you did."

"I will. I promise."

Tom and Regina Cooper are mostly silent for the better part of an hour as they sit together. Then, after waiting until the last possible minute, Tom stands and says goodbye to his wife.

"Okay, I'll see you later. Call me if you need me."

"I will. I will."

As Tom leaves for work, Regina sits and waits, but she's not the only one about to receive an uninvited visitor.

Joseph Robinson is sitting in the kitchen drinking coffee and reading the newspaper when he hears the doorbell ring. Opening his front door, he's taken aback to see a female police officer.

"Mr. Robinson?"

"Yes."

"Mr. Robinson, my name is Tina Shaeffer. I'm with the sheriff 's office. I wonder if I could come in for a minute."

"Sure, what's this about?"

Without sitting, she wastes no time in relaying the news she came to deliver.

"Mr. Robinson, there's been an unfortunate occurrence at the food kitchen where your wife was working."

"What happened?"

"A man walked in about 1:30 this afternoon with a gun and started shooting. Unfortunately Louise was one of the three people who were hit, and I'm sorry to say, she did not survive."

"What?"

"I'm very sorry to tell you this."

"... Oh my God, no, no I can't ... I can't believe this. I sat with her this morning ... Are you sure it was her?"

"She was matched with her driver's license."

"No — no. I was with her this morning. I didn't want her to go. That goddamn place. Some low life derelict murdered my wife. Is that what you're telling me?"

"I'm so sorry to have to tell you this."

"Those low life bastards, all of them."

"Sir, I have to ask you if there are other family members who need to be informed."

"... Just her sister that's all."

"We can get in touch with her, if you prefer not to."

"No, no I'll tell her. I can't believe this."

With a dazed expression of disbelief, Joseph Robinson staggers to a chair and sits. His muted incoherence prompts officer Shaeffer to break the uncomfortable silence.

"Mr. Robinson, we have bereavement counselors who can help you get through this. I'll leave their phone number here if you'd like to talk to them. I urge you, not to try and get through this alone."

"Who was it that did this?"

"He was a 42 year old man who allegedly had a grievance with the people who ran the food pantry. That's as much as I know."

"Where is he?"

"He's been arrested."

"Low life scum, I would've killed him with my bare hands if I was there."

"If it's any comfort, they said it happened so fast she didn't suffer."

"I... I can't get my head around this."

"Do you have friends or relatives that can help you get through this? Maybe you should have someone come over tonight. I think it would help."

"What good's that gonna do?"

"Mr. Robinson, I have to ask you, are you gonna be all right?"

"...Yeah ... I'll be all right."

"Are you sure? I could have someone come here and sit with you."

"No, no."

"Some people react to bad news by doing something they otherwise wouldn't do. Please don't do anything rash, okay?"

"Yeah, right."

"There's one more thing, Mr. Robinson. You'll be asked to go downtown for a positive identification and to sign some release forms. They'll call you when they're ready for you, probably tomorrow sometime. Are you sure you're gonna be all right?"

"I'm not sure of anything right now... Thanks for coming over."

"Well, I'll show myself out. Here's the phone number if you want someone to come over and sit with you. We have people trained to do this. It can really make a difference."

Hearing no response Officer Shaeffer asks, "How about if I stop by tomorrow to see how you're doing? Would that be all right?"

"... Sure."

"Once again, Mr. Robinson, I'm so sorry. I'll see you tomorrow."

Moments later Joseph Robinson is alone and staring blankly into the empty space in front of him. As the terrible magnitude of his loss seeps into his thoughts, a slow, numbing psychological paralysis comes over him. Louise was the perfect helpmate.

The thought of never seeing her again is simply too painful to consider. Joseph feels utterly lost and alone. Immersed in a flood of grief-stricken sorrow, he sits in silence and begins to weep. Joseph Robinson will remember this night as the worst might of his entire life. He won't rise from his chair for another seven hours before grief and exhaustion finally yield to the intercession of merciful sleep. Joseph Robinson is now and forever a changed man. The sudden loss of his dear wife Louise is an emotional trauma from which he will never completely recover.

Though less tragic, the trouble that afflicts Tom and Regina Cooper's residence is very serious and escalating. Still struggling to find a way to avoid being evicted from their home, they are now grappling with a dilemma that has now become a crisis. After being at work for nine hours, Thomas Cooper is beside himself, galled because Scott Palmer was in his home while he was gone. Resentful and agitated, he and his wife Regina are not in accord as to what they should do next. After waiting for their daughter Angela to go to bed, Regina tries to soften her husband's unpleasant mood.

"It wasn't that bad. He wasn't here very long."

"I just don't like the idea of him being here when I'm gone."

"Don't let it bother you, Tom."

"It has been bothering me. It's been bothering me all day long. I've made a decision."

"What do you mean?" asks Regina.

"We can't stay here, Regina. If we stay here, this guy will make it miserable for us. I just know it."

"Where can we go?"

"For now, we can move in with my uncle."

"You mean in Ohio?"

"Why not?"

"What about Angela? She's not done with school yet."

"She'll make the adjustment."

"Oh, just like that, huh? This is the only home she's ever known, and the only neighborhood she's ever lived in."

"Look Regina. We don't have a choice. We have to do something."

"Fine, let's make sure it's also the smart thing to do."

"That's what I'm trying to do."

"I think you're overreacting, Tom."

"No, I'm not. I'm being a realist."

"You mean you're ready to walk away from the ten years we've lived here, all the time and money we put into this place?"

"I hate to leave this place as much as you do, but we have a mortgage of $72,000 that we can't pay. We'll just have to start over."

"I have a problem with moving to Ohio, Tom."

"Please don't make this any harder than it already is."

"If we quit this house, there's no coming back. You need to think about this."

"You think I haven't? That's all I've been doing. We only have two options: we either leave or stay. To stay, we need to come up with $72,000. How likely is that? That leaves us with only one option. We simply have to leave, and the longer we put it off the more difficult it will be. That's how I see it."

"It sounds like you've made up your mind." "I have. I'm sorry."

After a tense minute of silence, Tom gets up and with passive resignation tells Regina, "I'm tired. I'm gonna get some sleep."

As their unhappy conversation comes to its close, neither Tom nor Regina Cooper are aware that their daughter Angela, has been quietly sitting at the top of the stairs listening to every word. When she hears her father leave the kitchen, she silently slips back into her room.

Moments later, Regina Cooper is sitting alone pondering her family's dilemma. Moving to a farm in rural Ohio is distinctly unappealing and the thought of pulling her daughter out of school is crossing a line too far, and too final, for her. In her mind, packing everything up and moving to Ohio seems more like panic than strategy. As she quietly sits alone in her kitchen, she tries to make sense of what's happening to her family. The unfortunate combination of Tom losing his well-paying factory job only weeks before Regina became seriously ill has brought them to financial insolvency. It happened more quickly than she would have ever thought possible.

Recounting the previous six months, Regina Cooper can find no instance where serious misjudgment or wasteful spending played any role in producing this crisis. Tom and Regina Cooper have always been careful with their money, but their modest savings were no defense against being blindsided by simultaneous financial emergencies. What could they have done? What could any family have done? Regina Cooper stares passively at the floor and wonders what tomorrow will bring.

Meanwhile, 17 miles to the north, Charles Beckler is in his pajamas and ready for another night of sleep. He ends his day as he usually does, with a gentle kiss to his wife Connie. After turning out the light he settles in for a night's rest, and within minutes is submerged in a mantle of tranquil sleep. Before drifting off, he thinks again of the dream he had last night and wonders if it will return.

Chapter Ten: Angela's New Friend

Louise Robinson's dreaming soul awakens, and she finds herself in a place at once both warm, familiar and strangely surreal. She opens her eyes and recognizes the back seat of her parents' station wagon, the same one that so often used to carry her to and from high school many years ago. Looking out the window, she sees a beautiful deep blue sky with soft billowy white clouds drifting slowly through a warm sunlit afternoon. She sees her mother's profile in the front seat and hears the local AM radio station playing just as it had so long ago. All looks and sounds as it did when she was a schoolgirl. Louise decides this must be a dream.

She remembers being at work. There was a loud noise. Something happened. Then she remembers being picked up by her mother and getting into the station wagon to go back home. How can this be? Whatever this place is, it certainly feels comfortable, secure, and reassuring. A strong feeling of contentment and belonging wells up within her as she watches her home town scenery roll by. Then Louise hears something she hasn't heard in nearly fourteen years; her mother's voice.

"We're almost home, Louise."

Through her wandering thoughts, Louise concludes this has to be a dream, but if she is dreaming why does everything seem so vividly real? She hears her mother's voice again.

"We're having shepherd's pie for dinner tonight. That's your favorite."

Louise sees her own reaction to what's happening as decidedly curious. She evinces no surprise at the sound of her mother's voice and feels completely at ease with her surroundings. An abiding sense she's exactly where she should and needs to be, consumes her. She looks at her hand and unmistakably sees the hand of a woman in her fifties. Is that the illusion or what she sees around her? Louise Robinson is observing what's happening as a 55 year old woman, while simultaneously experiencing what's happening as the child she once was. Overarching this inexplicable contradiction are profound feelings of love and complete acceptance.

Louise looks again at her mother in the front seat and asks, "Where am I?"

"You're home, Louise. You're home, and we couldn't be happier. Your father wants to see you. We're gonna have a nice dinner, then Brianna will come by for you later."

The name Brianna rings a bell for Louise. She remembers from her dream last night the strange woman named Brianna. Is this the same dream? As the station wagon slows and safely rolls into the driveway of her childhood home, Louise observes her father's face as he waves at her with a welcoming smile, just as he did so many years ago. Louise Robinson has somehow come home again.

Meanwhile, back in the temporal world of the living, Charles Beckler sinks deeper and deeper into a heavy slumber and soon awakens within his dream. He finds himself once again standing on a dock near a large body of water. He sees the fishing pole and the large basket of fish with their shimmering bodies reflecting the bright sun of a warm summer day. Charley recalls this scene from his prior dream, and he remembers the strange woman named Brianna who told him she would send someone to help him carry his basket of fish, but he sees no-one.

He feels the heat of the sun and recalls Brianna's words: "If any of your fish rot, then part of you will also rot." Charles looks at his fish and tries awkwardly to shade them with his arms. He looks around again and sees no one approaching. He's alone, waiting for something or someone to help him do something with his basket of fish, but what that something is, completely eludes him. He remembers how hard he struggled in his dream to catch those fish, how he was beside himself in a frenzy of enthusiasm as he pulled them in, in rapid succession, but looking at them now, they appear as a burden and even a worry. Charley looks again at his basket of fish, so heavy he can't lift it.

The dead fish with their gleaming eyes seem to look back at him and whisper, "A putrid waste of rotting death seeding your dreams with polluted breath." Once again, he looks around and sees no-one approaching. He feels the warmth of the midday sun and tries to cover his fish as best he can.

As Charles Beckler sleeps in his bed, captive to his enigmatic dream, two beings are continuing their journey together as teacher and apprentice. Calvin and Brianna walk along a beautiful country path. Calvin fully understands and accepts that he's now in a place where conventional logic and expectation have no place. As they continue on in silence, he ponders the incredible things he's witnessed. He thinks back on his mortal life of 84 years. Seeing that life now from the other side, it seems a pale imitation of something much deeper, as if his physical life was an aberration, a temporary departure from what is actually normal, real, and permanent. Above all, Calvin senses a calming, powerfully tranquil energy permeated in and through everything around him. Calvin Milner knows profoundly that he's in the close presence of a transcendent reality.

As they walk along together in silence, Calvin sees a gentle smile on Brianna's face as if she's somehow privy to what he's thinking. Looming in the distance, a large lake can be seen ahead of them.

As they approach, Calvin sees a man standing on a dock next to the water and asks, "Do you know who that man is, Brianna?" "That's Charles Beckler."

"Will you talk with him?"

"No, that will be the job of our next arrival."

"Who's that?" Calvin asks.

"Her name is Louise Robinson."

"She's the woman you mentioned earlier."

"That's right."

"Does she know what to do or say to him?"

"Of course. It's what she's been doing all her life."

"What did she do?"

"She volunteered, helped others, and always tried to give good advice, just like you did, Calvin. She's a perfect match for the work we have for her."

"What's that?"

"She'll be a dream sentinel."

"What's a dream sentinel?"

"It's someone whose left their earthly life and earned the privilege to return and counsel the living by appearing in their dreams."

"She must have a lot of wisdom," Calvin says.

"That, and something better."

"What's that?"

"The inclination to share it," says Brianna. "Where is she?"

"She's with her parents, renewing a primal bond."

"Just like I did."

"That's right. Are you curious about this woman?"

"Yes, I am. Will I meet her?" Calvin asks.

"You'll be present, but won't interact with her. Like the others, you need only observe in silence. They're completely unaware of you, anyway. Are you ready?"

"Yes."

"Let's go then and see this good lady."

Calvin sees his surroundings instantly melt into nothing and just as quickly he and Brianna are walking down a typical neighborhood street with houses on each side. Calvin notices no change of expression on Brianna's face and says, "Things change quickly here and without warning."

"That's right. Do you know where we are?"

"I would guess we're going to meet our new arrival."

"Yes, we are."

As they continue they see a woman standing on the porch of one of the houses. It's Louise Robinson, and she's with her parents. The moment she sees Brianna, Louise embraces her mother and father and bids them a temporary goodbye, and walks toward her.

"Hello Brianna."

"Hi Louise."

"My parents told me you were coming."

"I know. Did you enjoy your visit with them?"

"I did. It was as if all the joy, and all the happy days of my childhood were concentrated into one afternoon, as if the timeline of my life had been purged of all but the sweetest moments of joy, and then compressed into a few hours of complete ecstasy."

"How sweet, I love the poetry of your words. They speak to and from the human heart. I'm happy for you but for now, there's work to do."

"I know. I wanna help as much as I can."

"That's the reason you're here, Louise. Come, your first assignment is a man who needs help with a basket of fish. I'll tell you all about it."

Meanwhile, in the temporal world of the living, Charles Beckler sleeps undisturbed in his bed at home, but his conscious mind is somewhere else. Still captive to his dream, he can't seem to leave the dreamscape scene of standing on the dock with his basket of fish. He looks around again, and this time sees a figure approaching. It's a woman. He wonders who it could be. Moments later he sees the smiling face of a middle-aged woman.

"Did that woman send you here?" he asks.

"You mean Brianna?"

"Yeah, that's her name. She told me you were coming to help me."

"That's right, Charley. That's why I'm here. You have too many fish in your basket."

"I know. I can't lift it."

"I know a child who needs some of your fish, Charley. She's hungry. Do you want to give her some?"

"Yes, yes, of course, where is she?"

"She doesn't live very far from you Charley. I'll show you how to get there. I'll give you directions."

"What's her name?"

"Her name is Angela."

"Well let's go give her some fish. I'm ready."

"Let's do that, Charley. You grab one side of the basket and I'll grab the other."

As they lift, the basket suddenly seems as light, as if it were empty. Charley feels instantly relieved and even carefree. He looks over at the woman on the other side of the basket and asks, "What's your name?"

He looks to see the woman's face and hears her say with clarity and emphasis,

"My name is Louise, and yours is Charles Samuel Beckler."

Hearing his full name seems to summon Charles Beckler's conscious mind to awaken. He hears it as a cue and call for action and instantly opens his eyes. The bedside clock reads 5:41.

After sitting up he turns and looks at his wife still sleeping soundly, then quietly puts on his bedroom slippers and makes his way into the kitchen. After pressing the button on the coffee machine, he sits at the table and thinks about his dream. He has no difficulty remembering every detail, and clearly recalls the woman named Louise who helped him carry his basket of fish. As he pours his coffee, he recalls what she told him, about the child named Angela who needed some fish from his basket. He pauses and wonders, Why am I thinking about this? Does it mean anything? Then he remembers Louise telling him that the nine year old girl lived not very far away, on a street named Briarpoint, wherever that might be. He pauses for a moment and then picks up the cell phone on the table.

As he squints to see the numbers without his glasses, he hears his wife's voice. "Who are you calling this early?"

"I'm trying to get in touch with John. I need him to drive me into town for something."

"Here, let me dial it for you."

After giving the phone back to her husband Connie says, "You look more like a caveman every day Charley. I'm, going back to sleep. I'll see ya later."

"Sure honey, go ahead."

Hearing his driver's voice on the phone, Charles speaks. "Hey John, I'm sorry to call you this early, but I wonder if you could take me into town this morning. I need you to help me find an address. Great, uh, this won't take long. I'm not even dressed. I probably won't get out of the car. I'm just curious about something. Thank you John."

Charles Beckler turns off his cell phone and waits for his driver to bring the car around.

Meanwhile, miles from Mr. Beckler's home, at the Cooper residence, Regina Cooper wakes to find that Tom has for some reason left the house early. As she comes downstairs and looks out the kitchen window, she sees the reason why. Parked in the driveway is a large yellow moving van. Tom has rented a vehicle, intending to leave for Ohio. Is this what he meant when he said he'd reached a decision? Regina asks herself. She immediately braces herself for the argument that she's sure will come.

Minutes later, Tom opens the front door, walks into the kitchen and is confronted with a question. "What are you doing?"

"I'm trying to solve our problem."

"How, by running away from it?"

"I'm not running away from it. I'm facing it head on."

"Is that what you call this?"

"Look Regina, we can't stay here. You don't seem to be willing to face that fact."

"What upsets me as much as moving is the fact that you would rent a truck and start moving stuff without telling me first."

With his voice rising, Tom says, "Well, what have we been talking about for the last two weeks? Are you so surprised?"

"Yeah, I am surprised. I'm surprised that you would do this without letting me know."

As Tom and Regina's argument continues, their daughter Angela sits at the top of the stairs listening. She finds it difficult to hear what's being said, and in a psychologically instinctive act of simple retreat, she quietly makes her way down the steps and out the front door.

Distracted by their acrimony, neither Tom nor Regina notice her leaving. Still carrying her teddy bear, Angela walks past the large yellow moving van. It looks ominous. She reads the words on the side, For All Your Moving Needs and, in her mind, it verifies everything she's heard her parents talking about. Angela is faced with the reality of knowing she'll be leaving the only home she's ever known. It might even be today, she thinks.

Filled with apprehension, she continues down the sidewalk, and within minutes turns a corner and is out of sight. As Angela wanders further away from home, someone else has left their home, and like Angela is not clear in their reasoning as to why or where they're going.

Charles Beckler and his driver John are several miles away searching for something that has as yet eluded them.

"I don't know John. We might be wasting our time."

"There's just one more to check sir. It's Briarpoint Lane. We've gone to Briarpoint Avenue, and Briarpoint Cove, so Briarpoint Lane is the last street by that name."

"Well, let's check it out," Mr. Beckler says.

Riding in the front seat of his Mercedes Benz in his pajamas, still sipping his coffee, Charles Beckler feels foolish as they drive onward. He looks at the street ahead and sees nothing as he hears his driver's voice.

"This is Briarpoint Lane sir."

With every passing block it feels increasingly as if he's wasting his time. Why am I doing this? What will he tell Connie when he gets back home? How can he explain searching for a child he doesn't know because a woman in his dreams told him to do so? Feeling somewhat ridiculous he tells his driver, "Let's go home John. I'm wasting my time and yours. I ought to go to a barber shop and get a shave, start being sensible again."

"Should we find one, sir?"

As John asks the question, Mr. Beckler glances across the road and sees a young child sitting on a bench. It's a girl.

"Hey, John, turn around when you get a chance and head back. I wanna see something."

Two minutes later, after finding a safe place to turn around, the car is heading back the way it came, and once again Charles Beckler sees the girl sitting on the bench.

"Slow down, John."

The child is sitting alone sobbing, clearly lost and forlorn with her teddy bear. It's Angela Cooper.

"Pull over, John."

As John parks the car, Mr. Beckler places his coffee cup on the dashboard. He reaches to disconnect the seatbelt, and as he opens the door, his hand knocks over the half-filled coffee cup, spilling the contents on his pajama pants.

"Oh hell," Mr. Beckler says.

"I have a towel in the trunk, sir."

"That's okay. It's not that bad. I wanna talk to that girl over there."

"Should I stay here, sir?" "Yeah, I won't be long."

Seconds later, Charles is standing a few feet away from the child. "Hi, my name is Charley. What's your name?"

"Angela."

"Your name is Angela. What's wrong Angela?" Hearing no response, he asks, "Where are your parents?"

"They're home."

"Do they know you're here?"

"No."

"What's wrong Angela? Please tell me."

Mr. Beckler quietly sits beside her and as Angela meekly sobs out her story, he listens without interrupting. The two of them sitting together make an odd looking pair. Charles, in his coffee stained pajamas with an eight day beard, and nine year old Angela with her teddy bear sit for a few minutes and then, with a motion of his arm, Mr. Beckler summons his driver.

As John approaches, he stands and meets him halfway. Just out of earshot from the child, he tells him, "John, I'm gonna walk this child back home. She only lives a few blocks away. She's scared, and I think getting into a strange car might upset her, so why don't you stay here and watch the car. I should be back in about twenty minutes."

"Will you be all right sir?"

"I'll be fine. I'm just gonna walk her back home."

"Yes sir."

Moments later, with Angela clasping his hand and showing the way, Charles Beckler begins walking back to her home a few blocks away. As Angela and her new-found friend make their way, Tom and Regina Cooper are still unaware of their daughter's absence.

A tense stalemate hangs in the air as Regina tries to dissuade her husband from what she sees as a rash mistake, and she's ready to stand her ground.

"I have to take Angela to school. I don't know what you plan on doing here, but if you put stuff in that van make sure it's just your stuff. Don't touch anything that's mine or Angela's. I mean it, Tom."

"Regina, we don't have a choice. What do you want me to do?" Tom pleads.

Almost as an exclamation point to Tom's question, Regina hears a car door slamming shut. She looks out the window and sees their nemesis Scott Palmer standing in the driveway. The added aggravation of dealing with Palmer at such a stressful time might have rattled and flustered someone else, but Regina Cooper is not intimidated by the situation.

She tells herself, This is still my home. I'm not gonna be chased off by anyone. I don't care who it is. A resolute calm comes over her as she turns to her husband.

"It's Palmer. Look Tom, I have to run Angela to school. Please don't get into an argument with him."

"What the hell is he doing here this early?" Tom asks.

"I have no idea."

"I can't deal with that man right now."

"Let me go see what he wants," Regina says.

As she leaves the kitchen, she calls up the stairs to Angela.

"Angela, we have to go."

Thinking her daughter is upstairs in her room, Regina walks outside to see why Scott Palmer is here. She says nothing as she sees him taking pictures of the house.

"Mrs. Cooper, I'm just here to get some pictures of the outside of the house. It'll take about twenty minutes and I'll be gone."

"Okay."

With the quick exchange over, Regina turns and goes back into the house and tells her husband, "He's taking pictures of the outside. He'll be gone in a few minutes. So why don't you just relax, stay inside, have some coffee. When I get back, we can talk this over, okay?"

"Yeah, sure."

"Good, I'll see you later."

Regina takes the car keys from the kitchen table and walks to the stairwell.

"Angela, we have to go ... Angela."

Hearing no response Regina goes upstairs and knocks on her daughter's bedroom door.

"Angela, Angela."

When Regina opens the door, she instantly sees the room is empty and suddenly fears that her daughter is not in the house. After a quick room to room search, she comes downstairs and tells her husband, "Angela's not upstairs."

"Where is she?"

"I don't know."

"She's probably outside."

Quickly going outside, they both look and see only Scott Palmer still taking pictures. Regina calls to her daughter as Tom looks down the street in both directions.

"Angela, Angela!"

Fear becomes something closer to panic as they hear no reply. "Maybe she's in the garage," Tom says.

"Go look."

As Tom hurries inside to check the garage, Regina takes another look both ways down the street and sees nothing. It's not like Angela to leave the house without saying something. If Tom doesn't find her in the garage, then it's time to call the police. As Tom looks, Regina checks once more behind the house and still sees nothing. After returning to the front yard, she starts back to the door, and sees Tom coming out.

"She's not there. We have to call the police," he says.

Tom turns and goes back inside to make the phone call. As he does Regina looks once more down the street and sees her daughter making her way up the sidewalk with an older man she's never seen before. A powerful intuition seems to assure her that her daughter is perfectly safe. She calls to her husband, who is unaware of Angela's approach.

"Tom, It's okay. She's here."

"What?"

"It's okay. Here she comes."

As Tom returns outside, he sees Angela walking hand in hand with a bearded man in his pajamas and reacts predictably.

"Who's that guy she's with? I'm calling the sheriff."

"Don't do that."

"Look at him. He's a derelict."

Regina sharply tells her husband, "Don't do that. Trust me."

Within seconds, Angela and her new friend are standing in front of the house. After embracing her child, Regina asks, "Where did you go? We were worried sick about you Angela."

"Are you all right honey?" Tom asks his daughter.

"Yes."

"I found her sitting on a bench a few blocks away. She looked like she was lost, so I walked her home," Charles explains.

"Well thank you, we appreciate that," Regina says.

"Angela tells me you're having trouble."

"Well, it's nothing you can help us with, but thank you for bringing our daughter home. We're very grateful."

"Your daughter told me you're losing your home. Is that true?"

"I'm afraid it is," says Regina.

At that moment Scott Palmer comes from behind the house still taking his pictures, and Charles asks, "Who's he?"

"He's from the bank. He's the one handling the foreclosure," Tom says.

"Is that why you have this moving van parked here?"

"Yes, it is."

"Well, what's your preference? To move somewhere else or stay here? Your daughter certainly wants to stay."

"We'd much rather stay of course, but we can't afford it," answers Regina.

"You have a mortgage on this house, don't you?"

"Yes."

"Which bank?"

"First Capital."

"First Capital holds your mortgage?"

"Yes."

Pointing to Scott Palmer, Mr. Beckler asks, "And you say he's in charge of your account?"

"Yes."

"What's his name?"

"Palmer, Scott Palmer," Regina says.

"Well he's the man we wanna talk to."

Directing his attention to Scott Palmer, Charles calls to him from across the lawn.

"Mr. Palmer, can I talk to you please?"

Tom and Regina exchange uncomfortable glances as he approaches.

"Yes."

"You're handling the foreclosure on this house as I understand it. Is that true?"

Annoyed by what he regards as an impertinent question, Scott Palmer eyeballs the figure standing on the sidewalk ten feet away. He sees an older man in coffee stained pajamas with an eight day beard and disdainfully asks, "Who are you?"

"I'm Angela's friend. That's all you need to know. You work for First Capital. That's Jack Pearson's bank. I'm on the Board of Directors at First Capital."

"You're on the Board of Directors at First Capital?" Palmer asks incredulously.

"That's right."

"Oh really, and my name is Abraham Lincoln. Look I'm busy, if you'll excuse me." Scott Palmer turns to Regina and says, "I guess someone left the asylum door open this morning."

His mocking humor finds no response, and as he turns back to the house, Mr. Palmer sees an impeccably clean, black class E Mercedes Benz smoothly pull up beside the bearded man in pajamas, who takes little notice of the luxury sedan. Surprised, all focus their curious attention on the neatly dressed driver as he emerges from the car, all except Charles Beckler who tells him, "Hey John, I'm glad you came."

"I thought you might need me, sir."

"I do, thanks." Turning to Tom and Regina, Mr. Beckler says, "This is my driver. He keeps me from getting in trouble. John, can you get Jack Pearson on the phone? I don't wanna use the car phone. Get him on your cell phone if you can. Do you have his number?"

"I'm sure I do, sir."

"Good, call him at home. He never leaves his house before ten."

As John takes out his cell phone and dials the number, it's becoming abundantly clear that the odd-looking man in coffee stained pajamas is much more than he appears to be. Tom and Regina Cooper say nothing as Mr. Beckler takes the phone from his driver, and as he does, an uneasy apprehension comes over Scott Palmer when he hears Charles Beckler say hello to the president of the bank where he works.

"Hey Jack, how are you? I'm doing all right. Listen, this is not the reason I called but I wanna say again how much Connie and I enjoyed ourselves at your daughter's wedding. Absolutely, it was a beautiful ceremony. Oh, I know. Now you tell that new son-in-law of yours that if he ever needs a job to come see me. Well, you tell them both good luck for me. Listen Jack, the reason I called is, I'm standing in front of a residential property that your bank holds the note on. What I'd like to do is to pay off the balance. I know you don't have the paper work in front of you so, uh huh, That's great Jack I appreciate that. So, you know my driver John. Right, I'll have John bring this young man to your office and you can take care of it, if you would please."

Covering the phone with his hand, Mr. Beckler looks at Tom and asks,

"What is your name?"

"Uh, Tom Cooper, but sir, we owe $72,000 on this house."

"His name is Tom Cooper, Jack. No keep it in his name. I have enough to keep track of. Thanks Jack. No, we'll get them over there right now if that's convenient for you. Well, I'm not exactly dressed for it. If you have any papers you want me to sign just send them back with John, and we'll take care of it. I'm really grateful Jack. I appreciate that. Hey, when are you and Mary coming over for dinner again? I hope so. Really, yeah, Connie wants to go back to Australia for a few weeks. Oh I know she deserves it. That'd be great. Okay, thanks again Jack. Oh, I almost forgot. Do you have a man working for you by the name of Abraham Lincoln? I'm serious that's what he said his name was. Well he's standing right here. You wanna talk to him? Here he is, the one and only Abrahaaaaaam Lincoln."

Scott Palmer is visibly nervous as he takes the phone from Mr. Beckler.

"Good morning Mr. Pearson. Yes sir. My name is Scott Palmer. Yes sir. Oh that, well sir, we were just kidding around. Yes sir, I will sir. Yes sir, goodbye."

As Scott Palmer hands the phone back, he says to Mr. Beckler, "Well, uh, if I can do anything to help…"

"No thanks, we don't need your help," Mr. Beckler says dismissively, and then tells his driver, "John, I want you to take Tom over to Jack Pearson's office at the bank. He's expecting you both. Pay off the balance on his mortgage, and if uh, Abraham Lincoln here was due a commission on the sale of the house, pay him off too."

"Yes sir, will I be taking you home first?"

"No, I'll have Connie come by and pick me up in her car. She won't mind."

"I have to ask you. Why are you doing this? You don't even know us," Regina says.

"You're right. I don't know you. What's your name?"

"Regina, Regina Cooper and this is my husband Tom, and our daughter Angela. What's your name?"

"My name is Charles Beckler. Well, now we do know each other. As to why I'm doing this, I have too many fish in my basket Regina, and now I have a few less. Tom, have you ever worked in a warehouse?"

"Yes, yes sir, I have."

"I need a warehouse manager. I don't know if you'd be interested or not but —"

"Yes, I would certainly be interested."

"Good, then we'll talk about it later. Right now, you and John need to get over to the bank and get your business done, and I need to get home." Mr. Beckler directs his attention to his driver, "John will you call Connie and tell her to come get me? You'll have to give her directions."

"Mr. Beckler, I'd be happy to take you home. Please, after what you're doing for us, please let me at least do that for you," Regina asks.

"Well, sure, it's about twenty miles way. I'm on the lake off of Diamond Point Road."

"It's no problem at all."

"All right, you can meet my wife. Hey, let's do this, since you'll be taking me home, after Tom and John are done at the bank, they can come over and we'll all have lunch together," Mr. Beckler says. Then after looking at Angela who is smiling broadly, he checks himself. "Oh, I forgot. Angela has to go to school."

"Mommy, I wanna go."

Reaching to embrace her daughter Regina says, "Well, this is a special occasion, so today we'll make an exception."

"Well good, it sounds like a plan to me. John, I'll see you and Tom later."

"Yes sir."

Tom Cooper, who's been mostly aloof, asking himself, is this really happening? suddenly feels the urge to speak.

"Before we go, I wanna say thank you Mr. Beckler for what you're doing. You don't know what this means to us. This is like, it's like a dream come true. I can't, I can't tell you how much I appreciate this, how much we appreciate this."

"I understand," Mr. Beckler replies.

"I wanna start paying you back as soon as I can sir," Tom says.

"We'll work it out later, Tom."

Tom offers his hand to Mr. Beckler. "Thank you Mr. Beckler, thank you so much."

"You're welcome Tom, you and your family. Listen, you and John better go, and we'll see both of you at the house later on."

"Thank you again sir."

"It's all right. Well Regina, do you need a few minutes before you run me home?"

"I'm ready Mr. Beckler, anytime you are."

"Okay, well let's go then."

"Please come in for a minute while I get the car ready," she says.

As John and Tom walk toward the limousine, and Mr. Beckler, Regina, and Angela move to the front door, Charles Beckler stops and looks over at Scott Palmer who's been passively witnessing what has taken place. He then walks over to him, leans and whispers in his ear.

"You know what? I knew when I first saw you that you weren't Abraham Lincoln."

With this parting witticism, Mr. Beckler turns and walks away.

After John and Tom drive off, and Regina, Charley, and Angela go inside, Scott Palmer remains standing alone on the lawn. Moments later, he gets in his car and drives away.

Meanwhile, in that world imperceptible to the senses, Brianna and Calvin are walking on the same path by the lake they took before, but this time heading back in the direction they came from earlier. They again pass the dock where they saw Charley standing with his basket of fish, but Calvin sees the dock is now empty.

"There was a basket of fish on that dock when we passed here before. It's not there now."

"That's right, Calvin. It isn't. Charley and Louise have carried it away."

"Where is Louise?"

"She's visiting another dreamscape and another dreamer. Her work is just beginning. She'll give her counsel to hundreds in a single night."

"How is that possible?" Calvin asks.

"We're in a place where a thousand lifetimes can pass in an instant, and the briefest moment can take a lifetime to pass. Linear time doesn't pertain here."

"It's remarkable. Louise is now a dream sentinel."

"That's right."

"Will most of the dreamers she visits take her counsel?"

"Most will not."

"Why is that?"

"In the temporal rush of their passing lives, most people are too distracted to harvest the meaning of their dreams."

"Well, I know I have a lot to learn." "We all do, Calvin. Love and knowledge, which is another way of saying spirit and mind, grow in these two things and you'll live in harmony with your destiny."

"I think I have a long way to go," Calvin says. "The journey is the destination Calvin." "Where are we going now?" he asks. "We have to meet our next arrival."

Chapter Eleven: The Racist

Another beautiful afternoon is unfolding for Tracy Freeman at her rural home twelve miles west of Blakely in Early County, Georgia. Mrs. Freeman and her husband Tyler live a comfortable life of retirement and have resided in the same small rural community for their entire lives. Living only minutes from the Alabama state border, the Freemans have deep roots in a traditional southern culture that goes back for generations on both sides of their marriage, with ancestors who fought in the Civil War. In the 20th century, Early County was anything but quick to accept the changing politics ushered in by the social protest movements of the 1950s and 60s for expanded civil rights. By choice and preference, the pace of change for those living in this southern rural county has always been slow.

Tyler Freeman and his family have always played a prominent role in county politics and have wielded considerable influence in what and how things get done in Early County. Tyler Freeman's great grandfather made his fortune in textiles and provided a comfortable legacy for his descendants. Deeply conservative, the Freemans have always been active in their local church and, with like-minded members of the congregation, have resisted any changes in their local government. This meant stiff, unyielding opposition to any effort to expand the civil rights of minorities. Tyler Freeman has chosen to accept his ancestors' disdain for the ideals of racial and economic equality. His influence and ardent participation in local politics ensures that any prospective candidate who hopes to be elected is well advised to ask for his endorsement, and today he's expecting a visitor who's coming for that very purpose.

As Mrs. Freeman returns to the house after retrieving the mail, she sees a car pull in with a young man driving. After parking to the side, he climbs out and she greets him.

"Hello, you must be Mr. Edmonds."

"Yes ma'am, please just call me Bill."

"Well it's nice to meet you. My husband's expecting you. Come on up."

"Thank you ma'am, I appreciate that."

Seconds later after following Mrs. Freeman to the porch, she introduces Billy Edmonds to her husband.

"Tyler, this is Billy Edmonds."

"Hello young man, sit down please."

"Hello Mr. Freeman, it's good to meet you sir."

"Well what's on your mind today Billy?" Mr. Freeman asks.

"Well, to get straight to the point; I'm givin' serious thought to runnin' for sheriff here in Early County and I'd like to get your opinion on that, if you'd be good enough to tell me."

"Why sure, be happy to, I don't know if you're aware of it, but my grandfather used to be sheriff here in Early County."

"Yes sir, I did know that."

"He was the best sheriff this county ever had. Nathan Bedford Freeman was his name. He didn't put up with any nonsense. They used to hang trouble makers back then, Ku Klux Klan was very active."

"People never talk about the good things the Klan did, do they Mr. Freeman?"

"Oh, I know. They helped a lot o' people, kept the niggers well-behaved too. My grandfather was a member all his life. If he ever needed to deputize someone, it was always a Klansman."

"How long was he sheriff of Early County?"

"Not quite twenty years, from 1912 to 1932, he got disgusted when FDR came in."

"I take it your grandfather didn't like Roosevelt."

"That's right, he didn't, me either. That's where all this civil rights hogwash came from; Roosevelt started all that. Back when my grandfather was sheriff, the niggers knew their place. Now, you can't even call them niggers. The NAACP has completely infiltrated the federal government, them and the communists."

"I completely agree with ya," Billy says as Mrs. Freeman returns to the porch with a cup of coffee for her guest.

"Here ya go, Billy."

"Thank you, ma'am. I appreciate that."

"You want some more, Tyler?"

"I'm all right, thank you."

"Let me know if you need anything," says Mrs. Freeman as she returns inside.

"Thank you, ma'am," Billy says as he and Mr. Freeman continue their conversation.

"Yeah, times have changed since your grandfather's day."

"Sure have, blacks today are so brazen. They don't know what it was like to live back then. 'Bout every three or four months, the Klan would hang a nigger, usually a trouble maker. You can say what you want but I'll tell ya what, that kept things nice and quiet."

"Hell, in the long run it was probably cheaper that way than usin' the courts," Billy says.

"Sure it was, more effective too."

"I believe it."

"That's the way he ran this county. That was my grandfather, Nathan Bedford Freeman. Can you guess who he was named after?"

"I would think it's Nathan Bedford Forrest."

"That's right, one of the greatest southerners who ever lived. That's a fact."

"He started the KKK."

"Yes, he did. He was a general in the Civil War. After that he founded the Ku Klux Klan. Just say his name and a nigger would start shakin."

"He was a great man, no doubt about it," Billy nodded.

"Those days are gone forever. This is the modern age, and if you're gonna run for office, you need to know this, rule number one: you can't call a nigger a nigger. If you do, your campaign is finished. They'll splash it all over TV and radio like you committed murder or somethin."

"Isn't that the truth? I know exactly what you mean, Mr. Freeman."

"You don't say niggers, you say blacks. That's okay 'cause I hate blacks as much as I hate niggers."

"Oh absolutely, that's what freedom's all about."

"That's right. Well Billy, you sound like a reasonable man. You just might have a future in politics."

"I hope so."

"I'll tell you what, we'll talk again in a few weeks and see what happens. Maybe I can introduce you some of our church members who can help you. You have my number don't cha?"

"Yes sir, I do."

"Give me a call, say by the tenth of next month."

"I will, Mr. Freeman, and I wanna thank you for takin' the time to talk with me today."

"That's quite all right."

Looking at his watch, Billy says, "Wow, it's after seven. I need to get home."

"Well I'm glad you came by."

After a courteous and final goodbye, Billy Edmonds gets back in his car and within minutes, he's driving back to his home 36 miles away. The beautiful, warm, clear day is ideal for driving, but ten miles into his trip, he hears an unusual noise coming from the front end of the car and it's getting louder. It's a flat tire. As he steers his slowing vehicle to the side of the road, he glances at the time on his cell phone. It's 7:48pm. Though it will be dark in a half hour, he's convinced it won't take long to change the tire and get back on the road. After getting out and confirming the problem, he sees the flat is on the driver's side of the car and only five or six feet from the rush of passing traffic. He knows he must be careful.

Minutes later, he tries to loosen the lug nuts on the tire rim and finds them so tight that his best efforts are unsuccessful. He remembers when he had tires put on several months ago, the mechanic used an air gun to tighten the lug nuts, and tighten them he did. After repeatedly trying, he finds it impossible to break them loose. He stands up, looks at his problem and pauses for a moment. Then, he sees a pickup truck slowing down and pulling off the road ahead of him, with the driver showing a clear intent to offer help. Billy Edmonds sees a man of color who looks to be in his mid-20s approaching him.

His smile and friendly wave precede his words. "Hey, I saw you tryin' to get them lug nuts loose. I have a big four way wrench. If you push down on one side, an' I pull up on the other, we can get your tire changed."

"I don't need your help. You get on out o' here."

"Okay." After hearing the rude rebuff, the young man simply turns around and retraces his steps back to his truck.

Edmonds says nothing as he watches the man get back in his vehicle and drive away. Confident he can change the tire with no one's help, he returns to his task. Billy Edmonds has no way of knowing that within minutes he'll be leaving the world and the life he's known for 37 years.

Meanwhile, Brianna and her apprentice are proceeding alongside the same road, close to Mr. Edmonds. Cars and large trucks whip by, unnerving Calvin with their passing rush.

"What's wrong, Calvin?"

"Those big trucks make me nervous," he says.

"There's no danger. You could walk in front of them and they wouldn't harm you or even see you. Why don't you give it a try?"

At that moment, Calvin feels the noisy blast of air from an 18 wheel tractor-trailer as it passes. The huge truck thunders by at 70mph and is a menacing presence. The thought of stepping in front of one runs counter to every instinct for basic self-preservation but Calvin thinks to himself, this might be a test, perhaps a test of faith.As he walks along the highway thinking about it, Brianna says nothing. Another large truck roars by and shakes the ground as it passes. Calvin is more than a little reluctant to walk deliberately into the traffic lane a few yards to the left. Despite the incredible things he's seen and experienced and knowing he now exists in a non-physical realm, Calvin Milner's mind is still subject to a deep, primal instinct for avoiding any possible life-threatening danger. Another truck goes by and still Brianna says nothing. As Calvin looks at the road with its intermittent white lines, he thinks to himself once again, this must be a test. What else could it be? A choice between faith and fear.

Then Calvin starts walking out onto the road and is soon well inside the traffic lane. Moments later he hears the sudden approach of a car coming fast from behind. In an instant, he sees the flash of something passing through and all around him and just as quickly he sees the back end of a minivan speeding into the distance in front of him. Seconds later, Calvin hears the roaring approach of a large truck behind him and, as before, he sees something completely pass around him as if he were traveling backward through a tunnel, and as before, he sees the vehicle's rear end suddenly pulling away from him, receding in the distance ahead. In this case the truck was empty and a momentary but unmistakable image of the truck's interior flashes through Calvin's mind. He's intrigued by the strange experience and, as he returns to Brianna, she smiles at him.

"That was incredible. I actually saw what was inside that truck. It was empty. I could see inside the trailer. There were pallets. It went by so fast, but I could see inside it."

"I'm sure you could."

"Wow! That was a strange experience."

As they continue, Calvin sees a car parked alongside the road ahead and a man sorting through the trunk.

"Somebody has a problem up there ahead."

"He has a flat tire. That's Billy Edmonds, but that's the least of his troubles."

"Is he our next arrival?"

"Yes."

"But he's still alive."

"Yes he is, but not for long."

"Are you gonna speak with him?" Calvin asks.

"Just briefly."

"Will he be able to see you if he's still alive?" "He'll be able to see me but not you, Calvin. You're still the invisible apprentice."

"I understand."

As Billy Edmonds takes the tire jack and spare from the trunk of his car, he's aware that he must be careful. Then he looks behind him and sees someone in the distance walking toward him. Within minutes, the discernible figure is recognizable. It's a woman.

As she approaches, Billy Edmonds sees a dark-skinned woman with straight black hair and disdainfully whispers under his breath, "Niggers everywhere today."

A few moments later she's standing only a few feet away. As she looks at him without saying anything, he doesn't try to hide his annoyance.

"What are you lookin' at, lady?"

"I'm looking at a man with a problem."

"Yeah, well, there ain't nothin' you can do to help me, so get goin.'"

"I didn't mean your flat tire."

"Where are you from lady? I've never seen you before."

"I was born in North Africa."

"North Africa huh, well, well, well."

"Why didn't you accept the help that young man offered you a few minutes ago?"

"That's none o' your business, but since you asked, I'll tell ya. I don't need no help from a nigger like him and I don't need no advice from a nigger like you. Go back to Africa. How's that? Does that answer your question?"

"Would you turn away a hand pulling you from being drowned because of its color?"

"Yeah, if it was black I would."

"Why?"

"Why? Cause I'm a white man. That's why."

"What do you mean?"

"Are you stupid or somethin'? I said I'm a white man. Don't you have eyes?"

"Yes, I do, and they see very clearly. Maybe you should have yours checked."

"What the hell are you talkin' about?"

"You don't look white to me. I've seen white clouds, white cotton and white snow but I've never seen a white man."

"Well, you're lookin' at one now."

"Your skin isn't white. It has color just like mine. You're a colored man."

"You wish."

"I'm just stating the obvious."

"No, I'm white and you're black. That's a fact."

"My skin is brown, not black. Between the extremes of black and white, I'd say both of us are closer to the middle. So that makes me a colored woman and you a colored man. We're basically just two colored people. Don't you think?"

"You're crazy. I'm white. I'll always be white. That's how I like it."

"You really don't want white skin, do you?"

"Yes I do, whiter the better."

"Why?"

"Cause I'm a white man. Now go away. I don't have any more time to waste talkin' to you."

"Well, you must be a white man Mr. Edmonds, and you will be a white man. Rest assured."

"How do you know my name?"

Before he can hear an answer to his question, Billy Edmonds hears something else, the loud air horn of a tractor-trailer whizzing by to remind him of where he's standing. He turns to see the semi quickly receding in the distance. When he looks back at the strange woman who was standing only a few feet away, he sees nothing. Her sudden disappearance is mysterious and the question of how she knew his name is strangely unsettling. He stands for a moment and wonders who she could be but the abrupt sensation of a speeding car going by prompts him to shake off his thoughts of her and return to his immediate task. Besides, it's getting dark and time is passing. He resolves once more to break loose the over tightened lug nuts. Once that's done, the tire can be changed in minutes. He doesn't want to call for a service truck and have somebody else do something he thinks he should do for himself, and so he makes one final attempt. He has just enough light left in the day to change the tire and get back on the road and that's what he intends to do.

As he gets into position, he remembers that his four-way caution lights are not on, but thinks little of it because if he can't loosen the first lug nut, he'll have no choice but to call for help. He'll know in seconds what he has to do. He's confident that this last exertion will get it done. Placing the lug wrench in position, he summons his physical strength and lifts with all his power. Then, at maximum strain, the wrench slips off center and all the pent up force of his strength is released.

The sudden impact of his right hand finger hitting the unyielding metal of the wheel well is excruciating. The pain is immediate and searing in its intensity. He reacts by jumping up and back and, in an unthinking reflexive response to his pain, makes a fatal error in judgment. Billy Edmonds turns to see the headlights of the truck, but it's too late. The driver simply doesn't have enough time to avoid the catastrophic impact, an impact that is sudden and fatal. As a result, the earthly life of Billy Edmonds comes to its close.

In a remote corner of a dry, arid landscape that looks very much like the desert regions of the American southwest, a man lies recumbent on the ground as if in a deep torpor of sleep. His motionless frame appears lifeless, but as a gust of wind washes over his face, he opens his eyes. Billy Edmonds wakes to find himself in a hot, dry landscape devoid of any trees or green plants. The sun is intense, and the air is bone-dry. Looking around him, the recognizable shapes of a few cacti in the foreground can be seen. Billy Edmonds knows he's in a desert, but how and why is beyond him.

Through his blurry vision, he spots someone in the distance - or is it a mirage? Maybe it's just the play of floating heat waves dancing in the air, but as he stands and focuses, a visible human form becomes discernible. As the figure gets closer, he sees an older man walking toward him. His face seems strangely familiar, though it's not clear why. Minutes later, he's face to face with him.

"Hey, how are ya?" the stranger says.

"I don't really know. Where am I?"

"You're in the desert."

"I can see that but where? What desert?"

"They're all about the same, aren't they? Does it make a difference?"

"It does to me. I wanna get back home. How did you get here?"

"I don't know. It's been so long, I don't remember."

"Who are you?" Billy asks

"I'm just an old southern boy like you who's tryin' to get home."

"Well, that makes two of us. I wanna get back home too. You know the way out o' here?"

"Sure do. There's a road right over there in that direction. All we gotta do is flag somebody down who's drivin' through and get a ride to the nearest town."

"Good, then we can find out where we are and get back home."

"What do ya think?" the stranger asks.

"Yeah sure, sounds like a plan to me. How far is that road?"

"It's about two miles away."

"Well let's start walkin'. We should be there in about 30 minutes."

Billy Edmonds looks down at his feet and sees for some reason he's not wearing any shoes. He knows the two mile walk will be anything but easy and within minutes it becomes increasingly painful as he trudges onward.

"Is it far?"

"Bout another 15 minutes."

"My feet are killin' me. I don't know how much farther I can go."

"We'll make it."

"I don't know how I lost my shoes," Billy says.

"After we get a ride into town, you can get another pair."

"Yeah, I hope so. You say you're a southern boy, whereabouts?"

"I was born in Georgia," the stranger says.

"Oh really, that's where I'm from. Where at in Georgia?"

"Southeast, near Alabama."

"Well, you must know Early County. That's where I'm from."

"I sure do. I know Early County real well."

"What's your name?" Billy asks.

"Williams, Ed Williams."

"What a coincidence; we're from the same place. Have you seen anyone else around here?"

"Just people on the highway drivin' through. That's one good thing about this place."

"What do ya mean? I don't see anything good about this place."

"I'll tell ya what's good about it: you don't have to put up with anyone botherin' ya like they do in the city, all them niggers runnin' around, goin' wild. Ain't no niggers out here. I'll tell ya that, only scorpions, rattle snakes and spiders."

"Yeah, isn't that nice? How do you manage by yourself?"

"I get by. Nobody likes me, but that don't bother me. I'd rather live out here with the rattle snakes than livin' in some apartment with a bunch o' blacks for neighbors."

"I can't say that I blame ya," Billy says.

"That's cause you're a white man. We think alike. You an' me, we could straighten this country out. Any nigger that don't volunteer to leave the country should be shot."

"That would solve a lot o' problems, wouldn't it?"

"Sure would. I got a simple rule I live by: if it's black, it's evil. The bible even tells you that."

"That's right. It does. I have to agree with you on that," Billy says.

"That's cause you're a white man, a good white man."

"Well you are too. We have a lot in common."

"I'm sure o' that," the stranger says.

With his attention diverted, Billy Edmonds doesn't see the piece of dead cactus lying on the ground, but he certainly feels its sharp jab as he steps on it.

"Shit!"

"What's wrong?"

"I stepped on somethin'. Damn it!"

"What is it?"

"Looks like a cactus spike. What am I gonna do now?"

"Can you walk?"

"I think so... Yeah, I guess I can. Damn it, that hurts. How far is the highway?"

"It's right past those dunes over there."

After another five minutes, the pain in Billy Edmonds' foot is too sharp to continue.

"Hey, Ed listen; I can't go any further. I need to stop. My foot's startin' to swell up."

"We're almost there. The road's only a few hundred feet away, right there."

"I see it. I can see it," Billy says.

"Look, you stay here an' I'll flag down the first car I see. Then we can get out o' here."

"Great, I'll sit down and rest. You go and try to get a car to stop. I'll be okay."

As Billy Edmonds finds a spot on the ground, he sees his new companion, Ed Williams, walking toward the road, a few hundred feet away. As if on cue, as soon as he reaches the highway, he sees a black sedan stop, what a lucky break. Now finally, this strange nightmare should be over. As Billy gets up and limps toward the road and the black sedan, he sees his strange new companion inexplicably getting angry at the driver and shouting at him. The car quickly pulls away. Crestfallen, and at a loss to understand what he's just seen, Billy hobbles over to Ed Williams.

"What happened?"

"Did you see that bastard?"

"No, what happened?"

"Oh that pisses me off, Billy."

"What?"

"He expected us, two white men, to ride in his big black limousine, bastard. I told him to go to hell."

"What are you talkin' about?"

"Well didn't you see it?"

"See what?"

"The car, that's what, bumper to bumper solid black, black as the ace o' spades. Even the interior was black. You didn't see what I saw. Trust me."

"So what if it was black, what's the problem?"

"That ain't fit for no white man, Billy. You know that."

"Are you out o' your mind? We're stranded in the desert and you turn down a ride because the car's black? You idiot, I have an injured foot. What's wrong with you?"

"Ain't nothin' wrong with me, you wanna put up with somethin' like that you go right ahead. I ain't ridin' in any big, black limousine, ain't gonna happen. What's the big deal? There'll be another car comin' by, and this time it'll be a real pretty white one. You watch. Don't worry Billy. We got it covered. A real pretty white one, that's what we need."

"Look, I can hardly walk. I need to get out o' here. I can't believe you did that."

"I don't know what you're so bent out o' shape for. Somebody else'll be comin' soon. Billy, we're gonna make it. Don't worry."

"My feet are in pain, serious pain. Don't you understand that?"

"Just go back and sit down. We'll get out o' here. Don't worry."

"That's all I can do. I don't believe it. Please don't do that again."

After sitting in the hot sun for a few minutes, Billy Edmonds leans against a boulder and closes his eyes. The heat brings a weary drowsiness to the moment, and he drifts into a light sleep. Vague recollections of a journey on a highway from somewhere, an interrupted journey for some reason, slip in and out of his memory. In an instant he suddenly opens his eyes after hearing a loud shouting voice.

"You son of a bitch, you get the hell out o' here. Get out o' here you bastard. If I had my shotgun, I'd blow your ass away. You think I'm kiddin'? You get your ass out o' here."

As the tirade ends, Billy Edmonds sees a man with a backpack walking away and his irate friend, Ed Williams, staring angrily at his departure. He stands and makes his way over to his strange companion.

"The nerve o' some people. You won't believe it."

"What? What happened?"

"You know what that son of a bitch did? That bastard I just ran off."

"What?"

"Lemme tell ya what happened. When you were restin' over there, this guy comes walkin' by. I started talkin' to him and I told him your feet were hurtin'. You know what that bastard did?"

"What?"

"He told me he had an extra pair o' shoes he didn't need, had socks too. Billy, I told this guy that's exactly what you need. He

opens up his backpack and wanted me to take them. They were as black as coal. I mean, black as coal. The socks too, black as coal. Even the laces were black. I wanted to kill that bastard. If I had a gun, I'd a shot him. The nerve of the son of a bitch to think he could give somethin' like that to a white man."

With his mouth hanging open in stupefaction, Billy Edmonds looks down at his blistered and bloody feet with his right foot swollen from the puncture wound. Searching for words, he simply asks, "Are you insane? Look at my feet, you idiot."

After calling to the man disappearing into the distance who continues onward, Billy Edmonds hears his companion once more.

"Don't worry about him. We don't need someone like that around here."

"You must be a lunatic. My feet are bleeding and you turn away someone who wants to give me shoes, just because they're black? You must be out of your right mind."

"Look, I know you need a pair o' shoes but I saw them shoes. You didn't. There wasn't a speck o' white on them shoes, as god is my witness, as god is my witness. I swear! I looked inside and out, Billy. They were black, black and more black. Trust me. You'd a done the same thing. I mean there's only so much a white man can take!"

"What's the difference if they're black, blue, purple or green or any other color of the fucking rainbow you idiot? Shoes are shoes!"

"Calm down. Calm down. Let's do this, that guy said there was a gas station just down the road a few miles. If we start walkin', we can get there in an hour or so. I think that's our best option."

"I can't believe this is happening, stranded in this awful place, my foot's bleeding and now I'm getting hungry. I hope this place serves food. I need to get something to eat."

"I'm sure it will. I'm gettin' hungry too. We'll make it. I'm here for ya Billy. You don't mind if I call you Billy, cause I think we have some kind o' personal connection here. I really feel that."

"Well, I don't feel that at all. This is ridiculous. What is this place?"

"Come on now Billy, a couple o' white, southern boys like us, we got to stick together. You don't have to worry about nothin'. I'll be with ya every step of the way."

Ed Williams puts his arm under Billy's for support and they set off once more. Billy Edmonds looks over at his newfound companion as if he were his executioner. The two men make their way down the road and within minutes every step becomes a labored agony for Billy, until his ordeal becomes unbearable.

"That's it. I need to stop. My feet — it hurts too much. I have to rest... I'm so hungry."

"Okay, we'll stop for a minute. Hey Billy, do you see what I see?"

"What?"

"Down the road on the right-hand side, it's a house. I'll bet somebody lives there. I see a car parked outside. Let's see if we can get some help. Come on Billy. You can do it."

"How far is it?" Billy asks.

"It ain't that far. We can be there in five minutes. Come on. I'll help ya."

"Okay, I'll try. I hope we can at least get something to eat."

Ten long minutes later both men are standing across the road from the small, one story house. The car parked in the driveway is a sight that offers the first real hope of deliverance from this painful, nightmarish place. Billy Edmonds allows himself to think this terrible experience is about to end.

"Look Billy, You're all bloody and dirty. We don't wanna scare anyone, so you stay here, and I'll bring ya some food. That's what ya need first. Then we'll ask if we can get a ride into town."

"I'll go with ya."

"You better not. Your feet are dirty and bloody. You might scare these people and then we get nothin'. Lemme knock on the door first and ask for some food."

"Okay, yeah get some food. I'll wait here."

As Billy Edmonds sits, his companion crosses the road and into the yard of the modest, one story home. Moments later, Ed Williams knocks and within seconds an elderly woman opens the door.

"Yes,"

"Sorry to bother you ma'am but I have a friend here who's very hungry. He's in a real bad way and I wonder if you could spare a bowl o' soup or somethin' to help him out."

"Absolutely, I've been here for almost 40 years and I've never turned anybody away, not one time."

"Well God bless you for that, ma'am."

"Don't you worry about your friend. You wait right here, and I'll fix him a plate. We'll get him some food and anything else he needs."

"I really appreciate that ma'am. Lemme go tell him that and I'll be right back."

"Go ahead and I'll bring you both somethin' to eat."

Seconds later Ed Williams tells Billy the good news.

"Guess what, Billy. This lady answered the door, and she's gettin' us both somethin' to eat and you know what else she said?"

"What?"

"She said she'd give us any other kind o' help we need."

"Really?"

"That's what she said. That means a ride into town Billy. I think we made it."

"Finally, this nightmare is ending. That's great. I don't know why I'm so hungry."

"I know you are. She's gettin' our food ready so lemme get back. She might think we left. We'll eat first, then see if she can run us into town."

"I hope so," Billy mutters.

As Ed Williams walks back across the road to receive the offered food, he hears Billy's voice.

"Ask her if we can get a ride into town."

Billy sees his counterpart lift his hand in acknowledgment and watches as he again approaches the woman's front door. A deep feeling of relief comes over him as he sits waiting. She appears at the door carrying a tray with two bowls and two spoons, a small sign of hope at last for Billy Edmonds. Then he sees Ed Williams, without any apparent reason, take the tray from the woman, violently throw it on the ground and storm away in a rage. His seething words are bitterly angry.

"I should o' known better. I should o' known better. Bitch!"

Amazed at his sudden, and unexpected anger, she steps out of her door and rails at the man's ingratitude.

"What the hell's the matter with you, mister? You come to my house and ask for food. Then you throw it on the ground right in front o' me. I oughta call the sheriff on you."

"You can go to hell, lady."

By now, Billy Edmonds is on his feet and hobbling toward the house and the lady standing at her front door. Seeing his approach, her reaction is immediately unwelcoming.

"What the hell is wrong with you? You look like a ghost. You must have some kind o' disease, mister. Both o' you get out o' here before I call the sheriff."

"What are you talkin' about? Look ma'am, please, I need some help, please."

"You got some kind o' disease and I don't wanna catch it. I want you both off my property right now."

"Come on Billy. We don't need her."

"What happened? What made you so angry?"

"I'll tell ya but we got to get out o' here, get away from this hag."

"No, I'm not leavin' for somethin' you did. I need help."

"If you two don't get off my property, I'll let my dogs loose. You'll leave then. I got two German Shepherds in the back yard. I'll set my animals loose on ya. I mean it."

"Come on Billy. She's crazy. Let's get out o' here. It's gonna get dark soon."

"Just tell me what happened."

As the two men walk away, Billy hears his companion's reason for what just happened.

"You know what that old hag did to us?"

"What did she mean about me having a disease? What was she talking about?"

"She was just spoutin' off. She's crazy. That's all."

"What happened?"

"I was real nice to 'er. I told 'er we were hungry. We just wanted somethin' to eat. So she comes back with two bowls o' beans and

what I saw turned my stomach. They were solid black, the whole bowl. Not one o' them beans were white, not one. It made me sick. You think she could o' put at least a few white beans in that bowl. Every single one was black, every one. She did that on purpose. I know she did."

"Are you serious? That lady wanted to help us and you throw a tantrum because she served you black beans? You must be insane. You idiot, I can't believe you did that. She had a car in her driveway. She could o' helped us. What's wrong with you?"

"We don't need someone like that helpin' us Billy. I mean, come on. I've been insulted before, but that was over the top. I think she saw us comin' and just wanted to be hateful. Why else would she do that? White beans don't cost any more than black beans. Do they? She did it on purpose. It's obvious. She's just a mean old woman, Billy."

"What on earth are you talking about? What is this ridiculous thing you have about black? We could die out here and all because you have this fucked up idea about anything black. You turned down a ride because the car was black. My bloody feet are covered in blisters because you wouldn't take a pair o' shoes from some guy because they were black and now we might starve because you don't wanna eat black beans. You're nuts, mister. You are crazy and I'm stuck out here with ya."

"We'll make it, Billy."

"No, you're crazy. What is this thing you have about black? What's the difference between a black car and a white one? What's the difference between black shoes and white ones? There is no difference. The color doesn't matter, you dumb ass."

"Are you sayin' that it doesn't matter if something is black? Is that what you're sayin'?"

"That's right. It doesn't mean anything. It's just on the surface."
"Look Billy, I know you don't mean that. This is your first day here. You're confused. You're upset. I understand that but I want you to think about somethin'. What if them black beans that lady wanted us to eat were poisoned? What then? Then you'd be thankin' me for savin' your life. Wouldn't ya? Don't you think it's strange that

201

one minute she wants to feed us and the next she wants to sic her dogs on us? That ought to tell ya somethin.'"

"Wow, you're really out there. You're really out there. Aren't you?"

"No, no, I'm here. I'm right here with you Billy, doin' my best to protect you. That's where I am."

"Protect me, are you crazy? It's because o' you I'm in this condition."

"I know you don't mean that because god knows I'm doin' my best for ya. Lemme ask ya, how far do you think you'd get with your feet bein' like that? In case you haven't noticed, you can't walk without my help. Don't get me wrong. I'm glad to do it."

"This place is a nightmare."

Look we'll be okay. We just gotta keep walkin' till we get to that gas station. Then we can rest."

Billy Edmonds stares blankly into the distance and wonders when this agony will come to an end. As the sun sets, his companion puts his arm underneath his and both men start slowly walking down the road.

"It's gonna be all right Billy. We'll make it. We're in this together. Don't ever think I'd abandon you Billy, That ain't gonna happen. You know what? I feel as though we're like twin brothers. I really do. That's God's honest truth. So, you don't worry about anything. I'm not goin' anywhere."

"Gee, thanks, what a relief."As they hobble off together, Billy Edmonds gazes at his counterpart with a suspicious, even alarming curiosity. Looking on him as strangely as if he had seven heads, he wonders who he is and where all of this is leading. Onward they walk with no sign of any human activity until finally, his blistered feet are too painful to ignore.

"That's it. I have to stop. I can't do it any more... Shit! What am I doing here?"

"Okay, it's gettin' dark, anyway. Let's find a place to rest. We'll be all right."

After finding a place a hundred feet or so from the highway, both men sit and, as complete darkness enshrouds them, it starts to get cold, very cold. Sleepless, shivering and with his feet throbbing in pain, Billy listens in bitter silence to his companion's senseless prattle.

"She shouldn't a give us those beans like that, Billy. That was uncalled for. It really was. I know she did it on purpose... It's gettin' cold out here. I think it's gonna get down in the thirties tonight."

With his shivering body curled in a ball, Billy Edmonds listens to his nemesis drone on with his neurotic fixation.

"It makes you wonder why people would do somethin' like that. A white man can't get any respect. That's what it comes down to. I'll give ya an example, just yesterday this lady comes up to me cause she knew I was sleepin' out here in the open. She tries to give me four or five blankets, and wouldn't ya know it? They were all black and brown, every one, every single one, not a white one in the bunch, not one. I asked her don't you have any white blankets? She didn't say nothin'. I knew right then what she did. She thought I was dumb, Billy."

Shaking with goose bumps, Billy mockingly whispers, "I wonder what would make her think that."

"You know what she did Billy? She gave all her white blankets to her uppity friends. Then she thinks she's gonna pawn them black blankets off on me. You know what I told her? I said, "Lady you can take them blankets and stick 'em in your ass." That's what I told her. You'd a said the same thing, Billy. I know you would've. We could a used those white blankets Billy, but no, she had to give those to her fancy friends. Now, we gotta suffer. It ain't right, Billy. It just ain't right.

Shivering on the ground with his teeth chattering, Billy Edmonds knows he's in for a long, dark, cold night and if that wasn't enough, the neurotic chatterbox sitting a few feet away from him shows no sign of fatigue.

"Man, it's gettin' cold. Hey Billy, Billy."

"What?"

"You ever gone skiin'? I'd like to try that sometime, all that white snow and everything. I'd like that. Course, I'd have to learn how to stand up with them skis on my feet, but I think I could do it. You ever gone skiin'? The reason I ask is because maybe you could teach me. We could go skiin' sometime. I mean it's just a thought… Hey Billy… Billy are you sleepin?"

"No."

"I usually stay up all night. I sleep in the day time. Hey Billy, you know what I think?"

"Why don't you tell me. I can't wait to find out."

"I don't think that lady had any German Shepherds in her back yard. You know why? I didn't hear any dogs when I knocked on her door. Did you? Billy, did you hear any dogs when I knocked on that lady's front door?"

"No."

"That's cause there weren't any. You know how I know that? You know how I know that, Billy?"

"Why?"

"'Cause I had a cousin who had three German Shepherds, and every time I'd go over there, them dogs would bark, every time, every single time. That's how I know."

As Billy lies shivering on the ground, he knows sleep will be impossible tonight. With his feet still blistered and bloody from walking through the day and the cold now adding to his general misery, he wonders how he'll get through what promises to be a hellishly long and miserable night. Dozing off for a few minutes at a time until the cold wakes him again, he tries to ignore the intermittent strain of his companion's convoluted monologue. The night passes ever so slowly. Occasionally, looking at the stars making their imperceptibly slow transit across the sky, they seem to be fixed and stationary in their unchanging positions as the minutes pass. Every second seems to dwell forever in the perfect misery of his condition and sunrise seems like a hundred years away.

Chapter Twelve: The Lynching

After an interminably long night of discomfort, pain and sleepless agitation, Billy Edmonds open his eyes to see a faint glow of dawn in the eastern sky. The raw grip of this long, difficult night is finally ending. Tired, cold and hungry, he waits for the warming rays of the new morning sun, and when they come he feels as if he's been reborn. The flood of light and warmth are an immediate comfort and revive his hopes of returning home from this unfamiliar world. As the sun gets higher and stronger in the sky, Billy Edmonds feels his strength gradually return, and with gathering resolve prepares himself mentally for what might be another long day of walking through the desert, but for now, it's enough to just sit up and take in the warmth of a new day's sunlight. After passing a dismal, restless and bitterly cold night, not even the sound of his chatty companion can blunt the rejuvenating surge of energy he feels in this golden moment.

"That sun feels good. Doesn't it Billy?"

"It sure does."

"You know what I did?"

"What's that?"

"See that ridge up there. I walked up to the top o' that ridge an' you know what I saw?"

"What?"

"I looked down the road, an' you can see the gas station from up there. It ain't far at all."

"How long will it take to get there?"

"I don't know, ten minutes at the most."

"Let's go then. I'm ready," Billy says.

Buoyed by the prospect of what might be the end of his grueling ordeal, Billy stands and gathers his determination to move forward. Even his feet seem a little less painful this morning as he takes his first few tentative steps.

Meanwhile, less than a mile away, at the gas station they're trying to reach, the morning brings another day of business for Mike Hollister who's starting his early shift behind the counter. After pouring himself a cup of coffee and getting ready for a new day, he looks out and sees two men approaching the front door. The glaring sun, still low in the eastern sky, makes the two men appear as dark silhouettes and he puts his hand above his eyes as a visor, squinting to see them. Moments later, the door opens and Billy's companion Ed Williams, walks in.

"Sir, I wonder if we could use your rest room."

"Sure, it's right around the side of the building. It's unlocked."

"Thanks."

Within seconds, Billy Edmonds accompanies his companion around the side and opens the door to the bathroom. As he enters and turns on the light, he looks in the mirror and gasps in disbelief at what he sees. His face and hair are completely white, as white as the whitest snow. Even the pupils of his eyes are white. Transfixed by the image he sees in the mirror, an unnerving silence comes over him. He barely recalls from his memory the words a woman once spoke to him. "You must be a white man, Mr. Edmonds, and you will be a white man. Rest assured." But that was only a dream, he tells himself. This is real. This is what that lady back there had meant when she had said, "You look like a ghost." The spell of his panicked thoughts is broken when he hears his companion's voice.

"How are your feet doin' Billy?"

"You ask me how my feet are doin', look at my face! Why didn't you tell me I looked like this?"

"What do you mean? You look fine."

"What do I mean? Look at me. Look at my face and hair! I'm white as a sheet! No wonder I scared that lady back there. Why didn't you tell me this?"

"Tell you what, that you're a white man?"

"What's happened to me? I have no color. Even my eyes are totally white. What's wrong with me? I look like a ghost."

"I think you look fine Billy, look like a white man to me."

"Are you crazy?"

"I don't understand. Don't you wanna look like a white man?"

"No! I need color, you idiot."

Staring back at his image, Billy Edmonds tries to reason his way through this strange predicament.

"What should I do? I can't go anywhere like this. I need something to — wait a minute, shoe polish, yeah, that might help. Yeah, that's what I need. Look, ask that guy, the clerk inside, if he has any shoe polish. I need the kind you rub on, not the liquid. It comes in a can like car wax, you know the kind I'm talkin' about?"

"Yeah, I know. What are you gonna do, Billy?"

"Just do it please, Ed."

"Okay, I'll ask. I'll be right back."

When Billy Edmonds looks back at his own image, he once again sees a face and head completely devoid of any color. He turns on the water and washes his face thinking his strange appearance might somehow rinse off, but no amount of effort helps. Opening his jaw, he sees that even the inside of his mouth and tongue are as white as his face and hair. What's happening to me? His silent consternation is interrupted by the sound of a voice calling from the outside.

"Hey Billy, can you come out for a minute?"

"Did you get the shoe polish?"

"Not yet."

After opening the door and tentatively peeking, Billy Edmonds returns outside to his companion.

"What's the problem?" Billy asks.

"You want me to get shoe polish, I don't have any money."

At the same time Billy sees the station attendant come around the corner of the building but now, instead of looking into the glare of sunlight, Mike Hollister has the sun behind him and gets an illuminated, full-on view of Billy Edmond's face.

"Man! What the hell happened to you? You're as white as a sheet!"

"Look, I'm sorry to bother you but I need some shoe polish, some tan shoe polish, the rub on kind. I, I know this sounds crazy but —"

"You're the weirdest thing I've ever seen. You must have some kind o' disease, mister."

"No, no, I'm all right. I just need some shoe polish and maybe an old pair o' shoes if you have any. That's all, please."

"I might have an old pair in the backroom you can have. I'll see if I can find some shoe polish. Then both of you can move on. You'll scare my customers."

The station attendant turns to Ed Williams.

"You can come get it," and turning to Billy says, "you stay outside. I don't want you in my store. It's nothin' personal, but you could have some kind o' contagious disease. I'll give the shoe polish to your friend and then I'm gonna lock that bathroom door."

"I need to use the bathroom," Billy says.

"Do you want this stuff or not?"

"Yes, yes I do."

"Okay then, after I give it to ya, ya both leave. It's either that or you both leave with nothin'."

"Okay, okay."

After following the attendant back in the store, Billy's companion returns with an old pair of tennis shoes and a small can of brown shoe polish, dark brown shoe polish and gives the items to Billy.

"This is what he gave me, Billy. Is this what you wanted?"

"Yeah, great, and a pair o' shoes."

After putting them on Billy looks at the can of shoe polish. "Did he give you a rag or paper towel or something?"

"No, he didn't. He said he wants us out o' here."

"I'll have to use my hands. I wish I had a mirror."

"What are you gonna do?"

"What do ya think I'm gonna do? I'm gonna put some color on my face. I can't walk around like this. I'll scare people. Didn't you see how he reacted when he saw my face?"

"What on earth are you talkin' about Billy?"

"I just told you. Are you blind?"

Billy Edmonds opens the can and rubs the dark brown shoe polish on his face. Having no mirror, he makes doubly sure to get

every possible square inch of his face, neck and scalp until no trace of white skin is visible. Ed Williams is repulsed at what he sees.

" ...I can't believe this. I can't believe what I'm seeing. Have you gone crazy?"

"No, you're the one who's crazy. I'm doin' what I have to do to get out o' here."

"Well, I'm not gonna stand here and watch you do this. I just can't."

"Then look the other way."

"This is disgusting. You know what you look like? You look like a white man who turned himself into a nigger. I'm not gonna be part o' this. This is where you an' I part company. I should a known better. I try to help you, an' you turn crazy on me."

"No, you're the one who's crazy. This thing you have about black is what's crazy. I'd be out o' here by now if it wasn't for you. There's nothin' wrong with me. It's you. You're the one who's crazy. Why didn't you tell me what I looked like? I'm better off without you."

"Are you forgettin' who's been helpin' you get through this place? You couldn't even walk back there without my help."

"Yeah, well now I have some shoes and my feet are better, so —"

"You may not know it, but you still need me. You don't even know where you're goin'."

"I'll find my way. I don't need you. You're a lunatic."

"It's a good thing you don't have a mirror, Billy. You'd see what I'm seein' and what I'm seein' is pathetic. Adios, black face."

Billy watches in silence as Ed Williams turns and walks away. As he does, he sees something inexplicable. The receding figure of his erstwhile companion is less than 15 feet away when it melts into the thin air and completely disappears, leaving Billy Edmonds to wonder exactly who was the strange character who crossed paths with him. The warm sun and dry wind quickly remind him of his predicament, and he starts slowly walking away, but he's not the only one traversing this seemingly desolate stretch of highway. Brianna and her apprentice Calvin are walking toward him, and when he's a few hundred yards away, Calvin's sharp eyesight sees his figure in the distance.

"There's someone walking up there ahead."

"It's Billy Edmonds," Brianna says.

"He's the one we saw back there changing his tire."

"That's right, but that world is now behind him. He's on his way to his new destination."

"What destination is that?"

"That's something only he can decide."

"What will determine that?"

"Well, if he's ready to invite a gentler strain of music into his heart, then he'll go accordingly."

"And if he doesn't wanna hear that music?"

"Then he'll still go accordingly, but to a very different place."

"Do you know which way he'll choose?"

"It's impossible to know. That choice is inviolable. If it wasn't, then human freedom wouldn't exist. Only Mr. Edmonds can choose his destiny."

"What if he doesn't choose anything?"

"That's not possible here, Calvin. In this place, not making a choice is the worst choice of all. He'll declare himself. They always do."

"How will you know?" "I'll sift his words and draw him out." Brianna looks over at Calvin and says, "You'll soon be doing what I'm doing. It's good to hear you ask these questions."

"I hope I'm learning."

"You are, just be silent and observe."

"Will he be able to see me?"

"No, it's not time for that yet. It's coming."

As Brianna and Calvin continue walking forward, their counterpart is now aware that he's not alone on this endless highway. Billy Edmonds looks ahead and sees a figure beside the road, moving closer. Within minutes, he sees a woman approaching him and, as he gets closer, he recognizes her as being someone he recently met, but he can't recall exactly where. Seconds later she greets him.

"Hello, Mr. Edmonds."

"Who are you?"

"My name is Brianna."

"Do I know you? I've seen you somewhere."

"Yes, we met along the road before."

"Yeah, I remember you, the lady from Africa. You were there when I was fixin' my car. Then somethin' happened. I remember. I heard a loud horn. There was somethin' bright in my eyes... I was in some kind o' tunnel. After that, I woke up in this place. What is this place? Where am I?"

"You're in a landscape of your own making. You built this world."

"This place is a desert, lady. Why would I make a place like this?"

"It's not a friendly place, arid, dry and unyielding, very much like the barren hospitality of a human heart clenched with bigotry and race hatred, don't you think? You're not in Georgia any more, Mr. Edmonds."

"Well, where am I then?"

"You're on the other side."

"What do you mean?"

"Do you know what happened when you were changing your tire a few nights ago along the road?"

"What?"

"You died, Mr. Edmonds. You died to the life you knew. There was an accident. It was sudden, violent and fatal. Your earthly journey ended. You were killed."

"Then how come I don't feel like I was killed?"

"Well, how did you think it was supposed to feel Mr. Edmonds?"

"What I mean is, I don't feel like I'm dead. Look at me. I'm breathin'. I'm alive,"

"And so you are."

"You say I was killed, but I'm still alive. If I didn't die, then what happened?"

"Nothing uncommon, just another page being turned in another book of countless chapters, Mr. Edmonds. That's all."

"Yeah, well, I don't wanna read any books right now lady, but a road map would be nice. Do you know the way out o' here?"

"Of course."

"Tell me which way that is."

"The path out of this place leads into your own heart."

"Oh, come on. What's that supposed to mean?"

"It means you have a choice Mr. Edmonds. You can come with me. If you do, the way will be hard at first, but the journey will make you wise and strong, or you can return to the world you came from, or one very much like it. That path is quick and easy."

"That's the one I want."

"Are you really sure that's what you want?"

"Yes, I'm sure."

"I'm curious. Why would you want to return to the narrow minded bigotry of the life you had? That's going backward, not forward."

"Because that's who I am. It's my life not yours. Look, how I live my life is none o' your business. You can call it racism or whatever you want. I don't care. I wouldn't wanna live any other way. You think I'm bigoted, you should o' heard the guy that was here with me before. You just missed him. He left before you came. He was a lunatic. You should be talkin' to him, not me."

"I am talking to him."

"Now what are you talkin' about lady? That guy was a lot older than me."

"Yes, he was."

"Well that means you're talkin' to me not him. He's a different person than I am."

"No, he isn't. He is you and you are him, distilled to the very essence, or to put it more accurately, he is what you'll become in twenty years. Your soul's mirror image with twenty years added, matches perfectly to your erratic walking companion."

"He doesn't even look like me."

"That's only the surface. His appearance was an illusion. Only the presence of his corrupted soul was real. Another twenty years and your bigoted fixation on race will grow into his neurotic delusions about the color black. He is what you'll become in time. You're already both joined at the hip."

"You're crazy lady. I'll never be like that nut case. He was a lunatic."

"Did he tell you his name?"

"Yeah, Williams, Ed Williams, so what?"

"Ed is short for Edmond. His formal name is Edmond Williams. Your name is William Edmonds, or if you like, just call me Billy; a mirror image wouldn't you say? You might say it's like two sides of the same coin."

"This is — This is all crazy talk. I don't believe any of it. How do you explain my face bein' so white? Since you have all the answers, what do you know about that?"

"No mystery, Mr. Edmonds. You're a white man, a proud white man. You said that yourself. Don't you remember?' The whiter the better', those were your words. You wanted to be as white as possible. Isn't that what you said?"

"That's not what I meant, and you know it."

"Oh, you meant it Mr. Edmonds. You meant it, and now you have what you wanted."

"This is nuts. I'm goin' back where I came from. I have a life back there. I have things I have to do. You're looking at the next sheriff of Early County."

"It's too late for Early. I mean Early County, Mr. Edmonds."

"Not for me, it isn't."

"You should come with me instead."

"What kind o' crazy woman are you? You're tryin' to aggravate me and you're succeeding."

"You do seem to be getting angry, Mr. Edmonds."

"I am angry. I'm tired. I'm hungry. My feet are aching. I need to get out of this hell hole. You don't seem to understand that."

"The way forward is always difficult."

"Don't give me another sermon lady. I don't know what you're talkin' about, and I don't care. This place is a nightmare and, as far as I'm concerned, you're part of it. I'm not the problem here, you are. All this talk about race, who's white, who's black, I couldn't care less about it. I like my life the way it is. I'm not gonna change for anyone."

"Can life choose not to grow and evolve, Mr. Edmonds?"

"Grow and evolve, what kind o' silly shit is that? Evolve into what, something you think I should be, so we can all be brothers and sisters and hold hands? No thanks, you might think black is beautiful, well it ain't beautiful to me. You know what black is to me?"

"Why don't you tell me, Mr. Edmonds?"

"I will. Black is dumb. Black is uncivilized. Black is ignorant. Black is ugly, always was, always will be." He glowers at her with his face still thoroughly darkened with shoe polish.

Brianna replies, "You may have a point."

"So black is definitely not my favorite color. How do ya like that lady?"

"I'm actually very fond of lavender."

"Well why don't you go an' pick some? You're just like this other idiot I was with, askin' me these stupid questions. Get lost lady. I'm goin' back where I came from."

"I'm not the one who's lost, Mr. Edmonds."

"Yeah, and once I get back home, I won't be either."

"Are you sure that's what you want? There's still time to make a different choice."

"You don't get it. Do ya? I'll have to spell it out real plain. I said I don't want your world. I wanna go back to people who think

like me, who talk like me, who act like me and who look like me. You know what? It wouldn't bother me if they were all in the KKK. How do ya like that?"

"You talk lightly about those who terrorize innocent people. You surely wouldn't want to return to a world like that, Mr. Edmonds."

"Wow, you really are dense, aren't ya? Maybe you don't understand English. Did you hear what I said?"

"Yes, I heard you, and I understand all languages."

"Well, lemme be more blunt since you don't seem to get my meaning." To underscore his words, he takes a step closer to Brianna and looks directly into her face and says, "I'd rather go to a KKK lynch party and watch a darkie get strung up than stand here and listen to you talk about your equality and civil rights."

"Do really mean that, Mr. Edmonds? Please think carefully before you answer."

Raising his right hand as if pledging an oath he says, "I swear to God I do. So you're wastin' your time lady, and mine."

"You seem to mean what you say."

"Every word."

"Why then, it seems you've just made your choice, Mr. Edmonds. We don't usually send people back, but in your case we'll make an exception."

"I don't know, and I don't care what you're talkin' about lady."

"Well, if you're sure you want to go back to the world you just described, then all you have to do is walk up that path that leads over the hill, and it will take you where you apparently want to go."

Turning away from the strange woman, Billy Edmonds sees the path leading away, then looks back for a moment to see the woman named Brianna is no longer there.

Minutes later, he's making his way up the pathway. As he does, it seems to open up in front of him as if pulling him forward, and he soon reaches the crest of the hill. As he continues walking, he sees the landscape change with every step from the arid scenery of a sandy desert to the familiar, verdantly green countryside of his native southwestern Georgia. The path widens to become a rural, country dirt road and as he continues, everything around him becomes more and more familiar. The distinctive silhouette of pine trees against the background of a blue sky, the sight of cattle egrets foraging in a pasture and swaying Spanish moss draped from the branches of a Magnolia tree convince Billy Edmonds that he's back home, or at least close to it.

He continues onward, then looks ahead and sees a strange looking vehicle approaching him. As it gets closer and closer, its color and shape become recognizable. It's a Model A Ford. Through the windshield, the driver's white gloves can easily be seen as he works the steering wheel back and forth, trying to keep the narrow tires of the car in the well-worn ruts of the dirt road. The curious sight of this odd-looking vehicle is made even more bizarre by what he sees as it passes.

With the car moving at less than 20mph, Billy Edmonds has enough time to get a clear view of its occupants. The driver is a middle-aged man with round, wire-rimmed glasses. He's accompanied by a woman seated beside him wearing an ankle-length dress fully buttoned from the neck down. Their unusual attire appears strangely out of date. The woman's full-length dress and the straw boater hat of the man seem reminiscent of a bygone era. As the car passes, the driver's unfriendly sneer is a disconcerting reminder that Billy Edmonds is not yet sure of where and what this place is. Seconds later, the Model A recedes into the distance and he continues walking. After covering several miles, he sees a house near the road and as he gets closer he notices a man sitting on the front porch. Cautiously entering the front yard, he sees an old style well pump handle along the side of the house and off to one side what looks to be a small outhouse. A powerful apprehension takes

over his thoughts. He remembers the Model A Ford that passed him on the road earlier, and the dated apparel of the car's occupants. Billy Edmonds wonders not only where this place is, but also when this place is. He stops and quickly glances in every direction. He sees no electric wires or telephone poles and no antenna or satellite dish on the roof or anywhere else in the yard. The odd notion he's somewhere in an earlier time is becoming compelling.

As he approaches, the man sitting on the porch intercepts him. "What do you want boy?"

"What's the name of this place?"

"That's a dumb question. Don't you know where you are?"

"No, tell me."

"You're in Early County boy."

"Early County, I know this place."

Billy Edmonds notices a small table with a newspaper on it. Looking more closely, he reads its headline: 'President Wilson Pledges Neutrality In Europe's War', then he looks at the top of the page and sees the date. It reads June 17th 1915. His mind boggles for an instant and races with questions. Is this real? How can this be happening? He incredulously asks the man. "Is, is this 1915?"

"That's right. Who are you boy? I never seen you before. I know you ain't from around here. You have anything to do with Sheriff Freeman's horse gettin' stole?"

"I have no idea what you're talkin' about."

"Is that so? Get out a here nigger, git!"

"What do you mean, nigger?" Looking at his hands, Billy's reminded of the shoe polish still smeared on his skin. "No, this is just shoe polish. I'm a white man."

"I said get out a here nigger!" As the man angrily reaches for his shotgun and points it at him, Billy Edmonds backs away.

"All right, all right, I'm leavin."

Moments later, Billy's walking down the dirt road again away from the irascible stranger who threatened him. He stops for a moment to glance back at the man and sees him in his front yard. With him are at least six men on horseback and several dogs barking excitedly. As he strains to see what they're doing he sees the man he spoke with pointing back at him, directing the men on horseback. Then he sees one horsemen give a quick, sharp command to the dogs and the entire pack starts running full pitch in his direction.

The sudden, unnerving realization that he is now being hunted is driven home by the sight of a half dozen men on horseback in hot pursuit behind the clamorous barking dogs chasing him. Billy Edmonds runs as fast as he can, but his only option is to find a tree to climb and hopefully stay out of reach of his pursuers. He sees one that looks suitable and heads for it. As he reaches the trunk and climbs, the dogs are less than a hundred feet behind him. Fueled by adrenaline, he quickly scales the lower branches and precariously lodges himself ten feet off the ground. Exhausted and clinging to safety, he hears the raucous frenzy below as the dogs bark incessantly. Their threatening snarls are an intimidating sight, but when the men on horseback arrive, their actions and demeanor are even more alarming. Dreadful expressions of burning revenge and hateful anger signal their deadly intention louder than any words.

"That's the nigger who stole your horse, Nathan."

"I know it."

Still panting and exhausted, Billy Edmonds tries to explain.

"Look I'm not who your lookin' for; I swear. You're makin' a mistake. This is just shoe polish. I swear."

"Shut up, nigger."

After being pulled from the tree and manhandled by three husky men, a fearful panic sets in when Billy Edmonds sees the rope with a ready-made noose on one end.

"Please, please, I'm a white man. I'm a white man."

With his hands tied behind his back, Billy Edmonds feels the snug fit of a rope being put around his neck. As he sees the other end being thrown upward into the tree, the terrible realization seizes him: he's only seconds away from being lynched. One man takes the other end of the rope, pulls out the slack and ties it to his saddle. Without warning, the rope tightens and Billy Edmonds feels his feet being lifted off the ground. As he slowly chokes to death, one of his killers taunts him.

"You take a good look at me, nigger. You know who I am? My name is Nathan Bedford Freeman. I'm sheriff here in Early County, so when you get to hell ya can tell all your friends who sent ya, damn, thievin' nigger."

As Billy Edmonds feels the twitching, involuntary nerve spasms in his legs, his last tormented thoughts are laced with a cruel irony. He instantly recalls the conversation he had earlier with Tyler Freeman, who said his grandfather was the sheriff of Early County and his name was Nathan Bedford Freeman. Through his final agony he remembers the newspaper dated 1915 and the Model A Ford. It all adds up. Billy Edmonds has come back to Early County, but a full century before his time, and the sheriff who's just hanged him is the same sheriff he wanted to pattern himself after when he became sheriff of the very same county. The bitter, twisted irony of his suffering is sharpened with one final taunt. While hearing his own neck bones breaking, he sees the smirking grin on the face of Nathan Bedford Freeman as he spits tobacco juice from his mouth and says, "You have a real nice day now, nigger." With one final agonizing convulsion, his entire body twitches, consciousness ebbs and then darkness and oblivion.

On a stretch of beach in the Caribbean Sea, two beings casually walk together in the twilight hours of early evening. The sun is well below the horizon and its fading afterglow bathes the sky in the warm colors of sunset. All seems idyllic but this beautiful setting conceals a grim reality.

"Do you know where we are, Calvin?" Brianna asks.

"We're on an island somewhere."

"Yes, we are. This is Cuba, but it's not the Cuba most people know about."

"What do you mean?"

"Look out into the bay."

Calvin looks out across the water and, barely visible in the distance, is the unmistakable silhouette of a sailing ship with its tall mast conspicuously etched against the horizon.

"That's a sailing ship."

"It's more than that, Calvin. It's a slave ship. Cuba is a slave colony in the year 1826 and we are now in that place and time."

223

"The Spanish ruled Cuba at that time."

"And ruled with notorious cruelty. This island is a collective prison. Innocent people had their lives stolen from them and were brought here to be worked to death in the fields growing sugarcane. A terrible inhumanity reigns here. Cruelty teaches us to shun it, but not everyone learns the lesson. This place and the madness that governs it is what happens when people don't."

"Is this the destination for Billy Edmonds?"

"Yes, sadly it is. Only moments ago, a child was born a few miles away from here and was christened 'William' but all will know him as 'Billy'. As a child with dark skin, he'll quickly come to be trained for a life of bonded servitude. His body will feel the stinging lash of the whip and his life will slowly measure out countless hours of forced labor and grieving resentment. He'll live out his days and die in this awful place, and perhaps that will be enough."

"Enough for what? Calvin asks."

"Enough for empathy to be born through the crucible of human suffering, enough for Billy Edmonds to finally learn something every person must learn."

"What's that?" Calvin asks.

"To see himself in others."

"Do you think he will?"

"I hope so."

Chapter Thirteen: The Warrior

Another afternoon is passing for Heather Crosby and her family in Amherst, Virginia, a small town about 85 miles west of Richmond, where she and her two children,

a son and a daughter, have lived for over ten years. Mrs. Crosby's husband, Tom, a captain in the Marine Corps has recently returned home from multiple tours of duty overseas, including three years in Iraq. It's been nearly a month since his reentry into civilian life, and the domestic routines of family and household activity. The adjustment is proving to be far more difficult than Tom Crosby thought it would be. Since he's been home, a noticeable tension seems to hang quietly in the air. Everyone in the family has known for some time that his return would mean adjusting to a new reality, but since that new reality has arrived, the mood and emotional landscape of the Crosby residence has not been the same.

Tom Crosby joined the Marines 12 years ago and, for nine of those years, he was overseas. The extended absence of a husband and father has had the effect of forcing Heather Crosby and her children to find interests and activities they could do on their own, independent of a father's participation. For 17 year old John, this means singing and playing the piano and for his younger sister Sara, it means dance lessons. Neither of his children identifies with their father's profession, and Tom Crosby can't understand why. His rigid ideas and deeply held beliefs are seen as inflexible and even abrasive, and his pro-military, ultra-conservative views don't seem to resonate with his children, who accept more liberal viewpoints.

This is especially true regarding the Iraq War. At seventeen, Tom Crosby's son, John, has become an ardent critic of the war and America's involvement in the debacle. This and other things have prevented Tom Crosby from making a smooth reintegration back into family and civilian life. He knows he's an odd fit in this new world, but in his mind he's already forged a possible solution to his problem. He's scheduled an appointment to be interviewed later today for a position as a security contractor and, if he's accepted, an overseas assignment will follow. His wife Heather is unaware of the real purpose of the interview and has been told by her husband it's for a local civil service job. Heather Crosby and her children assume that Tom is now home for good, and things will eventually work out for the best.

As Mrs. Crosby sits with her son in the kitchen, she brings up the touchy subject of having his father back in the house again.

"So how are you and your dad getting along?"

"We're doin' okay."

"Are you sure?"

"I don't know. I don't think he likes my music."

"Did he say that?"

"Not in those words but, it's like the other day he asked me if I wanted to go to the gun range with him. When I said no, he said, "Oh you rather play pretty notes on the piano, huh?" It was like some kind o' put down. I mean, why would he ask me to go to a gun range? I told him I hate guns. I guess he thinks I'm weak or something."

A knock on the door cuts into their conversation before John's mother can respond. It's Benjamin Keely, their elderly neighbor and friend of the family.

"Hi John," says Benjamin. "The reason I came over is because I forgot to pay you for doing my lawn last week, so I have a check for you."

"Oh, that's okay. You didn't have to do that. I would o' caught up with you."

"No, no, you always do such a good job. I wanna make sure you get paid on time."

"Well, I appreciate that Mr. Keely," John says.

As Mr. Keely hands the check to John, Heather Crosby sees her husband's truck pull into the driveway.

"Your father's home."

"I'm gonna go practice." Rising to accept the check, he says, "Thanks Mr. Keely. I'll see you on Saturday."

A moment later the kitchen door opens as Tom Crosby enters. "Hello Tom."

"Hi, Mr. Keely. How are you, sir?"

"I'm doin' okay. How are you?"

"Pretty good, had to go to the parts store to get some things for my truck."

"Well, I need to get back home. Rusty will be waitin' for me."

"How's he doing Ben?"

"I took him to the vet yesterday. They said he checked out okay, so —"

"That's good."

"He's getting' old like me. What can you do?"

"How old is he now?"

"He's sixteen. That's old for a retriever. Anyway, it's good to see ya both."

"Good to see you Ben," Tom says.

As the door closes behind Mr. Keely, Tom Crosby pours himself a cup of coffee and sits at the table across from his wife.

"Where are the kids?"

"Sara's in her room and John's in the basement."

"Piano practice again?"

"That's what he said."

"A waste of time."

"He doesn't think so."

"I do. When do they start back to school?"

"September third."

"It's his last year of high school."

"That's right."

"What's he gonna do after that, play piano in the basement?"

"He'll be okay."

"I told him last week he should enlist in the Marines. He wouldn't even consider it."

"It's not for him."

"Well, what is? If he's not goin' to college, what's he gonna do?"

"He wants to be a musician."

"Oh, come on. That's not practical. He needs discipline, not tinkling at the piano."

"He has discipline. I've seen him sit and practice for hours at a time, every day. He never misses."

"So what? So he can play fluttery notes some composer wrote down?"

"He writes his own music."

"Seems like a huge waste of time and energy to me."

"Have you ever heard him play? He's good, a lot better than you give him credit for."

"So we have a piano player and a ballet dancer in the house now."

"I guess we do. What's wrong with that? I encouraged Sara to take dance lessons and besides, it's not that expensive."

"It's not the money."

"Then what is it?"

"People who go to watch ballet are snobs. It's for intellectuals and the elite."

"That's not true."

"Sure it is. If you took a poll of these people, they'd mostly all be liberal."

"So what if they are? If you polled the people at the VFW, they'd be mostly conservative."

"There's a big difference. Conservatives love their country and liberals don't."

"Do you honestly believe that?"

"It's true."

"You're so dogmatic. It's too early in the day for this, but since we're on the subject, I wish you wouldn't get into these heated discussions with my father. He has a heart condition. His blood pressure gets too high."

"I'm just tryin' to set him straight. Someone has to challenge all this liberal propaganda he's gettin' from newspapers and TV."

"I have another bone to pick with you. Why do you wake me up so early? That's three days in a row now."

"It's always good to get an early start."

"Six thirty is early enough for me."

"I'm used to gettin' up at five every day."

"You might be used to it, but I'm not. What time is your interview today?"

"One o'clock this afternoon."

"What kind o' job are you being interviewed for?"

"I don't know, some kind o' civil service work. They'll let me know what's available."

"Well, good luck."

"Thanks... well I'm gonna change the oil in my truck before heading to Richmond. What are you gonna do?"

"Take a nap, a nice long nap."

Without responding, Tom stands, puts his coffee cup in the sink and, without looking at his wife, exits through the kitchen door. His mind is focused on his interview today. Despite his artful prevarication in answering his wife's questions, Tom Crosby has no intention of applying for any civil service job or any other work he's unaccustomed to; his sole aim is to be hired as an overseas security contractor and return as quickly as possible to the only world he's known for the past nine years, a world of armed conflict and insurgency.

The prospect of moving from that world to the placid normalcy of nondescript family life is increasingly unappealing for Tom Crosby. He's thought about this question for some time and once believed he could transition to civilian life with little difficulty, but since his return home he feels increasingly out of place. Years of living in a war zone with its prolonged exposure to the chaos and violence of battle have changed him. What he once looked on as abnormal and incomprehensible, he's come to accept as commonplace. Like so many others, war has changed Tom Crosby's personality. After adapting to its callous disregard for life, the capacity to live and thrive in a world of peace and community is, for some men, not attainable or even desirable. Tom Crosby is one of them.

Meanwhile, seven time zones and a world away from Amherst, Virginia, an Iraqi man is coping with another day of survival in the capital city of Bagdad. Omar al Shaliki has watched his country descend into chaos and complete anarchy since the American invasion in 2003. He was there when 'Shock and Awe' lit up the night skies of Bagdad in March of that year. He watched as Saddam's statue was toppled in Firidos Square, and he lived through the terror of death squads and militia rule that surged in 2006.

Omar al Shaliki was an engineering student at Bagdad University in the late 1990s, when Iraq was living under austere international sanctions imposed for its invasion of Kuwait. As a result, a downward spiral in the national economy meant having a degree in engineering was relatively useless. Omar had lived with his parents and two sisters when the war started, but within two years his mother and father had been killed, and when militias ruled the city a year later, tragedy returned when one of his sisters was murdered. Now, only he and his remaining sister are left. The grim struggle of surviving over a decade of war has deepened the bond that Omar al Shaliki has with his sister Adara. They are the only members of their original family of five that are still alive. Omar and his sister often talk about reuniting with their departed family in the next life. The cumulative trauma of living so long and so close to the intimate chaos of war's indiscriminate brutality has fostered in both an almost carefree indifference to the serious danger that still remains for them and the people of Bagdad.

Bomb blasts are a daily occurrence for the seven million residents trying to put the pieces of their lives back together after so much conflict. The horrific aftermath of the war's upheaval is a nation whose civil institutions have been ripped from the center of public life. While residents of Bagdad struggle to reestablish some familiar patterns of association that once flourished in Iraqi society, the perilous uncertainties of the time make only the most immediate needs important.

The worst day of the war for Omar al Shaliki came in August of 2005 when he learned that his parents had been killed at a military checkpoint just outside the city. To find out how and why they'd lost their lives, he went to the place where they had been shot to death by U.S. Marines. After hearing an effusive apology, he was told through an interpreter that the car they were riding in was traveling at high speed and the driver had failed to stop or slow down when warning shots were fired. He was then offered a claim card and told to fill it out and was informed that he might be eligible for a 'condolence payment' if it was approved by a third party.

The policy was well known by Iraqis, who were sometimes paid an average of two thousand five hundred dollars for the wrongful death of a family member, but only if military officials authorized the payment. This meant that Omar al Shaliki might receive in compensation for the death of his mother and father the rough equivalent cash value of a cheap second hand car, but if and only if the claim was approved. When he was told this, he looked back at the interpreter and the Marine captain who was holding the offered claim card in his hand, and after a moment of icy silence, he asked in broken English, "Did you kill my parents?"

Hearing the question asked in English surprised the American military officer and instantly locked him into silence.

At that moment, Omar al Shaliki intuitively knew he was looking at the man who had killed his parents. No answer was given to his question on that terrible day in 2005, so he took the claim card, tore it into pieces and walked away, but he made it a point to remember the name of the Marine captain who ignored his question. It was Crosby, the same Tom Crosby who years later would return to his family and their safe, secure home in Amherst, Virginia.

For Omar al Shaliki, this horrific event was far more painful than anything else that occurred over a decade of war and civil bloodshed. That mayhem was general; the death of his parents was, and still is, bitterly private and personal. From that day on, the life of Omar al Shaliki was permanently shattered.

When one of his two sisters was murdered 14 months later, the news didn't seem to evoke the sorrow it should have. It was as if his human capacity to experience emotional anguish had already reached its limit. Looking back now at that awful day, he vividly remembers the long walk home from the place where the lives of his mother and father had been taken. As he walked over the Old Diyala Bridge, he paused halfway across to look below at the slow moving water, thinking it might calm his distracted mind.

It reminded him of happier times when he would go with his parents and sisters for a picnic by the river, but the recollections of a happy memory were short lived. As he stood there watching the river that day, he saw something floating downstream moving in his direction. Moments later, the object revealed itself to be a severed human head. The floating decapitated skull slowly made its way downstream, and it soon became clear what exactly he was seeing.

Someone had mounted a human skull facing upwards, tying it in place on a square piece of wood to float it securely downstream and beneath its black and rotting flesh were the words: 'Death to the Infidel, God is Great'. The murdered man's skull had no eyes. Birds had already pecked them out and consumed the soft tissue. As the hideous object got closer, Omar al Shaliki found it impossible to look away. He remembers how the eyeless head had passed directly beneath him on that day. It seemed to him as if that skull was a perfect symbol for the life and death struggle of his country to survive. A nation, or what used to be a nation, marred by war and pointless death, severed from its history and identity, seemed to be drifting blindly into its own future like the sightless, pathetic object that floated beneath him.

Since that painful day in 2005, only one thing motivates Omar to keep struggling, and that's his younger sister, Adara. He sees it as his personal duty to take care of her in every way possible. Despite all the personal anguish the war has brought him, Omar al Shaliki sometimes thinks if things get better, just maybe he'll be able to use his engineering degree to find work, provide for his sister and help rebuild his war torn country. But for now, because of the shattered economy, he can only stand on a public street corner every morning and hope to be chosen for an occasional menial job.

Today, Omar and his sister are going to Monsour Mall, and though they don't have enough money to buy anything, the meager sum they have is sufficient to buy lunch, and for them, that's enough. But there's a deeper hunger that draws them out into the public spaces of their capital. It's a hunger for normalcy, a hunger for civil order and peace, a hunger for healing and renewal. By visiting and spending time in public places, Iraqis can show each other they're not afraid and they're ready for a better future. Omar and his sister believe they must play their part in helping to make this a reality. Hope, faith and little else animates their lives and gives them the strength to face another day.

Meanwhile, at an office park in a suburb of Richmond, Virginia, a man is parking his truck as he arrives for his scheduled interview. It's Tom Crosby. As he walks toward the front entrance to the four-story building, he sees a window cleaning crew working on a scaffold at the fourth floor nearly 40 feet above. With painting and landscaping crews also working, it's evident the building is undergoing a serious renovation. After passing a crew working on the front of the building, Tom Crosby makes his way to the elevator. His appointment is on the fourth floor. When the elevator door opens, he sees five or six people removing dozens of folders from filing cabinets and packing them into cardboard boxes. A cursory look around the room reveals this office with all its contents is being moved to another location.

Despite the activity, the neatly dressed receptionist offers a welcoming smile as Tom Crosby approaches.

"Yes sir, can I help you?"

"My name is Tom Crosby. I have an appointment to see Adam Fischer."

"I'll let him know you're here."

"Thank you."

"Mr. Fischer, Tom Crosby is here to see you. Yes sir, I will. Mr. Crosby, you can go right in. It's the second door on your right."

"Thank you."

Within seconds, Tom Crosby is inside a spacious, elegantly furnished office. Behind the large mahogany desk near the window, a middle-aged man who's looking through the contents of a folder places it aside and rises to welcome his guest.

"Mr. Crosby, I'm Adam Fischer. It's good to meet you finally. Please have a seat."

"Thanks, I'm glad to be here."

"Sorry for the mess out there. We're in the process of moving to another building."

"Yeah, I see that."

"Well, that last time we spoke, you were still the property of the U.S. Marines. How do you like civilian life?"

"To be honest with you, Mr. Fischer, I can't say that I like it much at all."

"Call me Adam. Yeah, I know what you're talking about. It's called 'culture shock.'"

"People in the states don't have a clue about the rest o' the world. All they know is their little bubble."

"That's all they wanna know."

"They're never asked to sacrifice anything. That's why. My family's a case in point. I have a son who spends hours every day tinkling at the piano and a daughter who takes ballet lessons. They have no idea that the freedoms they take for granted are threatened."

"Most Americans don't think twice about it," Mr. Fischer says.

"Yeah, that's something I learned since coming back home. My son is seventeen. I told him the other day that we're at war, that this nation, right now, is at war. He looked at me like I was crazy, started spouting off some nonsense about the 'War Powers Act.'"

"When these terrorists start setting' off bombs every day in this country. You'll see a lot o' people changing their tune."

"Yeah, I hate to say it, but it'll have to come to that."

"Anyway, so the last time we talked you were not completely sure you wanted to go back overseas. Have you made a decision?"

"Yes, I have. I'm ready to go back."

"You wanna go back?"

"That's right."

"Well, we can sure use you. Global Security Solutions is a great company to work for. We're in seventeen countries. Most of our personnel are in the middle east."

"That's where I'd prefer to be placed."

"I was looking at your military record. You did two tours of Iraq."

"Yeah, I got there in 2004 and stayed until October of 2007."

"I see you had an E.O.I., escalation of incident, in 2005. What happened?"

"That happened in August 2005 at a checkpoint east of Bagdad. We set up a security checkpoint looking for weapons, explosives, you know the routine."

"Sure."

"Around two in the afternoon, this car starts coming toward us. We signaled for it to stop but it just kept coming, so we did what we had to do."

"Sounds like you didn't have a choice."

"Turned out it was a man and his wife. We had no idea it was two civilians. The next day their son came to see what happened. I told him. He wasn't too happy. I offered him a claim card. He tore it up and walked away. So —"

"You did the best you could in the circumstances."

"Three days before that, two guys were killed by an I.E.D. about four miles from where we were. I wasn't takin' any chances."

"You did the right thing, could o' been a car bomb," Mr. Fischer says.

"I'm mean, I'm sorry it happened, but what are you gonna do?"

"You were cleared of any wrongdoing by your commanding officer. That's all that counts. I wouldn't worry about it."

"I don't. I made a judgment call. When something like that happens, you have to let it go and move on," Tom Crosby says.

"That's all you can do."

"Okay, so let me ask you, if GSS hires me, how soon can I go back overseas?"

"As soon as you want, certainly within two or three weeks. It's really up to you. Some guys wanna leave immediately. Others need more time."

"A couple o' days is all I need."

"Well, looking at your military record, I can tell you right now that we can use you. I'll have to run it by my supervisor, but I'm sure he'll okay it. So it's up to you when you wanna start."

"That job in Kuwait that we talked about; is there any word on it yet?"

"Not yet, if it's available I'll know by next week."

"Okay, I guess we'll wait and see then, but if it isn't, I still wanna be overseas within a month, preferably sooner than later."

"Sure, that's fine. We can do that. Well, that's it for now, that's all I needed to hear from you. I'll get your paperwork lined up. Like I said, I have to run it by my supervisor. Once he signs off, I'll write up the contract, you can have a final look at it and we'll go from there. That's about all we can do today. Why don't you call me next Thursday? We'll at least have your paperwork ready."

"Sounds good, Adam."

"Good to see you, Tom."

"Thanks."

"I'm glad you came in today, so we can get the ball rolling on this."

"So am I."

"I wanna get you all squared away before we get moved," Adam Fischer says.

"When will that be?"

"We'll be completely out of this building in one month."

"Is that why the work's being done outside?"

"That's the reason. As soon as they're done this building goes on the market."

"Yeah, you said you were moving to Washington."

"That's where the action is. If you're a military contractor, you almost have to be there."

"Makes sense. Will you buy another building in D.C.?" "We'll sign a lease for a year before we decide."

"Pretty expensive I'll bet."

"You wouldn't believe what office space costs in Washington."

"Selling this place should help," Tom Crosby says.

"Not really, we'll be lucky if we break even when we sell this place. We bought it in March of 07, when real estate was through the roof, market's cooled off since then. This building is almost 40 years old."

"Someone'll buy it. Just wait for the right price."

"Oh, it'll sell. We just can't wait too long. It's costing us a fortune. We're cutting every corner we can, trying to save money and it's still costing us a fortune."

"I'll bet."

"All this work, inside and out, has to be completed in three weeks. That's our deadline. Those work crews you saw outside have been at it seven days a week for over a month now."

"That's getting it done."

"It sure is."

"Okay, well I guess I'll call you on Thursday Adam."

"Please do. Maybe I'll know something by then. If I find anything out about that job in Kuwait, I'll call you. I have your cell number. Thanks again for stopping by Tom."

After a handshake and a polite goodbye, Tom Crosby exits and, within seconds, is in the elevator. As the door closes his thoughts turn to how he will tell his wife that he'll soon be leaving to go overseas again, and whether to tell her anything at all. A tempting thought comes to him; why not leave unnoticed and write her a letter explaining why he made this choice? He knows that doing so would be less than honest, but it would avoid something that Tom Crosby finds very uncomfortable. That is a long and candid discussion between a husband and his wife about feelings, about shared emotions and commitment, but most importantly about future intentions.

Years of living in a war zone have deadened his capacity to experience and consequently express any normal degree of emotional sensitivity. It's simply a language he'd prefer not to speak. Tom Crosby knows if he tells his wife he's going back overseas, it will spark a long and emotionally unpleasant conversation, a conversation he would prefer not to have, so he pauses and says to himself, I'm goin' overseas. I'm not goin' through some heart to heart discussion and spill out my guts because somebody else wants me to. His thoughts are jumbled, tossing between what he should do and what he wants to do. When the elevator door opens, it returns him to the present moment, and he walks to the front door to leave.

As Tom Crosby thinks about the upcoming changes in his life, Omar al Shaliki and his sister Adara have just finished a meal together at the food court in the Al Monsour Mall in Bagdad. The familiar scene of mall-goers walking by as others casually enjoy their meals is a welcome respite from the usually grim difficulty of living in a war zone. All seems perfect as they sit and observe their surroundings. Seeing people interact naturally, hearing occasional laughter and the innocent banter of children, even the taste of their Chinese food, seems to infuse the very air with a sense of optimism and reinvigorated hope for a peaceful future. Though they finished their meal fifteen minutes ago, Omar can see in his sister's eyes she'd prefer to dwell just a bit longer. The open stores, the human activity, the sights and sounds of people socializing again are all so reassuringly normal.

The quiet smile on Adara's face is undimmed when she hears her brother say, "We have to go."

"I know. Thank you Omar for this wonderful evening. God willing, many more will come."

"Next time we come, we'll go to the movies."

"You need to save your money."

"What I need is a job. I need to be hired to do what I was trained to do."

"You will."

"The government needs engineers to rebuild this country. I should've been hired a year ago."

"Be patient. It will happen with God's will."

"I hope," Omar says as he glances at a wall clock in the distance that reads 9:15.

"Are you ready?" Adara asks her brother.

"Yes, if you are."

After one more leisurely walk around the food court, it's time for them to head back to their home in al Washash, nearly four miles away. Within minutes they've passed back through security checks and are soon in the warm open night air of Bagdad. Once they go through the last security check point at the entrance to the mall's parking lot and walk the open streets of Bagdad, they know and feel more vulnerable to danger. Despite the possible risk, Omar and his sister feel a surge of confidence and optimism as they make their way back home. Perhaps they and the people of Iraq have reached a turning point in their patient struggle for the return of normalcy. If only for this passing moment, all things seem to be possible.

Back in Richmond, Virginia, Tom Crosby is ready to make the two hour return trip back to Amherst. As he leaves building, he looks at his watch. It reads 2:24. Outside, work crews are diligently trying to complete their various tasks before the allotted deadline in a few weeks. A strategy of allowing only one work crew to occupy any one side of the four-story building minimizes the risk of accidents. The window cleaners with their 32 foot high scaffold have completed the entire front side with its 38 windows, and are disassembling the 42 foot long scaffolding frame to move it to the other side of the building.

The top down process of disassembly is uncomplicated but requires careful and sustained attention. Today, like most days, that job belongs to Paul O'Malley, a man who's worked with and on scaffolding for 19 years and knows the routine well. As he removes piece by piece, the long pole like metal sections and carefully sets them aside, Tom Crosby is walking toward his truck in the parking lot to begin his trip back home when he hears his cell phone ring. The voice he hears is Adam Fischer's, the same Adam Fischer he's just had a conversation with in the building behind him. He's calling Tom Crosby with unexpected news. As Tom Crosby answers the call, he notices the time. It's now 2:27.

In Bagdad, nearly 6,300 miles away, it's 9:27 in the evening and Omar and Adara al Shaliki are strolling home after a rare treat of having dinner at the Al Monsour Mall. The pleasant experience is still resonating in their thoughts as they walk on together in silence. Omar knows of a cafe along the way, and has just enough money to buy himself and his sister a cup of coffee. What a perfect way, he thinks, to end an enjoyable evening. Since the city-wide curfew has been lifted, a growing number of shops have been open at night, despite the intermittent power supply and the serious risk of terrorism. Omar knows this cafe is usually open and seeing its lights from a distance they know tonight is no exception. Two gasoline-powered generators provide a back-up source of power for this well-lit cafe and, because of that, it's known as reliably open for business to its patrons. As Omar and his sister enter the open air cafe, Adara takes a seat and Omar walks to the counter to buy two cups of coffee. The clock on the wall reads 9:34.

The local time is 2:34 in the afternoon for Tom Crosby in Richmond, Virginia. The cell phone call is from Adam Fischer, who has just learned that the contractor job in Kuwait is available.

As their brief conversation continues, Tom Crosby, standing only twenty feet from the building where the call is originating from, moves closer to it to stand in the shade and within seconds is only a few feet from the metal scaffolding.

Meanwhile, working over 30 feet above, Paul O'Malley is unaware of Tom Crosby below and continues removing the metal poles and braces one piece at a time from the scaffolding frame. Below him, at the corner of the building, he sees landscapers working at a hurried pace. They, too, are working under the pressure of a deadline and trying to complete their work as soon as possible.

With his attention focused on his work, Paul O'Malley doesn't see the landscape worker get into the dump truck loaded with mulch and expects nothing awry as he loosens and removes a ten-foot bracing pole. He moves carefully to set it aside when a powerful jolt knocks him to his knees. The landscaping truck has accidentally backed into the end section of the scaffolding with enough force to dislodge the ten-foot long metal pole from Paul O'Malley's hands. As it tumbles downward, one end of the metal pole wedges in the bracing of the scaffolding frame and the other end continues to fall until it strikes a utility line carrying almost seven thousand volts of electricity. Instantly anticipating the danger, Paul O'Malley quickly moves to the safest place on the scaffold. He huddles on the wooden planks as far away from the metal frame as possible.

His unfailing perspicacity saves his life, but for Tom Crosby, still standing on the ground and only inches away from the now electrified metal frame, the danger is fatal. Unaware that death is only inches away, he casually lifts his hand to rest it on the metal frame. When he does, over 6,800 volts of electricity enter his body and instantly stops his heart. The electric wall clock mounted above the elevator doors inside the building's lobby marks the exact moment of Tom Crosby's death. It reads 2:39. An unlikely accident has brought his earthbound journey to its end. Tragedy waits for others in this world, and not only by accident.

In a cafe in Bagdad, Omar al Shaliki has just bought himself and his sister a cup of coffee to cap off their evening together. As Omar's sister Adara, glances at the clock on the wall, it reads 9:39, Bagdad time. She turns her head to see her brother bringing two cups of coffee to their table and notices his attention is directed out into the street. Omar is looking past his sister at a man whose fast approach is menacing and he has the look of another world in his eyes.

When he's only a few feet away, the man screams, "God is great!" and then the deafening blast obliterates everything within a hundred feet of the explosion. Another suicide bomber has taken his life, along with the innocent lives of those around him. Among the dead are Omar and Adara al Shaliki.

As bloodshed, bedlam and death visits its fatal confusion on another tally of innocent victims, in a different reality, one impervious to the mortal shock of murderous brutality and violence, two beings of radiant energy are casually walking along a paved road. Once again, it's Brianna and her apprentice Calvin Milner. Their nondescript surroundings give no hint about where they are or where the road leads. Calvin sees an intersection ahead and asks his counterpart, "Are we here to meet our new arrival?"

"Yes we are, Calvin. He's on his way."

As they walk toward the intersection Calvin sees a small gazebo off to one side and a pickup truck parked across the street from it. Within minutes they're only a few feet away from the wooden structure that seems placed solely for their convenience.

"Come Calvin. Let's sit down."

"Thank you, whose truck is parked over there?"

"That belongs to our new arrival. His name is Tom Crosby."

When Calvin looks down one of the roads that leads into the intersection, he can see on the horizon the orange glow of a sky illuminated by flames. The rest of the sky is darkened, ominous and laden with smoke, and he sees something else. Two figures are approaching from that area, and toward the intersection where Calvin and Brianna are seated.

"There's someone coming. It looks like a man and a woman," Calvin says.

"Yes, it's Omar al Shaliki and his sister Adara. They're on their way to their next destination."

"What is that place behind them in the distance? It looks like a battle zone."

"That's what it is Calvin, a living hell of pointless killing and needless human agony."

"Is that where they came from?"

"It is, but not where they're going."

Within minutes, Omar and Adara are smiling at Brianna.

"Omar and Adara, hello to both of you and welcome," Brianna says.

Correctly assuming his presence is not perceived, Calvin says nothing.

"Where are we?" Omar asks.

"You're home, Omar and Adara. You're both home."

"What is this place?"

"It's a place of renewal and new beginnings, a place where you both belong."

"Who are you?" Adara asks.

"My name is Brianna and your name is Adara al Shaliki." "How do you know us?"

"I know all who come this way, where they came from and where they're going."

"We came from a terrible place," Omar says.

"I know that. The darkness you came away from is behind you now. Don't look back at it. It's time for you both to move forward. You are loved here by those who are waiting to see you again. Look there on the road ahead," Brianna says as she points onward.

As Omar and his sister both look, they see three figures a few hundred feet away waving invitingly at them from the road in the distance. They both instinctively know it's their departed parents and younger sister. Adara's eyes well up with tears as she sees them.

"Go Adara, greet your parents with a kiss. Go Omar. Offer your tribute of love. Use your knowledge and engineering skills to build a new world of hope and possibility. This is the world you both wanted, and so now it is yours."

Without words, Adara offers her kiss to Brianna and Omar does the same. Then, buoyantly happy, they tearfully walk together to be reunited with their parents and sister. Brianna and Calvin watch as they make their way down the road and soon see the family's joyful reunion.

"They look happy," Calvin says.

"They do."

As Calvin watches the happy scene, something in his peripheral vision catches his eye. He looks to see a man coming down the road from a different direction.

"Someone's coming."

"His name is Tom Crosby," Brianna says.

"Is he our next arrival?"

"Yes he is, and we'll deal with him as his condition warrants."

As Tom Crosby approaches, Calvin notices something different in Brianna's demeanor. Her manner and countenance changes from the warm gentleness that was so welcoming to Omar and his sister just moments before, to something more stern and earnest. Calvin senses a confrontation is imminent.

After walking the distance to the intersection, Tom Crosby sees the gazebo and his pickup truck parked alongside the road. He also sees Brianna, who stands to meet him while Calvin, unseen and anonymous, observes.

"Who are you?" he asks.

"You should be asking yourself that question, Mr. Crosby."

"What are you talking about?"

"I'm talking about you, Marine Captain Thomas J. Crosby, veteran of the Iraq War and genuine military hero, a true master in the art of 'Shock and Awe'. Aren't those your credentials? I hope you'll pardon me if I don't say thank you for your 'service' as you call it."

"What's your problem, lady?"

"Oh, I don't have a problem, but you certainly do."

"What is this place?"

"It's the other side."

"What do you mean?"

"It's like a train station or an airport where people arrive from somewhere and make their connection to go somewhere else."

"I don't know what you're talkin' about. That looks like my truck over there."

"And so it is. You'll need it to get where you're going."

"And where is that?"

Pointing into the distance to the dark, smoky horizon illuminated by fire, Brianna says, "Right there, Mr. Crosby. That's your destination, the battle zone of war, and its attendant mayhem."

"I'm actually a peaceful man."

"Are you?"

"Yes, I am."

"I see. Well, I guess this is a case of mistaken identity and the next time I look at the moon, I'll call it the sun. A thing's intrinsic quality is not changed by re-naming it. If you're a man of peace than Jack the Ripper was a gynecologist."

"You can go to hell, lady."

"No, I'm afraid I can't do that. That's your next address Mr. Crosby, not mine."

"I did what I had to do."

"What was that?"

"I know what you're talkin' about, that day at the checkpoint when I opened up on those people in the car. If you think you can lay some guilt trip on me over that, you're wasting your breath. We fired warning shots, they never slowed down. What was I supposed to do, let my guys get killed by a suicide bomber? No, if you're dumb enough to charge up on a heavily fortified checkpoint, then you can expect to get ripped open. It's called war, lady."

"No one can be blamed for repelling what he thought was a deadly threat if that's what happened. Grievous as those killings were, they were the consequence of a more general crime, a crime that you freely conspired in when you took up arms and invaded a country that was no threat to you in any way, shape or form."

"That was not my decision, that was a political decision."

"No, it wasn't, Mr. Crosby. You and you alone made that decision. You weren't forced by anyone to do what you did. God grants all freedom of conscience, the gift is inviolable. It therefore follows, does it not, that you could've made a different choice?"

"Yeah, well it's not as simple as you make it out to be lady. What was I supposed to do? Maybe you think I should've changed sides or something and betrayed my own country."

"When you committed yourself to go to a foreign land and wage war, you betrayed your own humanity. War means blood, death and unspeakable agony. Knowing this, you gave yourself to its unholy rites. You knew it would be dark and beastly and you said count me in. That's your crime Mr. Crosby, committed well-before that act of sickening brutality when you needlessly slaughtered two innocent people."

"You don't know what you're talkin' about lady, and if you did I wouldn't care, anyway. I don't care about those two people. I did my job and I did a lot more than that. My country called and I gave my country my best service."

"Service, don't slander the word! Real service is godly. Real service is humble. Real service is offered through love. Your bloody work is something very different. Isn't it?"

"I don't care what you say. You don't know what you're talkin' about. I say it was service."

"Look!" Brianna says as she points. "This is your service."

Tom Crosby is startled to see, appearing instantly out of nowhere, a young Arab boy standing only a few feet away. Barefoot and plainly dressed, his face and chest is splattered with blood, but most unnerving for Tom Crosby, the young boy is crying hysterically. The screaming pitch of his inconsolable wailing is heart wrenching. As he looks at the child and the boy looks back at him, he hears Brianna's voice again.

"This is your service, Mr. Crosby. His name is Abdul. He's seven years old. He was riding in a car with his parents and watched as they were shot to death in front of him at a military checkpoint. The blood on his face isn't his. As you can imagine, when you're that close to two people who are shot over a hundred times, blood gets splattered everywhere, so as you can see, the tears on his face now mix with the blood of his own mother and father. This is your service!"

"I've never seen this child before in my life."

"That's right. You didn't pull the trigger. Not in this particular instance. What you did was help create the conditions that enabled it to happen. It's too bad you don't speak Arabic. Maybe you could explain to Abdul that the reason his mother and father were killed was because they were, as you say, "dumb enough" to charge a heavily armed checkpoint."

The intensity of the moment is unnerving for Tom Crosby. His breathing becomes shallow. He feels trapped and strongly impelled to leave this unfamiliar place.

"Lady, I don't know who you are or who this kid is. I'm not wasting any more of my time listening to you."

As he walks away, he turns and looks back at Brianna. "And since that's my truck, I'll take it with me."

"Yes, you really do need to go."

"I'll go where I wanna go, not where you say."

Tom Crosby gets into the truck and seconds later, pulls away. He sees the darkened sky in the distance and takes a road that leads directly away from it and is soon out of sight. Brianna walks over to Abdul, and in her gentle, calming presence, his tears subside. A quiet sense of ease pervades, and the child's mood becomes tranquil. Calvin has observed all and looks at Brianna.

"That encounter with Mr. Crosby was dramatic. I'm so sorry for this boy. I can't imagine the pain he must feel."

"By saying that, you've at least acknowledged it."

"I'm so very sorry for Abdul."

"So am I, Calvin." Tom Crosby is driving down a road that looks vaguely familiar. The countryside he sees is reminiscent of his native Virginia and as minutes pass, he becomes convinced this is a road he's traveled on before. After driving through a stand of trees that obscured his forward view, the road leads into an open field on both sides and he sees on the horizon directly in front of him, the ominously dark, smoke-laden sky he thought he was driving away from. He finds it odd that, though he's made no appreciable turns from the direction he's driven, he's still moving toward the threatening sky looming ahead.

He turns sharply onto a side road and hopes it will lead away from it, but within minutes, despite driving straight ahead, he sees again the dark forbidding horizon in front of him. After another turn, he comes closer to the darkness. He turns back in the direction he came from and thinks if he could just get back to the intersection where he started from, he could find his way out of this strange place. He drives on, but as before, it only takes him closer to what he wants very much to avoid. The road he's traveling on looks increasingly familiar and when he reads a sign that says, Amherst 17 miles, he knows why. He's heading back to his hometown.

How is this possible? He remembers talking on the phone with someone and then something happened. A connection was lost, permanently lost. Tom Crosby recognizes the road he's on as one he's traveled many times, but the landscape is different. Some homes he's driven past have been burned to the ground and, as he looks ahead, the dark sky is illuminated with the orange glow of firelight hovering directly over his hometown of Amherst.

An urgent thought seizes him. His family is in Amherst, and may be in some jeopardy. The noise of automatic weapons being fired in the distance is faintly audible, and its muffled intermittent clatter is a menacing sound. Tom Crosby feels a strong impulse to get back home and check on his family's safety. As he gets closer, the surrounding landscape looks increasingly battle scarred. He can see buildings burning and the sound of gunfire becomes more pronounced as he progresses. He's at a complete loss for an explanation of what he's seeing. This must be some kind of terrible dream. This place can't be the same familiar countryside he knew as an adolescent, years before. He recognizes a curve in the road up ahead, and knows that just beyond it on the right side is the Little League baseball field he played on so many times as a boy. Seeing it has always brought back happy memories, but after making the turn and slowing down, Tom Crosby sees something shocking: a line of six or seven men standing on the baseball field with their weapons raised are aiming in unison at a man tied to a wooden post. The man is wearing a black hood on his head and these are the last few seconds of his life. When shots are fired, his body slumps motionless and its dead weight becomes lifeless.

Utterly aghast and sensing danger, he quickly pulls away and is stunned to think about what he's just witnessed. He feels an imperative need to get home, to ensure his family's safety and, after seeing someone executed, perhaps his own safety as well. How can this be happening? Something must be terribly wrong. Now only a few miles from his house, he sees no-one in the street, but in the distance on both sides of the road, armed men in small groups are maneuvering around buildings and occasionally shooting at something.

Tom Crosby knows very well what guerilla warfare looks like, and that's exactly what he's seeing. He keeps driving and soon glimpses ahead of him a small building alongside the road with a metal barrier blocking the way. It's a checkpoint. As he gets closer, he's waved in by four men in uniforms with weapons. Tom Crosby becomes very uneasy and has no idea what to expect as he rolls his window down.

"I need to see your ID."As he reaches for his wallet, he can clearly see the two men watching him closely through the windshield on both sides of the truck with their weapons trained on him.

"Here's my driver's license. What's goin' on around here?"

"Insurgents are on the offensive. Okay, you can go."

With this curt reply the barrier lifts and the soldier in charge waves Tom Crosby through. He doesn't ask the guard any more questions as he pulls away, but his thoughts are buzzing with confused apprehension. What did he mean about insurgents on the offensive? This unsettling comment hastens his will to get back home quickly. When he approaches his old neighborhood, no one can be seen walking or driving in the streets. It's late afternoon, a time of day when human activity is usually at its peak, but what Tom Crosby sees around him is hauntingly empty. The sky is heavy with smoke and fires are burning in different places. His thoughts are increasingly apprehensive as the worrying sound of sporadic gun fire can be heard.

Minutes later, he's driving on his home street and sees his house, but it looks unfamiliar. As he pulls in the driveway, he sees the house has been painted black and cement blocks have been placed in the window spaces. Tom Crosby remembers his house looking very different, or was it a dream? He remembers driving to Richmond to keep an appointment, but doesn't remember why. Despite his confusion, he's certain that his home and his neighborhood have radically changed. Trees that were once in the front yard have been cut down and the sun-brightened landscape looks almost alien, but the dominant visual feature is its color. The entire house, including the roof, has been painted flat black. Even the yard, sidewalk and driveway have been darkened. Taken aback by what he's seeing, he sits for a moment in silence. Then the front door suddenly opens, and he watches as his wife Heather and their 17 year old son charge out with automatic weapons and quickly assume defensive positions. Without eye contact, they aim out into the street and visually scan in both directions as if expecting an attack from somewhere. His wife and son are dressed completely in black and move with the precision and speed of trained military proficiency.

Surprised at their sudden action, he looks at his wife and asks, "What's happening? What's going on here?"

"Better get your vehicle inside, sir," she says without looking back at him.

The garage doors unexpectedly open. The light-duty motor-driven aluminum door has been replaced with two large steel panels hinged on both sides that swing out from the middle, and pushing the doors open is Tom Crosby's daughter Sara who, like her mother and brother, is wearing a totally black uniform and carrying a weapon. Before he can think, Tom Crosby hears his wife's voice again.

"Get your vehicle in, sir."

Suddenly the sound of gunfire coming from a source close by is heard, and Tom Crosby scrambles to get his truck in the garage. As the doors close behind him, he hears the clang of heavy metal latches being bolted shut and after getting out of his truck, he sees his daughter staring back at him. Her joyless greeting is brief and impersonal as she salutes.

"Welcome back, sir."

Without waiting for a reply from her father, she walks back into the house with Tom Crosby following.

"What's happening, Sara? Why are you dressed like that?"

At that moment the front door opens and Tom Crosby's wife and son enter, shutting and locking the metal door behind them.

"What's happening here? What were you doing outside?"

"We were giving you cover, sir. Insurgents are now active in this area."

"What insurgents?"

"From intelligence reports, we think they're an offshoot of the DRF," Heather says.

"Who's the DRF?"

"It's the Democratic Revolutionary Front, sir. As far as we can tell, they're the militant wing of that organization. They splintered off when we killed most of their commanders in a raid last month."Tom Crosby sees his son John, and daughter Sara, exit the room as if returning to some unfinished activity.

"Where's John and Sara going?" he asks his wife Heather. "They're on duty, sir."

"What kind of duty?"

"They're spotting."

"Spotting?"

"Yes, sir."

"Why do you call me sir? I'm your husband."

"You're an officer. Our military protocol requires it, sir."

"What's happening here? This place looks like a war zone."

"Well, yes sir, as you know we're at war."

"This is crazy. What are you people doing?"

Before she can answer, a rifle shot is heard from inside the house somewhere upstairs.

"What was that?"

"It might've been a kill. Let's go see."

With this quick reply Heather, with her weapon still on her shoulder, briskly moves toward the stairs. Tom Crosby follows as they ascend and enter the main bedroom. He sees that the ceiling has been cut away and what looks like a loft with an observation platform installed. Large enough for two people, it's constructed with a narrow horizontal opening that looks out into the street below. Tom Crosby sees his son John descending the vertical ladder, while Sara remains above, looking out through the narrow slit with binoculars. As John comes down, Tom Crosby sees his son carrying a different weapon than the one he had before. This rifle has a mounted scope and a longer barrel and is designed to be used by a sniper. Seconds later, John is standing beside his parents with a self-satisfied smile and proudly says, "That's 19."

"Not 'til it's confirmed," Heather says and, looking up to Sara, she asks, "what do you see Sara?"

"Uh, so far no movement, a lot o' blood."

"He ain't movin'. I drilled him dead center. It was a clean shot. How much blood, Sis?" he asks his sister, who still has her binoculars trained on the freshly bleeding body.

"A lot, a lot o' blood. He's bleedin' out."

"That's right. I put one through his heart. My kills only take one shot," John says proudly.

"Well congratulations then, that's your 19. What's it look like, Sara?"

"He's in a pool o' blood, no movement. He's done," she says with a thumbs down gesture.

"That's good enough for me. You'll have to sign off on it, sir," Heather says to her husband.

"Sign off on what?" Tom Crosby asks. "Confirmation of a clean kill, sir," John says. "You've done this 19 times?"

"That number's for both of us. I have fourteen kills. Sara has five."

"I have six kills," Sara says in objection.

"No you don't. You have five kills, not six," John says to his sister.

"That's not true. I have six kills."

"You have five kills, Sara. Only five were confirmed," Heather tells her daughter, and turning to her husband, light heartedly says, "they have a bet between them over who can get to twenty kills first, sort of a sibling rivalry, you might say."

Aghast at what he's just heard, Tom Crosby turns away in disbelief.

"What's happened here? This is crazy. Have you all gone insane? What's changed you people? What happened to your piano music and ballet lessons? Don't you remember?"

"What are you talking about? Ballet lessons, there are no ballet lessons here."

As Sara comes down from her observation perch, she sees her mother and brother looking suspiciously at her father.

"Do you feel all right, sir?"

"Don't call me sir. I'm your husband."

"Yes, sir, whatever you say."

"Put that weapon down," Tom Crosby tells his son. "I said put that weapon down."

"Is that an order, sir? Because if it is, I'm afraid I can't obey."

"You people have gone crazy. The whole world's gone crazy. You're killing people, sniping people from your own home and joking about it. You're insane. You've all gone insane."

Heather, John and Sara look at each other with suspicion and alarm at the unexpected words they're hearing. Then, as if on cue. Heather says, "Listen sir, you must be a little tired after traveling all day. Why don't you take a quick nap and get some rest? Dinner's at 1800 hours. We'll call you when it's ready. Let's leave your father alone now so he can relax," she says to her children.

With this, Heather, John and Sara leave the room, closing the door behind them. Their exit seems curiously abrupt, and Tom

Crosby stands alone in the room. He sees the sleeping cot with its mattress a few feet away, but knows it would be impossible to fall asleep. His mind is racing with questions. What is this place? What's happening to his family? He looks around the room. The smell of the spent bullet cartridge his son fired to mark his 19th kill still hangs in the air, a sinister reminder of the brutality everywhere around him.

The room he's standing in used to be the master bedroom of the house, and holds personal memories for Tom Crosby. This is where he and his wife Heather once slept together through the early years of their marriage, before he went overseas. That was the happiest time of his life, but that world now seems a universe away. His drifting thoughts are quickly dispelled as he looks around the room with its altered surroundings. The room's windows have been covered with permanent steel plating. The light of large fluorescent lamp fixtures on the ceiling make the room unnaturally bright, but the most conspicuous change in the room's appearance is the construction of a sniper's loft in the roof area above him. The walls, once colored in soft pastels have been painted a drab gray, with no pictures or adornments of any kind, giving the stark interior space a sanitary, unwelcoming look. No trace of anything feminine or familial is in the room, or any other part of the house. Everything around him reflects the relentlessly masculine qualities of battle- hardened military life.

He remembers the strange woman named Brianna who told him earlier that this would be his fate, that he would inherit a world of unending war and killing. Tom Crosby is not afraid of battle. He's accustomed to armed conflict and knows how to survive its dangers, but this is something very different. Seeing his wife and children living, thinking and acting as battle hardened soldiers is a frightening paradox and the most disturbing element in this new inexplicable reality.

War, for Tom Crosby, is always something that happens in foreign lands, with its horrific trauma inflicted on other people, other families and other neighborhoods. He wonders how all this can be happening. He slowly walks over to the sleeping cot and sits. Slumped forward with his elbows resting on his knees, he tries to understand what he's experiencing. His drifting thoughts keep returning to Richmond. He remembers driving there, an appointment, and a call on his cell phone, then walking somewhere toward an intersection.

His muddled recollections are cryptic and indecipherable. Was he traveling on a train going through a long tunnel, or maybe walking through a cave toward a sunlit opening ahead? He can't remember. What Tom Crosby does clearly remember is what his family was like before he made his trip to Richmond. Can it really be since this morning that things have so radically changed? It seems like a lifetime away. Everything was normal, sane and predictable.

He remembers talking to his wife about their children, about John's piano music and Sara's ballet lessons. He remembers his gentle, elderly neighbor, Benjamin Keely, stopping by for a friendly visit. Tom Crosby intuitively knows that that safe, orderly world, with everything in its assigned place, is now gone forever. A life, a world, a future once rich with promise and expectation has been hideously transmogrified into a grotesque caricature of its former self. The full meaning of what the strange woman named Brianna meant is now terribly clear. Lying back on the cot, Tom Crosby reaches an impasse in his thoughts and surrenders to an impulse of weary resignation.

As he tries to relax, he looks up at the ceiling and in a tone of sober determination says, "This is crazy. I have to stop these people somehow. I have to stop this."

Minutes later, Tom Crosby hears a knock on the door and the sound of his daughter's voice.

"Sir, dinner's ready in five minutes."

Shaking off his distracted thoughts, he opens the bedroom door, but his daughter is already half way down the stairs and apparently not interested in spending a private moment with her father. The cold rebuff is not unnoticed by Tom Crosby. After following his daughter downstairs, he sees only his wife seated at the other end of the dining room table. Seeing that particular dining room table kindles warm recollections for Tom Crosby. He recalls the happier years of his marriage before he was deployed overseas when he was home for every holiday and the family meals that were served and enjoyed around that table. Its beautiful wooden finish is still in pristine condition. At least the table is still here, he thinks to himself. Tom Crosby will use the opportunity of a family meal to sort out this strange reality and somehow get things back to normal.

The smile on Heather's face seems encouraging as he sits opposite her. Though plates and utensils are placed and ready, the dishes are empty and no food has been served. Tom Crosby looks at his wife and thinks this is the time to press her for answers, but before he can say anything, Heather intercepts his speech.

"I want you to do something," she says.

"What's that?"

After pulling a .45 caliber service revolver from under the table and pointing it at him, she answers his question.

"Keep your hands away from the edge of the table so I can see them."

As he hears these threatening words, Tom Crosby sees movement off to the side and looks up to see his son, John, enter the room, pointing an automatic weapon at him. Then his daughter Sara enters with her weapon, also pointed in his direction.

"What is this? What are you people doing?"

"We're placing you under arrest."

"What?"

"Cue up the video Sara," Heather tells her daughter.

Tom Crosby watches as his daughter opens the sliding cabinet doors mounted on the wall fifteen feet away and sees no less than twelve contiguous viewing screens. Each one is providing a live camera view that continually monitors both the exterior and interior of the house.

"As you can see, we maintain surveillance 24/7, including upstairs."

With Sara operating the remote, he sees one screen descrambling its picture. The image he then sees is himself when he was lying on the cot upstairs minutes before.

"You had me under surveillance?" he asks in disbelief.

"That's right, and here's why. Turn up the volume, Sara."

Tom Crosby sees and hears himself saying the words he spoke only twenty minutes ago when he was lying on the cot, "This is crazy. I have to stop these people somehow. I have to stop this."

After hearing his recorded words, his wife asks, "What did you mean when you said, 'I have to stop these people'? That's what we need to know."

Glowering at her husband while still pointing the .45 caliber revolver, her icy stare dispels any hopes he may have had about resolving this inexplicable enigma.

"What's happening here? You're all insane. Look at you, ready to shoot your own husband, and you," Tom Crosby says turning to his son, "ready to kill your own father. You're all sick. This is insanity."

"You're the one who's behaving erratically. Ever since you've returned, your behavior's been strangely atypical. We'd like to know why. See, here's the problem: we don't know who you are, and until we do, we must keep you in a secure place."

"This is ridiculous. What are you people doing?"

"I want you to stand up slowly and keep your hands on the table, now."

Tom Crosby looks around and sees the cold staring eyes of his wife and children looking back at him, with weapons poised and ready.

"Keep your hands on the table. Back up two paces and spread your feet apart. Are you carrying any weapons?" Heather asks her husband.

"You people have all the weapons, not me. I can't believe this."

"Search him," Heather tells her daughter.

After the added indignity of being frisked by his own daughter, Tom Crosby is led downstairs to the basement. As he enters, he sees the space has been converted to four detention cells for holding prisoners. When he looks inside one, Tom Crosby is shocked at who he sees.

"Mr. Keely, Benjamin Keely, what are you doing here?"

"No talking."

"But he's our neighbor."

"I said no talking."

Seconds later, the jarring sound of hearing the cell door shut behind him, sharply underscores the incomprehensible madness of what's happening. After his captors go back upstairs, Tom Crosby looks across and into the cell that's holding his elderly neighbor, Benjamin Keely, who looks drawn and weak.

"What are you doing here, Mr. Keely?"

"I have no idea. Someone accused me of giving information to the insurgents. It's all a pack o' lies. They want me to confess to things I've never done. They want me to sign a confession, but I won't. I won't do it. I'll never do it."

"What's happening here? Why are they doing this to you?"

"Why don't you ask them? They're your children. Tom, I looked out for your family when you were deployed overseas. I was the one who checked in on your family, treated them as my own, and now they do this to me. If I had a gun, you know what I'd do when they come back for me later? I'd blow their cursed brains out right in front of you. I would. That wouldn't bother me at all after what they've done to me."

"What do you mean, when they come for you later?"

"They come every night, always at the same time. They want you to expect it. That way it wears on your mind."

"What do you mean, expect what?"

"What do you think? Torture, that's what."

"What?"

"They've water boarded me seven times now. They call it 'enhanced interrogation.' I guess they learned that from you. I'd kill them all if I could."

Stunned into silence, Tom Crosby turns away in disbelief and wonders when this bizarre nightmare will end. Wasn't it only this morning when his family and the world were normal? Before he can ponder the question, he hears the approach of someone coming downstairs, and moments later, sees his son and daughter walk over to Benjamin Keely's cell door.

"Okay Ben, you know what time it is. Why don't you tell us what we wanna know and we'll leave you alone?"

"I told you, I don't know what you're talking about."

"Come on, Ben. We know better."

At this point Benjamin Keely breaks down and sobs. "Why can't you leave me alone? I'm just an old man."

"And you're also an informant, Ben. We know that. Just tell us who your contact is with the insurgents and what you told them. That's all we wanna know."

"I told you, I never spoke to anyone."

Tom Crosby watches as his son walks behind the chair Mr. Keely's sitting in and sees him quickly slap his open palms against the old man's ears from both sides causing him to grimace in pain.

"What the hell are you doing? Keep your hands off him. You bastards. If I had a gun, I'd shoot both of you."

"Really? I'm sure you would. That makes you the enemy and a traitor doesn't it?" Sara says to her father. "Sit back and enjoy the show, traitor, cause you're next."

With an automatic weapon trained on him, Benjamin Keely is strapped into a chair, and his arms and legs are bound. After the chair is tilted back far enough, the old man hears the sound of water being filled into a bucket. He knows what's coming next.

"Okay Ben, this is the last time I'm asking you. Who's your contact?"

"I told you. I don't have one," Mr. Keely blurts out.

"Wrong answer, okay, you wanna do this the hard way."

Tom Crosby watches as his son wraps a towel around Benjamin Keely's face and lifts the bucket of water while his daughter holds his head securely. Mr. Keely's body becomes taut as he braces himself in panic and as the water pours over his face, he gags and arches his back, writhing in agony.

"Stop! You're killing him. What good will he do you then?"

"Shut up, traitor."

More water is poured, and a steady stream fills Benjamin Keely's mouth and nostrils. His convulsive gags and frantic desperation are unpitied as he chokes and struggles for air. His body's instinctive reaction to clear his airways provokes a reflexive and violent regurgitation response. Still choking and gasping for air, Benjamin Keely is now drowning in his own vomited stomach fluids.

Every skilled torturer knows the art of bringing his victims to the edge and then pulling them back before they go too far. Sara raises her hand, signaling to her brother to let the old man momentarily recover. Then John refills the water bucket. Tom Crosby looks on the scene in stupefied disbelief. A numb, muted incoherence seizes his thoughts as he wonders how this can be happening. The malevolent surrealistic intensity of the moment is too extreme to be real, he tells himself. This must be a dream. Then, as if to assure him it's not a dream, Tom Crosby hears a spray of gunfire coming from somewhere in the house above him.

He sees his children grab their weapons and rush upstairs, leaving Mr. Keely still bound and choking for air. A Violent commotion and another round of automatic weapons being discharged, followed by the sound of people rushing through the house is heard. Seconds later, four soldiers with weapons ready, storm down the stairs and find Benjamin Keely still choking and strapped to his chair. Then another soldier descends, and the demeanor of the others indicates that he's in charge.

"What's here, lieutenant?"

"This man's been water boarded, sir."

"Those bastards, he's an old man. We got here just in time. Cut him loose and take him upstairs. Do what you can for him."

"Yes, sir."

"We have another man over here, sir."

After walking over to his cell, the officer sees Tom Crosby looking back at him through a dazed expression of shock and confusion.

"You're lucky," he says to Tom Crosby. "Looks like you were next. Bring him upstairs."

"Yes, sir."

Within minutes Benjamin Keely is carried away. After Tom Crosby is freed and led upstairs, he's immediately confronted with a grisly sight. His wife and both children have been shot to death in the living room and their freshly bleeding bodies are sprawled on the floor. The appalling scene evokes no reaction from him. Tom Crosby no longer has the capacity to reason through the violent mayhem surrounding him, and is emotionally and psychologically bereft. He sees the same man as earlier giving orders in the basement, directing his men.

"Lieutenant, get two or three others, take these bodies out back and bury them."

"Yes, sir."

"Where's the old man?"

"Medics are looking after him sir. He has water in his lungs, but they said he'll make it."

"Good, that's good. So who are you?"

"My name is Tom Crosby."

"Why were they torturing the old man?"

"They said he was giving information to the insurgents."

"And what about you?"

"They said I was a traitor."

"Well, any traitor to their cause is a friend to ours. Do you have any military experience?"

"Yes."

"You should join us, for protection if nothing else. Think about it."

"Those three bodies."

"What about them?"

"Let me bury them."

"That's a strange request after what they were ready to do to you."

"Please, it's something I need to do."

"Is that all you wanna do to those bodies?"

"That's all."

"Are you sure you have the strength to do that?"

"Yes, I'm sure."

"Why do you wanna do this?"

"I have my reasons. Let me bury them."

"I guess there's no harm. Go ahead, if it means that much to you, but you need to know, we're movin' out in a few hours. I advise you to come with us. The enemy's completely infiltrated this area. It's not safe. You do what you have to, but we're movin' out at 1900 hours, with or without you."

Minutes later, Tom Crosby is standing in the back yard looking at the corpses of his wife and children. Their lifeless bodies, still covered in blood with their shoes removed, have been unceremoniously dumped to the side of the yard. After dragging them one by one to their resting place, he begins the dreadful work of covering their bodies. With grim resolution, he tries not to look as, shovel by shovel, each one of his family members disappears from view.

Several hours later his work is complete, and he stands in silence, looking at the place where his wife and children are buried. Tom Crosby has given up any attempt to make sense of what's happening around him, and doubts his own ability to separate what's real from what isn't. To dismiss this place as no more than a horrible nightmare seems trivial and incredulous. The blister forming on the palm of his right hand from digging suggests that this place is anything but a dream. The sound of gunfire crackling in the distance forces the question to the forefront of his thoughts as he asks himself, if this is not a dream, then what is this? Tom Crosby unexpectedly hears a woman's voice. "This is war, Mr. Crosby. That's what it is, my condolences on your recent loss."

After turning to see who's behind him, he sees a face he recognizes.

"You, I remember you. You were at the intersection with that boy from Iraq. You're the reason I'm here."

"I'm not the reason you're here. You made that choice, Mr. Crosby."

"What is this place?"

"You should know the answer to that question. It's a battlefield, or as you call it, 'a theater of operations', which is a nice tidy euphemism to describe a place where people get killed, usually civilians. This is your new home Mr. Crosby, a place of endless war and human conflict. This place is governed by the force of arms. Softer things like reason, amity, domestic peace, have no place here, but a man like you with your skills will fit right in."

"So you think I deserve all this because I'm a soldier? Is that what you're saying?"

"No, not because you're a soldier; a soldier is someone who sees war as a temporary interruption of normal life. A soldier wants to do his duty and get back to that normal life as soon as possible. You're something different, Mr. Crosby. You're a warrior. A warrior prefers the chaos of armed conflict. It becomes intrinsic to his identity. He feels a hypnotic exhilaration in the violent mayhem of war. That's who the warrior is, Mr. Crosby, and that's who you are."

"Why am I here?"

"Because you've molded yourself to this world and so now, this world has molded itself to you."

"I didn't choose to be here."

"You didn't?"

"No, I didn't."

"Do you remember the reason you drove to Richmond? It was to sign up for another overseas tour, and go back to a life and world that you apparently prefer. This is that world."

"Why did my family have to be part of this? They had nothing to do with the things I've done. Why involve them?"

"Because that's what war does, Mr. Crosby. It rips families apart with death and slaughter, but in your world and by your logic, that only happens to other families in other places. You need to learn that those who light fires in other neighborhoods shouldn't be surprised when they come home and find their own homes have been burned to the ground."

"I didn't burn anyone's house down. All I did was engage the enemy. I followed orders."

"There's that word again, that toxic word that war mongers love to hear. They know if they get enough people to call others 'the enemy', then a slow inevitable tilt toward war will follow.

Fear driven psychology will always need an 'enemy' to validate its paranoia, and you're no different."

"I followed orders."

"All warriors do that, even to the point of abdicating their own humanity."

"So, what happens now?""What else? You'll pack up a few things and be moving out at 1900 hours with your new unit."

"What makes you think I'll join these people? They're the ones who shot my family."

"Oh, you'll join them."

"How do you know?"

"Because a warrior needs a support team to be tactically effective. Group warfare increases the scope of strategic possibility. I don't have to tell you that, Mr. Crosby. You're the expert here."

Turning away, as if not wanting to hear, Tom Crosby looks back at where his family's buried and then hears the voice of one of the soldiers calling him from inside the house.

"Hey, Crosby, Commander wants to know what you wanna do. We're movin' out in 20 minutes."

He looks back at Brianna and hesitates. "Tell them-"

"Tell them what?"

"Tell them I'll be ready in ten minutes."

After looking once more at the grave site, he turns and sees Brianna has vanished. A stark and sober realization comes over him as he contemplates his predicament. Then, in complete psychological resignation, he walks back in the house to collect a few things and readies himself for his new life. Thirty minutes later the eight man military unit prepares to leave. A ninth member has been added to their number in the person of Tom Crosby. As they file out of the house, two spirits watch them leaving. Brianna and her apprentice, Calvin, stand unseen in the front yard.

"Where are they going?" Calvin asks.

"They're going on patrol. They have night vision equipment that works to their advantage, enabling them to hunt and kill in the dark."

"Who are they hunting?"

"Those who they call the enemy. Those three syllables are a notorious word trap, Calvin."

"What do you mean?"

"Words influence the human mind. Words we hear ourselves saying each day slowly pull us toward their implied logic. Enemy is a dangerous word. Once we accept the premise of having an enemy, ridding ourselves of that enemy becomes paramount, and war becomes the only option."

"Will war and killing ever end?"

"Yes, they have no evolutionary future."

"When will that happen?"

"When the young are no longer encouraged to be heroes and warriors."

"But there are so many who want to do exactly that."

"That's very sad for the peace of the world. Heroes and tragedies are always found together. Come, Calvin, this place is noisome and perilous. Better things are ahead. Let's walk from this malevolent realm into gentler regions."

As the militants move out and disappear into the urban landscape, Calvin and Brianna set out in the opposite direction. With every step they take, their surroundings change, and in only seconds the dark, foreboding, war torn battle zone is far behind them.

Chapter Fourteen: A Faithful Wife

Sights and sounds quickly change as Brianna and her apprentice Calvin leave the armed conflict of urban warfare behind them, and in only a few seconds a rustic vista opens before them as they make their way along an unpaved dirt road. In the distance, an unspoiled view of farms and houses gives the appearance of a world that is once again normal. As Calvin has learned to expect the unexpected, the sudden change elicits only a subdued smile in him, and he continues walking with Brianna. The blue sky and tranquil surroundings are a pleasant contrast to the strife-laden chaos of the world they just departed. The bucolic flavor of this new scenery is vaguely familiar to Calvin as he takes in the agreeable view.

"This place is beautiful. It reminds me of home."

"A place called Pennsylvania."

"Yeah, that's where I grew up."

"You were a happy child, weren't you Calvin?"

"Yes, very happy. We lived in a rural area, knew all our neighbors, it was good. When I was a boy, I used to go out at night in my backyard with binoculars and lie on the ground looking at stars. It was great. Sometimes I'd sleep out there with my dog."

"Your furry companion, Max."

"Yes, Max. I loved that dog."

"If you could name the happiest day of your life, which would it be?"

"Oh, that's easy. That would be the day I proposed to Clara."

"Your wife?"

"Yes."

"Tell me about that day."

"I remember it clearly. It was wonderful. We were both 18. We had just graduated from high school. After spending most of the summer together, I had to get ready to go off to college, so we had a picnic at our favorite spot. I found this beautiful place in the country where I used to set up my telescope. On the weekend before I left for college, I asked Clara to go there with me. This place was special, it's at the top of a hill with a 360 degree view of the sky. Astronomers liked to go there a lot, but that day we had the place to ourselves. There was a picnic table at the top. Clara brought sandwiches and fruit. When night came, I set up my telescope, and we looked at the moon."

"Clara brought sandwiches, but you brought something too. Didn't you Calvin?"

"Yes, I did, an engagement ring. That's when I asked Clara to marry me, and she instantly said yes. I can't think of a happier day in my life."

"That's a wonderful story, Calvin. Do you miss your wife?"

"Yes, very much."

"Calvin and Clara, even your names sound like they belong together."

As they continue onward, Calvin takes in the beauty of a countryside pristine with gently rolling hills and flower-laden meadows.

"This place is so lovely. Are we here to meet our next arrival?"

"Yes we are, Calvin, and then your apprenticeship is over."

"What do you mean?"

"This next arrival will be the last one we receive together."

"I'm sorry to hear that, even though I knew it was coming. You said we'd eventually part company. I'll miss you, Brianna. Have I been a good apprentice?"

"Yes, Calvin, you have."

"It's so strange, I feel like I've always known you and somehow always will."

"And so you have, and so you will."

"Will I be able to do this without you?"

"Yes, you will."

"I hope so."

"You needn't worry. Everyone that comes before you goes irresistibly to their appointed end. All you have to do is travel with them along the path a little, and then let them go."

Brianna and Calvin continue walking as the dirt road ends and a foot path begins an upward grade into a wooded area. Calvin recognizes the oak, birch and hickory trees around him and hears the familiar calls of finches, warblers and sparrows. All the sights and sounds of an Eastern Pennsylvania forest evoke powerful memories of the life he once lived. After many turns in the upward sloping path, the grade levels out and he sees a sunlit clearing ahead.

"It's time to meet our new arrival, Calvin."

"You said you want me to speak, to do the talking?"

"That's right."

"But I don't know what to say to this person."

"Just speak from the heart."

After entering the clearing, Calvin is stunned by what he sees. There, only 50 feet away, is a picnic table with a woman seated with her back toward him. A telescope, very much like the one he used so many years ago stands only a few yards away. As the woman rises and turns around, Calvin Milner sees the face of his beloved wife Clara looking back at him. Then, an added surprise, just as unexpected, presents itself. From behind the picnic table a golden retriever comes bounding out and, with unrestrained exuberance, runs over to greet his master. It's Max. In startled amazement, Calvin is completely taken aback and struggles for words.

"Clara, Clara and Max, are you, are you, real? I, I can't believe this."

"Oh, Calvin, Calvin I'm so happy to see you again."

"Oh Clara, my dearest Clara, are you really here?"

"Yes, yes I'm here Calvin, and we're together again."

"How can this be happening? Look at you. You're young again."

"So are you Calvin."

"I know this place. It's where I proposed to you."

"I remember Calvin. I'll always remember."

After a tearfully joyous embrace with Brianna looking on, Calvin says, "I'm overwhelmed. What's happening Brianna? Tell me."

"You're greeting our new arrival Calvin. That's what's happening."

"I don't understand."

"It's very simple. When your good wife Clara lived with you those many years, her secret wish was to be with you again after death, and now that wish is granted. What the heart is inclined to is where the soul is directed, either to friendly or unfriendly destinations. This is Clara's destination. Her devotion to you is why she's here."

As tears of joy flow down Calvin's face, he finds it hard to speak.

"This is, this is incredible. I'm speechless. I don't know what to say. Clara, oh Clara, I love you."

"Calvin, I love you too."

"Now your work begins Calvin, and you have a worthy companion to help you. Many thousands will pass before you. An unending journey of souls through their countless incarnations is the immutable destiny of collective humanity. Always remember that no matter what they've done or left undone, however grievous or questionable, there's always the possibility of redemption. Every individual soul is loved and valued by a supremely transcendent power. Remember this, and all good things will follow."

"I promise to do my best."

"I know you will. So now, your commission begins."

"Where do I start?"

"Just walk the same path that we walked, and they'll come to you."

"Where will you go, Brianna?"

"I go to meet my next apprentice and those new arrivals who come after."

"Thank you, Brianna. Thank you for everything. I love you. I'll never forget you."

"I love you too, Calvin. Goodbye, Clara."

"Goodbye Brianna, and thank you."

As Brianna walks away, she stops, turns back and points upward. "Look Calvin, the moon's in its first quarter. It'll be a good night for observing."

He sees the moon for a moment then looks back to Brianna, but she's no longer there.

"Is she gone?" Clara asks.

"No, she's never gone. She's on her way to receive another harvest, and then another and another. There is no end. Come Clara, my dearest Clara. Let's prepare for our work."

The End

Please review this book and others at Amazon books. Other works by Michael Mckinney include,

"The Invitation" "Three Dreams" "Does God Exist?" "Cassandra's Gift"